# DEATH IN DARK GLASSES

**George Bellairs** was the pseudonym of Harold Blundell (1902–1982). He was, by day, a Manchester bank manager with close connections to the University of Manchester. He is often referred to as the English Simenon, as his detective stories combine wicked crimes and classic police procedurals, set in quaint villages.

He was born in Lancashire and married Gladys Mabel Roberts in 1930. He was a devoted Francophile and travelled there frequently, writing for English newspapers and magazines and weaving French towns into his fiction.

Bellairs' first mystery, *Littlejohn on Leave* (1941), introduced his series detective, Detective Inspector Thomas Littlejohn. Full of scandal and intrigue, the series peeks inside small towns in the mid twentieth century and Littlejohn is injected with humour, intelligence and compassion.

He died on the Isle of Man in April 1982 just before his eightieth birthday.

# DEATH IN DARK GLASSES

## An Inspector Littlejohn Mystery

### GEORGE BELLAIRS

ipso books

This edition published in 2017 by Ipso Books

First published in 1952 in Great Britain by John Gifford Ltd.

Ipso Books is a division of Peters Fraser + Dunlop Ltd

Drury House, 34–43 Russell Street, London WC2B 5HA

*To the memory of Agnes Platt*

# CONTENTS

# CHAPTER ONE
# THE MISSING CLIENT

The defalcations of John Wainwright Palmer at Silvesters' Bank, Rodley branch, were of small dimensions compared with the hornets' nest of crime they set buzzing in the town. Only two hundred pounds, taken from the till and hidden in the accounts with moderate skill, yet in the mind of the dishonest bank cashier, they had assumed such enormous proportions that, learning the Chief Inspector of the bank was closeted with his manager and then being told the pair wished to see him in the private office, Wainwright Palmer bolted. In his panic and haste to the station, he failed to see a bus, fell beneath it and was picked up dead.

The Chief Inspector of the Bank had called to discuss Palmer's career with the manager of Rodley branch and they were about to offer the cashier promotion in the shape of the managership of a highly sought-after seaside branch. Beautiful, tragic irony of life!

It seemed obvious that Palmer must have had something on his conscience and that, to the bank, meant only one thing. An alarm was sounded which brought to Rodley a large team of investigators from headquarters. Had he lived, Palmer might, out of fear, hope or remorse, have laid bare his whole scheme of modest fraud. Now, the branch had to be turned upside down to trace the causes of the cashier's flight. The process was far from easy. The balances of all the clients who could be contacted were verified. It was proved that Palmer had forged cheques on rarely-used accounts to square his books. Finally, all the customers but ten had been covered. Seven of these were abroad and inaccessible; two were dead; and one would not reply to letters. It was thought better in these cases to call in a handwriting expert to examine the cheques drawn on their accounts. They had specimens of Palmer's writing and in a very short time had sorted out the whole affair. Entries were passed to make good the fraudulent withdrawals, the bank wrote off as bad the unlucky debt created by their faithless servant, and the manager of Rodley breathed again. But not for long.

Mr. Hoffman, the handwriting expert, was still uneasy.

"I can't make this out, Mr. de Lacy," he said, passing his soft white hand over his large bald head. He had a tic in one eye and winked at the manager, who, after weeks of strain, winked mirthlessly back. Mr. Hoffman placed three cheques on the official writing-pad.

"These are forged, too, if the specimen in your signature file is authentic," he said. "But Palmer didn't do it."

Mr. de Lacy slumped in his chair.

"My God!" he managed to say and he placed his hands flat on his desk and gazed blankly into space like a cataleptic.

The cheques totalled seven thousand pounds! They had been drawn to "Self" on the account of one Finloe Oates and they had exhausted the whole of his balance. Nay, with accrued charges, Finloe Oates owed the bank nine shillings and threepence.

After bracing himself by drinking most of the brandy in his first-aid box, Mr. de Lacy rang the bell.

"Bring me Mr. Finloe Oates's file ... ."

No sooner said than done. The file revealed that five letters, all unanswered, had been sent to this customer in the course of investigations arising from Wainwright Palmer's misdeeds. The manager, his eyes wild and his thin hair dishevelled from his tearing at it, ordered them to get the Chief Inspector on the telephone.

"Hullo, de Lacy.... How are you?" came a cheerful voice from Head Office.

"I'm not so well," answered the manager and fell unconscious under the desk.

The Chief Inspector arrived later that day and this time he was far from cheerful.

"Where does the man live ... this Oates fellow ...?"

He spoke as though poor Finloe Oates had himself caused all the trouble.

"Netherby ... about five miles away in the country ..."

They had given Mr. de Lacy more stimulant; so much, in fact, that he was a bit truculent.

"Why wasn't somebody sent out to see him when he didn't answer letters?"

"So busy and confused by all the fuss ... I mean, all the worry of the investigations, I quite overlooked it. And if I overlook anything, nobody else finds it. I'm not getting the support I ought to get from Killgrass ..." he said between paroxysms of nervous coughing.

"Very serious.... Very serious indeed. Seven thousand pounds! Whatever were you thinking of ...?"

The Chief Inspector might have thought Mr. de Lacy had himself put pen to paper and forged Oates's name!

"Send a man out right away ... ."

They rang for the assistant manager, Mr. Killgrass, who entered braced for the fray. He was a clean, bald, tubby man

with the folds of his heavy face set in lines of irony and disappointment. He objected to being assistant to a manager
like Mr. de Lacy. He felt he could manage better himself.
They told Mr. Killgrass the nature of his mission, waved
aside his expostulations, and meticulously instructed him
what to say and do, like potentates sending an emissary into
a distant alien land.

"We depend on you...."

Mr. Killgrass took a taxi in a show of efficient haste.
"The bank can stand it," he thought to himself, and, after
all, he was in a hurry.

Netherby is a small village which once boasted little
else than a pub for refreshment, stocks for evil-doers, a fine
church, and a few workmen's cottages. Now, however, it had
grown into a dormitory for Rodley's professional and mon-
ied classes. Large, imitation period-houses had sprung up
solidly in the middle of the village, surrounded by an outer,
more attenuated ring of pseudo-manors and sham-castles
in magnificent bad taste, like their owners. Most of the
wealthy elders of the community moved about it in large,
opulent cars and their offspring tore about it in racing models. Mr. Killgrass, after a pint and a few inquiries at the inn,
found that Mr. Finloe Oates lived in a bungalow named, for
some obscure reason, "Shenandoah," and situated about a
mile outside the village in a country lane, along with three
or four similar houses built by a speculative builder.

Shenandoah was closed. Nobody answered Mr. Killgrass's
knock. He looked around the place. It was a rustic-brick
structure; two living-rooms, two bedrooms and the usual
offices. Behind, a small orchard and a vegetable patch; in
front, what must once have been a very pretty lawn and
garden, but now it was a wilderness. The grass was like a
meadow, with coltsfoot and plantain romping merrily all

over it; the round rose-bed in the centre was running riot and sprouting burdock; the flowers on the borders had gone wild and were choking under the weight of stitchwort and coarse grass.

Mr. Killgrass was a man of imagination. He had read books by Walter de la Mare, Sheridan le Fanu and Ambrose Bierce. He believed in the benevolence or malevolence of bricks and mortar and knew that houses bore personalities endowed upon them by powerful occupants. There, on a hot afternoon, with no birds singing; with not a soul about but the taxi-driver snoozing in his cab, a fag dangling in his mouth; with somewhere the sound of water running from a pipe and falling from a height; he felt that the house was watching him and that the forsaken, desolate garden was trying to tell him something he could not interpret. He shook off the feeling, remembering that he was expected to return with an answer of some practical kind. He took the liberty—not without looking furtively around to make sure he wasn't overlooked—of peeping in through the windows. The living-rooms were tidy. Over the fireplace of one, a dark portrait in oils looking straight at him, made Mr. Killgrass recoil like one discovered doing wrong. The blinds of the bedrooms were drawn. The kitchen bore signs of habitation, but it must have been a long time ago. The table was laid. On a soiled cloth were the remains of a meal; dirty dishes, a half-empty jar of marmalade, a piece of mouldy cheese, and a loaf of bread turned almost to fungus. There was a mouse busy eating the cheese. Instinctively, the banker tapped on the pane with his finger-nail and the mouse bolted to a dark corner and was gone. The place obviously hadn't been occupied for weeks—nay months, and someone had left it in a hurry.

Mr. Killgrass then peered through the letter-slit in the front door. There was a small pile of letters on the floor and among them he recognised two of the bank's envelopes with the familiar crest on the flaps.

"Wantin' somethin'?"

Mr. Killgrass raised himself and spun round. As if in answer to a prayer, it was the postman himself, a little, stringy fellow, with mean, inquisitive eyes and a face like a wizened nut. His jaws rotated as he chewed and then he spat out a quid on the grass to facilitate articulation.

"I'm trying to find Mr. Oates...."

"Funny place to look for 'im. Ain't been 'ere for near on two months. Went away an' said nothin'. Not even left 'is address. Put a note on the door for the milk-boy. 'Gone abroad,' it said. As if that were any help. What's 'e want goin' abroad for...a feller of 'is age? Made 'is money in distant parts, but never bin away from 'ere since he married and settled down more'n a dozen years since. Seems 'is wife dyin' turned 'is 'ead, if you ask me.

He seemed affronted by the fact that the vanished tenant of Shenandoah had not taken him into his confidence before disappearing. He eyed Killgrass up and down.

"What you wantin'?"

Mr. Killgrass replied by another question.

"Do you still deliver the letters here, then?"

The postman's thin lips disappeared altogether as he compressed them in stubborn malice.

"Course I do. Can't do no other, 'cept burn 'em. Serve 'im right if I did. Why didn't 'e tell me? He could tell milk-chap. I'm more important than milk fellers, ain't I? So, as 'e didn't tell me, I keep on puttin' his letters through the slit in the door. Not that 'e gets many now. All 'is dividends stopped comin' a while since."

Mr. Killgrass started.

"What do you know about his dividends?"

The postman spat maliciously on the grass.

"Don't get no ideas as I opens 'em. I can tell divi letters. Smooth and sleek, like, with, like as not, name and address printed on 'em, 'stead o' written. Mostly circulars now, with penny stamps, or a letter or two from the bank. P'raps he got 'isself overdrawn. Anyhow, by the look o' things, bank'll 'ave to whistle for their money. Somethin' tells me we won't see Finloe Oates agen ...."

Mr. Killgrass looked at the postman with respect. His comments on the letters had been worthy of Sherlock Holmes himself! Perhaps he knew ....

"When 'is wife up an' died early in the year, Oates tuck funny. For a week or two after the buryin', he was normal. Nay, 'e was more chirpy than usual. As if his missus's death 'ad give 'im more freedom. Then, of a sudden, overnight like, he shuts 'imself up indoors and won't come out. I knew 'e was there. Saw 'im through the winder, moving round. Heard 'im, too. Letters went from behind door and milk was tuck in. I recollect parcels, too. Registered 'uns. 'Leave 'em on the mat,' 'e sez. 'Not me,' I sez. 'You got receipt to sign.' So 'e tells me to put it under the door; then 'e signs it and shoves it back without showin' 'imself."

"You didn't see him, then?"

"Not close to. But 'is writin' on receipt ... that was 'is. I'd know it anywhere. Gone queer with broodin' and bein' alone after Mrs. Oates got tuck ...."

He waved a grubby hand like a talon at the garden.

"Look at all that. Wrack and ruin. An' Oates that proud of it once. Nobody more proud. In it from morn till night till just after 'is wife died and 'e tuck funny. Even photographed it an' won prizes in ladies' papers for best gardens ...."

The postman spat again.

"Since she died...well...as I said, he was normal for a bit. Mowin' the lawns like mad and weedin' them beds like a good 'un, as if it comforted 'im. Then, he stopped, and never done a 'and's turn at it since. I can't understand it. You thinkin' o' buyin' this place, because I don't know whose goin' to sell it to yer if they don't find Oates...?"

Mr. Killgrass informed the postman he wasn't going to buy. He didn't quite know what to do. The thought that the taxi was still at the gate ticking away the bank's sixpences, spurred him to action, however. He bade the postman good-day and hurried off. Whereupon, the postman, assured that nobody was looking, went behind the house, cut a fat neglected marrow from a wilderness of nettles, grass and weeds, stuffed it in his bag, and made off as well.

"Hadn't we better have a word with the police about this?" said Mr. de Lacy to the Chief Inspector when Killgrass had made his report.

"I think so...."

An hour later the telephone in the lobby of Netherby police-house rang. P.C. Albert Mee, digging in his garden, rose to the perpendicular, dusted his hands, and lumbered indoors.

"Telephone, Dad," said his wife from somewhere upstairs.

"I know...."

P.C. Mee always knew. They called him "Johnny Know-all" in the village.

"Yes, Mee speakin'."

"Yes, but who is it?"

"You know very well 'oo it is.... What do you want?"

The man at the other end of the line laughed. It was a perennial joke. "The Super wants a word with you...."

"Yes, sir."

"I believe the bungalow, Shenandoah, in your village is deserted...."

"I know, sir...."

"Don't interrupt, Mee. It seems an official from one of the banks here called there to-day, couldn't get an answer, and said the place looks as if it's been empty for weeks.... The postman said the owner, a man called Oates, is abroad. Is that so?"

"Yes, sir. I knew that. Went away about two months since. I've been keepin' an eye on it."

"Do you *know* he's abroad?"

"Yes, sir."

"Did he tell you so before he went?"

"Not exactly, sir. He left word with the milk-boy. Wrote it on a card and left it.... Didn't want any more milk, sir."

There were tearing noises at the other end of the wire.

"Any idea where Mr. Oates went?"

"South o' France, I think."

"You think! Do you *know*?"

"Not exactly, sir. But 'e always talked of how easy gardenin' was there. 'E'd lived there, or somethin'...."

"Don't make wild guesses, Mee. Better go up and see what's going on there. Take a good look round and get inside if you can without breaking-in the door. Speak to me again if you don't manage it...."

"I'll get in, sir. I know 'ow...."

"Remember, no breaking-in without my permission. The chap may be dead or something, inside. I'm surprised you haven't seen to it before. Go right away...."

P.C. Mee was annoyed. Insinuating that he didn't look after his village properly, were they? He'd show 'em.

"I'm just going up to Oates's place, missus," he called upstairs. "Won't be long. 'Ave me tea ready about five...."

9

"Somethin's not right there," shouted his wife over the landing rails. "Miss Featherfew who lives next door..."

"I haven't time to listen to what old Featherfew thinks," said Johnny Know-all rudely and then relented, bade his wife a civil good-bye, and pedalled off on his bicycle.

On the strength of the message produced for his information by young Belcher, the milk-boy, P.C. Mee hadn't worried much about the absence of Finloe Oates. He'd heard about Oates becoming a recluse shortly after his wife's death. Well... he'd a right to his grief in peace, hadn't he? He'd get over it. He'd told one or two busybodies who'd wanted him to investigate matters at Shenandoah that. Leave 'im in peace with his memories and his sorrow. He'll get over it. And he'd been right. Oates had gone off for a holiday to the South of France. Or, that was where P.C. Mee imagined him, sporting on the beach with the pretty bathing girls like they showed on the advert. at the station. Maybe, Oates had seen the advert. for Nice on the station. Yes, that was it. Provided the bungalow was secured, hadn't been burgled, or set on fire, P.C. Mee thought he'd no cause to interfere. Besides, Johnny Know-all didn't miss much in his village. No, sir. He'd tell the Super a thing or two in his report. Returning from night patrol on his bike at five o'clock one morning, he'd seen Mr. Oates on his way to the station to catch the first train. You have to get an early train when you're going abroad from Netherby.... He'd shone his light on him.... Mr. Oates in his big coat and soft hat with his limp, too.... When the milk-boy told P.C. Mee, he'd been able to say "Yes, I know...."

Still pondering his case, P.C. Mee parked his bike at the gate of the bungalow. Funny, Mr. Oates hadn't told him properly, though. Always before, when Mr. and Mrs. Oates had been going away for a day or two, Oates had telephoned to say the house would be empty and if anything happened...well...Mee knew where the key was....

P.C. Mee boldly approached the rockery at the side of the house. Beneath one of the large stones was the hiding-place known only to the Oateses and Mee. He raised the rock, peered in the cavity, and brushed away a couple of woodlice and a centipede. Nothing there. Mee was annoyed. He moved a few more rocks without success. At this rate he'd shift the whole rockery! He rose and dusted the soil from his hands and knees. Funny; yet perhaps not. Poor old Oates had taken it on the chin when his wife died. Everybody in the village was sorry for him. The bobby looked round to see that nobody was looking and then carefully put the rocks back in their holes. Then he made no more ado, but took out a large clasp knife, opened it, went straight to a certain window and forced the catch with great ease. He'd done it once before when the Oateses went away and left the cat in. After that, they'd hidden the key for him, just in case. Mee winked to himself and climbed in.

"Pooh!" said the bobby as the atmosphere of stale air, food, yes...and mice...greeted him. He was in the best bedroom. Just as Mrs. Oates had left it apparently. Like the window of a furniture shop. Everything in order, the bed made, the place tidy, but very dusty. The lounge was the same. The other bedroom was the reverse. Bedclothes filthy, bed unmade, clothes—a man's—all over the place. He drew the curtains and started instinctively to flail at the moths which flew out. Dead flies on the window-sill.... P.C. Mee shuddered.

"Poor Finloe Oates.... All gone to pieces," he said.

Clocks stopped, dust everywhere, letters behind the door. P.C. Mee picked up the envelopes. Gardening circulars, a few other advertisements, a number of sealed letters from Silvesters' Bank, according to the name on the flaps … .

Oates hadn't been living in the dining-room either. He'd had his food in the kitchen; and what a pigsty! Grease and dirty pots all over the shop. Tins of food, stale bread, the remains of a meal … . P.C. Mee opened the back door to let in the fresh air. A mouse scuttered from temporary hiding and ran to a hole in a corner.

Mee wasn't an imaginative man at all, but he felt cold shivers run down his spine. He felt someone was watching him! He'd see about that! There was only one other place. He tugged a cord hanging from the kitchen ceiling and a door in the loft opened and a ladder descended. He tried the light, but they'd evidently cut it off. He climbed the ladder and struck a match. Nothing there except a lot of old junk. He didn't even go in. It was a small place, a room made of plaster-board and his matches illuminated it to every corner. He turned to descend and then … There, on one side of the little loft-room, was another door, a sort of entrance to the rafters beyond, where, like as not, the water tank was kept. He'd better take a look. But first he climbed down, took a candle from the kitchen window-sill and lit it. Then he went aloft again. The little door opened easily, and P.C. Mee almost fainted. The stench was appalling. The hair under his helmet rose as the bobby realised, knew for sure, that there was something dead there. He braced himself and entered.

The body was lying doubled in one corner and it was in an advanced stage of decomposition. There was no mistaking it, however. The blue uniform with the red stripe down the seams of the trousers, and the peaked cap with the initials C.R., Corporation of Rodley, on the front. Although the Electricity Board had taken them over now, the officials were wearing out their old clothes. It was Jack Fishlock, the electricity meter-man. He'd been a bit of a one for the girls, had Jack, and when he vanished and couldn't be found, they'd said he'd run off with one of them. His wife had sworn it....

P.C. Mee scrambled down the ladder, locked-up the house, was sick with dignity in the garden behind, and then mounted his bicycle. With limbs which seemed turned to water, he pedalled off to the nearest telephone.

# Chapter Two
# The Silent House

Mr. De Lacy began to think it would never end. First, the frauds and death of Wainwright Palmer; then the forgeries in Finloe Oates's account and the way he had vanished; and finally the dead body of the meter-inspector in Oates's house. It seemed as though somehow fate were intent on Mr. de Lacy's downfall. The police were in and out the bank all day.

Did Mr. de Lacy think this or that...?

Did Oates ever...?

These forgeries, Mr. de Lacy...did you...?

One after another, until he didn't know whether he was on his head or his heels.

"How long has this forgery business been going on, sir?"

It had started all over again. Now it was Inspector Montacute, of the Rodley police. The police station was right opposite the bank and Mr. de Lacy was sure that whenever the Inspector had a minute to spare or a fresh urge, he just crossed the road to pester him. He might have thought that the poor banker had no business to do other than concerning the crimes.

"Not that he's much use," Inspector Montacute told the Chief Constable. "I ask him question after question and I'm just as far away when I leave as I am when I get there.... "

The handwriting expert, Mr. Hoffman, had called in a second opinion and was now cock-a-hoop because Prediger, the new specialist, had confirmed his own findings. Their written reports had caused a terrible hullabaloo. Now, here was Inspector Montacute again.

Mr. de Lacy licked his dry lips and turned his tired, pouched eyes on the policeman. They protruded as though you'd come upon him suddenly and given him the fright of his life. The banker was a chubby, fresh-looking man of the old school with a tall, stiff collar, black coat and grey trousers, white shirt showing gold cuff-links, and patent-leather boots. He was due to retire on pension in eighteen months' time and nursed a grievance against the late Palmer for not waiting until he'd gone before putting a light to the powder barrel which had just exploded.

"How long has this forgery business on Oates's account been going on ...?"

"As far as I can gather from the experts, it was perpetrated over a period of a month or six weeks. It began about three months ago and ended suddenly.... Yes, what is it?"

A clerk entered deferentially and showed Mr. de Lacy a ledger and a cheque.

"Where's Mr. Killgrass ...?"

"At coffee, sir."

"He's always at coffee! Return the cheque 'Refer to Drawer'."

"Very good, sir."

The clerk departed with apparent eagerness to do as he was told.

"So, it ceased about two months ago?"

"Yes ..."

"H'm."

Inspector Montacute was a bit out of his depth, As a rule, police work in Rodley was comfortable and rule-of-thumb. Then, suddenly from the blue had dropped a levanting cashier who got himself killed; forgery in a local bank; a vanishing resident in a rural area; and now, to cap the lot, a nasty murder. Too wholesale by far! He'd wanted to call in Scotland Yard, but the Chief Constable had flown into a rage. They had their own C.I.D., hadn't they? What did they pay all that staff for, if they intended farming-out their tricky cases to another force? No....

Montacute was a nice fellow, tall, middle-aged, fresh-looking with a cheerful pug-dog's face. He was fond of gardening and taking his kids out for picnics, and murder wasn't much in his line.

"The cheques were forged by somebody who knew Finloe Oates's financial position and wanted to clean him up...?"

"Obviously."

The banker had no intention of allowing a policeman to tell him anything about finance, crooked or straight.

"Obviously. But there's more to it than that. Oates had most of his money in gilt-edged investments. These we were first instructed by letter to sell. Previous to that, Oates had a mere hundred or two in the account. We sent our usual form for his signature and he returned it completed...."

"Were all the letters hand-written, or typed?"

"Entirely done by hand; otherwise we might have suspected something...."

Mr. de Lacy was anxious to make a show of closing the stable-door now.

"...We advised Finloe Oates that the proceeds of the sales had arrived and he wrote at once to say he was investing in property and would be withdrawing the funds in two or three instalments and would require drafts on our London office in settlement. The drafts were ordered and issued and charged to Oates's account. They completely cleared the balance .... "

"Looks as if he might have been getting ready to bolt."

"How were we to know at the time? It all seemed straight and above board."

"And now ...?"

"All the letters, the orders to sell the stocks, and the cheques for the drafts were forged. Seven thousand pounds in all. It's nearly driving me demented. I can't make head or tail of it. I hope you'll be able to solve it all."

"What about the drafts you issued on London?"

"They were, as instructed, made payable to Finloe Oates, and their endorsements were forged ...."

"But who got the cash, and how?"

"They were paid into the account of Oates's brother, Lysander, at the Home Counties Bank, Pimlico ...."

"What?! Why wasn't I told? This is a valuable lead."

"Be reasonable, Inspector. We've only just got to the bottom of it ourselves. I've got the forged drafts here. They've just arrived and I was going to send them over to you."

Montacute almost snatched the documents from the manager's trembling hands. All this time wasted in talk, talk, talk, whilst there, on the desk ...

"Excuse me. I must be off at once."

Montacute suddenly smiled grimly. Pimlico, eh? Now, they'd *have* to call in Scotland Yard.

"How long has Fishlock been dead, Inspector? He was a customer here."

To crown all, the murdered meter-man had kept a small savings account at Silvesters' Bank! Mr. de Lacy had grown quite resigned to the repeated blows of circumstance. Probably he himself would be the next victim.

"Two months, the doctor says…."

"Then, he must…"

"Yes; he was in an advanced state of decomposition."

"Ohhh…. "

Mr. de Lacy groped for the new bottle of brandy in the first-aid drawer.

Poor Fishlock had been far-gone when his body was removed from the garret at Shenandoah. His wife had been eager to identify him and had been in a state of hysterics ever since. The police surgeon had only that morning handed to Montacute the report he would make at the inquest.

Dead two months; corroborated by Fishlock's meter-book, which showed his last reading at eleven-fifteen on May 4th; now it was July 7th. Death had been caused by a savage blow on the head and the heavy poker which had done it was found lying in the cold hearth of the kitchen. It looked as if Fishlock had disturbed Finloe Oates in something questionable and had been murdered for it.

Montacute went straight to the telephone and told his troubles to Scotland Yard and then took himself off to Shenandoah for a quiet browse on his own.

The experts had been busy at the bungalow. All they had found were the fingerprints of Finloe Oates and some which might have been those of his dead wife. The funny part of it all was, there were no recent prints. The dirty dishes, for example, bore none at all. Neither did a few circulars and disused envelopes lying on the sideboard after they'd eliminated the postmen. They found a pair of ordinary household rubber gloves on the table in the kitchen. For some reason, Oates must have worn them about the house in his last days. He'd even gone to bed in them, as the absence of recent prints in the bedroom indicated.

It was another hot, dry afternoon when Montacute reached the house. Once past the garden gate, it was like entering a land of awful silence. The abode of the Sleeping Beauty at the pantomime! He looked sadly at the neglected garden. Oates, they'd told him, had been fond of his garden, but the tale went that a short time after his wife's death, he'd shown a distinct aversion to it.

A beech hedge divided Shenandoah from the next house. The dead leaves of last year had given place to strong green shoots and to Montacute the whole place gave that inner flurry which warns the expert gardener that nature is winning in the battle between the wild and the cultivated.

The side door of the next house opened and a woman emerged with a basket of washing, which she started to peg on a clothes-line. A heavy-bosomed, thick-limbed woman, with a worried look and her grey hair looking wind-blown. She started when she saw the Inspector, put down her basket and sidled to the hedge.

"Have they found Mr. Oates yet? I saw them taking away poor Jack Fishlock...."

She looked down at the washing in the basket.

"Have to do all my own washing these days. Can't get help and my husband won't have the laundry. Washing your stuff along with other people's, he says, isn't hygienic. So..."

She was trying to convince him that this wasn't the sort of thing she'd been used to. It was her husband's fault.

"When did you last see Mr. Oates, Mrs ...."

"Mrs. Burditt. My husband's the Clerk to the R.D.C. You know him...."

"Of course. When did you last see Oates, Mrs. Burditt?"
She had it all pat.

"His wife's death turned his brain, if you ask me. Always together. For a week or two after she was buried, he seemed all right. I saw him about the place and spoke to him. He was busy keeping the garden straight. Then, of a sudden, he shut himself up indoors. I never saw him again in the daylight. The chimney was smoking and the milk taken in and I saw someone inside the house when I passed now and then. He didn't seem to want anybody about. I called and knocked to see if he was all right. There was somebody in ... you know how you can tell ... you sort of feel it. After all we've done for them.... "

"How long ago was that?"

"His wife was buried in February. He shut himself up about the end of March."

"You can't think of any reason?"

"He'd gone queer."

"And when Oates finally disappeared altogether, did anybody see him go?"

"Yes. The local constable, Mee, says he saw him on his way to the station very early, and the porter says he caught the first train. He didn't speak to either of them. Didn't even book a ticket...."

"Oates didn't let you know he was going away?"

"No. The milk-boy got a note. 'Gone Abroad' it said. That proves Mr. Oates had gone off his head. To go abroad without a word, like that.... It's not natural."

It wasn't natural. That was true about the whole set-up. Why murder the meter-man on top of it all and convert himself into a hunted man? That explained, of course, why Oates had fled. He'd got a dead man on his hands and didn't know what to do with him. He'd gone queer and was turning his assets into cash. But, no. That wouldn't do. Somebody else had done that by forging Oates's name....

"Were you wanting anything else?"

"Eh? Oh, no, thanks. I'll just go in and take a look round."

"Me and my husband are looking out for another house. I can't stand it here any longer. After what's gone on, the place seems haunted. It ruined everything for us. We hoped to settle here after Jim retires, but this has spoiled it all."

"Just one more thing, Mrs. Burditt. P.C. Mee tells me he knew where the key for the back door was hidden. The Oateses used to ask him to keep an eye on things when they were away or out and told him where the key was to be found in case of emergency."

Mrs. Burditt bridled and put her hands firmly on her hips.

"Yes; and I didn't like that. We were living here before the Oateses and we did all we could to be good neighbours and help them to get settled nicely. For all that, they couldn't trust us with the key to look round the place when they were away. It was Mrs. Oates, of course. Some women can't bear other women to see in their houses when they're not there themselves. But it wasn't right to let the bobby have the key and not us...."

"What I was asking was, did Fishlock know where the key was hidden?"

"Yes. He called a time or two to read the meter and found nobody in. It's a long way to keep coming. So they told him, too. Neither Fishlock nor Mee would tell us. Not that I asked them; just hinted. Yes, Jack could get in. Everybody trusted Jack except his wife."

She smiled to herself. Poor Fishlock must have had winning ways with the women!

Montacute left Mrs. Burditt pegging the clothes on the line. He entered the house with the key he had brought.

The place smelled of chloride of lime. Poor Fishlock! The Inspector walked round from room to room, eyeing this and that, gently touching objects as he passed. The house was terribly quiet in a ghastly way. He had known it at its best. He'd passed it in his car, driving his wife and little girl and boy for picnics in the country. The road led to some nice spots. They'd always said how lovely the garden looked and what a happy house it seemed to be. They'd wondered how it got its name, too. Now, more dreadful things even than Jack Fishlock's murder had gone on here. The very walls seemed impregnated with evil influence and terror.

Montacute, his imagination smoothly running, shivered.

Mrs. Oates.... They said she'd been under the doctor for stomach ulcers quite a while before she died. Then, one day, she'd been taken ill at the Women's Institute and died two days later. Finloe Oates, alone in the house, brooding, trying to forget in an orgy of gardening, and then going under. Shut himself up like a hermit and refused to see anyone. Meanwhile, someone started to forge his name and filch away his savings from the bank. Yet, the letters were dispatched from Shenandoah and the bank addressed its replies there. Surely, in that case, Oates was bound to find out what was going on....

The house seemed to be trying to give an answer to the riddle. Some little thing, a clue to the mystery.

Montacute was in the kitchen. The experts had gone over it all and left things as they found them. The Inspector turned his head from side to side and took it all in, like a moving camera. All the cooking utensils, pans, pots...a pair of rubber gloves on the draining board. He picked them up. Fingerprints! Then it dawned on him—swept over him like a swift revelation.

Why had Finloe Oates neglected his garden, suddenly lost all interest in it? Why had nobody seen him properly, although they said he was indoors all the time and signs of life went on in the bungalow? Why no recent fingerprints; instead, Oates had worn gloves?

*Because it wasn't Oates!*

It was someone else, posing as Oates. Someone else who had either frightened him away ... or murdered him.

Montacute was all keyed up. He nervously lit a cigarette. He needed three matches because in his excitement his hand wouldn't stay steady.

Oates had gone and someone started to draw his money from the bank, sell his investments, forge his name, and that done, stole away by the early train. Someone who looked like Oates in the half-light. The policeman and the porter had mistaken him for Finloe Oates.

"Are you still there?"

Mrs. Burditt was back. She couldn't keep away in spite of her antipathy to the place.

"I'm just going ..."

"You were very quiet. I wondered if you were all right."

"Did you think I'd been murdered, too?"

"Don't talk like that, Inspector. It's gruesome. One murder's enough."

Someone had been hiding there and Fishlock had taken the key from its hiding-place, after knocking and getting no answer. The intruder had been waiting for him with the poker ....

"Had Oates any other relatives beside his brother in London?"

"No. I never heard of any. There was only Lysander. I believe he was some sort of a commercial artist. Mr. Oates once showed me an advert. in a paper and said his brother had done it. It was for breakfast cereal. He seemed proud of it, though, I must say, I didn't see much in it."

"Did Lysander Oates ever come here?"

"Not to my knowledge."

"So you didn't know him?"

"No. There was a photograph of him with Finloe taken when they were younger. It stood on the mantelpiece in the lounge...."

She led the way quite possessively, horror overcome by curiosity.

"Well! It stood there.... But it's gone. So has the big photo they had taken on their honeymoon, Mr. and Mrs. Oates. He must have burned them. Perhaps it brought his grief home to him too much...."

"Is that an album on the whatnot there?"

A typical family portrait gallery. An album, heavily bound and with a brass clasp, backed in threadbare red velvet. Montacute turned the pages and the woman looked over his elbow. Out-of-date pictures of extinct relatives; views of places; costumes and dresses of bygone days. Some of the photographs had faded out; others were wooden, staring, ill at ease.... A rare old, fair old rickety-rackety crew of relations.... Some of the pages were empty.

"Someone's taken them out. There were pictures of all of them in here...."

Yes, they'd made a proper job of it. Not a single picture of Finloe Oates.

"Did you see the photograph of Lysander Oates?"

"Yes. He was a bit like his brother in build, but he wore glasses and a little beard. Finloe Oates was lame from the first war. He limped a bit.... I don't understand all this."

The drafts on London had been paid into Lysander Oates's account there. Lysander, whose portraits had been scattered about his brother's house and had suddenly disappeared.... He'd taken the photographs to prevent publicity.

"I say, I don't understand all this."

"No...."

Finloe had vanished and Lysander had...

"Have there been any signs of digging in the garden since winter, Mrs. Burditt?"

"No. Didn't I say...?"

"All the same, were there any signs? You would notice, wouldn't you?"

"We certainly would. We can see every foot of it from our house. The garden hasn't been disturbed since Mr. Oates buried the dog...."

"The dog?"

"Yes. The little fox terrier they had. Very fond of it, too. It died, poor thing, the day after Mrs. Oates. Fretted to death. As if Mr. Oates hadn't enough to bear without losing the only other living thing he was fond of...."

"He buried it in the garden?"

"I'll show you...."

They crossed the back lawn and along a path under the apple trees, which were already showing signs of a good crop later. At the bottom of the orchard, a clearing with a cold frame, a compost heap, some rhubarb, smashed plant pots and a broken barrow.

"There.... Here; what's happened?"

The earth had been disturbed some time in the past in a short oblong about the size of a small dog's grave.

"There was a mound here. It's gone. I remember watching Mr. Oates finish it. Carried the dog down wrapped in a cloth and buried it with the rubber bone and ball it used to play with. Cut me to the quick, he was that upset...."

More sniffing in the handkerchief.

"Is there a spade about?"

"You're surely not going to ..."

"I'd like a spade and then you'd perhaps better go. It won't be pleasant."

Mrs. Burditt knew all about it. There was a tool-shed among the trees. The key was hanging on a nail in the kitchen. "My husband sometimes borrowed his scythe and Mr. Oates used to give him the key to get it."

"What's behind the bushes at the bottom, Mrs. Burditt?"

"A narrow sort of spinney, and then pasture. If you go there, keep your eyes open for the dog. It's a wolfhound and Mr. Snapper, who farms the smallholding, lets it run free, especially at night. There was somebody prowling round there after dark, after his chickens, Mr. Snapper thought. It caught somebody a while ago, but they got away. I'll bet they left with its marks on them."

"Is that a pond in the spinney?"

"The drainage from the septic tanks runs off there. There are two little ponds. I've heard my husband say—he studies the local history—that a long time ago, more than a hundred years, there was a little tannery in the field and the ponds were the tanpits where they put the bark and tanned the leather .... "

"Well ... I'll do my digging now. I may call to see you again. Thank you for your help, Mrs. Burditt."

There was no dog in the grave. Someone had been there before Montacute. All he found was the rubber ball marked by the dog's teeth. But someone had taken the body .... 

Montacute had a headache from annoyance and frustration. Somewhere behind consciousness, the solution was knocking at the door. He pushed back his hat and stood there looking in the empty hole. Then, he pocketed the ball and carried off the spade.

Back at Silvesters' Bank, Mr. de Lacy groaned as he saw Montacute once more crossing the square to his office.

"I wonder if they think I did it...."

"Finloe Oates has disappeared, Mr. de Lacy. They say he's gone abroad. Did he let you know?"

"Certainly not. He couldn't have taken any money with him without our help... or another bank... Treasury Regulations... I'll check that."

Mr. Killgrass confirmed it. Nobody knew about Oates's going abroad. Killgrass almost winked at Montacute. It was fun watching the boss being grilled by the police every half hour.

"Very well. Thanks, sir. I'll probably be back again before long."

The manager smiled a sickly smile. He was sure he'd be back. He felt, somehow, his fate was sealed, his number up. Like a rabbit with a stoat.

"Take a gang of men with spades and grapnels," said Montacute to the huge sergeant on duty, when he got back to the police station. "Dig up the garden at the bungalow and drag the ponds at the back. Make a proper job of it. Finloe Oates has vanished. See if you can find him."

# CHAPTER THREE
# THE DISAPPEARANCE OF
# LYSANDER

"**I**s Mr. Lysander Oates at home?"

In response to the appeal for help from Rodley, Scotland Yard at first sent a constable round to Berkshire Mansions in Victoria, but he hadn't been able to make head or tail of what the woman in charge of the flats had told him. He knew that, according to what the Rodley police had said, Finloe Oates had gone abroad, and here was Mrs. Kewley saying Lysander had done the same.

"They must have both gone together," he told the Chief Inspector.

"Is Mr. Lysander Oates at home?" asked Littlejohn. If both brothers had vanished matters were serious and London looked like having on their hands a second instalment of the Rodley murder case, so it had been put in proper hands.

"I told the other man, no. He left one morning and said he was going abroad. I haven't seen him since."

Mrs. Kewley was a harassed little body, whose daughter, married to a van-driver in Putney, was expecting her first at any time, and she couldn't keep her mind on what she was doing.

"Which flat did Mr. Oates live in?"

"The studio right on top ... ."

"May I see it?"

"Really! Can't you call again. I'm that busy and bothered. The phone might ring any time to say my daughter Lizzie's been took with the pains and I'll have to go to Putney to 'elp. 'You've got to be there, Mother,' she said, 'else ...' "

"I won't keep you above five minutes, Mrs. Kewley, but I must see the place ... ."

"It's been let again. You won't find anythin' there."

"All the same ..."

"Oh, very well. Might as well go up as keep arguin'. This way."

Littlejohn was sorry for the woman. A little pinched thing, gallantly battling for existence with a block of second-rate flats. She wore an elastic stocking for varicose veins and panted heavily as she led the way.

"These stairs is killin' ... ."

Two flights leading to better rooms were carpeted in threadbare Wilton; then the carpet gave out and oilcloth began. It was a shame to toil the woman any higher.

"I'll go myself. Is there anybody in the rooms?"

"No. 'E's out from nine till six. You can take my pass-key."

Littlejohn mounted the rest of the stairs and he could hear Mrs. Kewley puffing her way back. The top-floor landing was of bare varnished boards. Outside the door of Lysander Oates's old flat lay a decent rug to make it look cosier. Mops, brushes and buckets piled together at the far end.

The Inspector turned the key and let himself in. He might just as well have saved his legs. After all, the new tenant would have cleared out all traces of the former occupant and put in his own stuff ... .

They were tolerable quarters. A bedroom, a kitchen, and a nice large living-room. In the latter a skylight had been fitted covering almost half the roof and sloping to within a yard of the floor on one side. You got a view all over Victoria Station and the roofs beyond. To anyone who liked watching trains come in and go out or philosophising over chimney-stacks it was ideal. Littlejohn walked from one room to another, touching nothing, trying to imagine what Lysander Oates was like. The only trace he found of his man was a watercolour over the fireplace in the living-room. A few washes with a brush, but very nicely done for all that. In the bottom left-hand corner the initials L.O.

"The picture over the mantelpiece in the studio-room, Mrs. Kewley. Did Mr. Oates do it?"

Mrs. Kewley was drinking a cup of black tea to sustain her. Her daughter's first accouchement was taking more out of her than any of her own; and she'd had five, with more than her share of subsequent complications.

"Eh?"

"The picture over the fireplace...."

"Oh, yes. He left it. It'd got behind the wardrobe some'ow. Mr. Brodribb, the new tenant, found it. Said he liked it. He's in that line himself, only scene-paintin' for theeayters. Keep it, I sez. No use to me. Though, I regretted it after. Mr. Oates told me at the time it was of the Isle of Man. The late Mr. Kewley came from there, though I never went myself. I'm a shocking sailor. Why, even to Margate...."

"He cleared-up completely before he left?"

"Yes, and we 'ad his room distempered and done up. Hadn't had so much as a coat of paint since before the war and the landlord said..."

"Did Mr. Oates leave any address where you could find him?"

"No. He come over queer towards the end. It all come on of a sudden, like. Went away for a few days' holiday and come home that different you'd hardly of reckernised him. Are you not so well, Mr. Oates? I sez to him. He was quite rude. I wasn't sorry when he went in the end. Is that the telephone?"

"No. We can hear it from here when it goes. Why do you say he was queer?"

"It might have been his work, you know. Might have changed his job, but never told me. Once he did all his work in his room. Did pictures for advertising things and he'd work part of the day and go out the rest to sell what he'd done, I guess. But later, his 'abits changed. He'd sometimes be off at five in a mornin'. Away perhaps a day or two and then back he'd come well after dark. He'd be up in his room at night, jumpy and pacin' the floor and then out early again in the morning. I couldn't make head or tail of it all."

"How long is it since this change came about?"

"I'd say three months ago. February or March ...."

"How long is it since he left you?"

"Two months or thereabouts."

Mrs. Kewley was on her feet clearing away her tea-things, fussing about, looking reproachfully in the direction of the telephone as though the instrument were holding-out on her.

"Did Mr. Oates end by just sleeping here and nothing more? Or did you gather he was working at night as well?"

"No, not workin'. When I used to do his room in the old days, he'd have pictures pinned on boards, half-done. After he started to go funny, I never saw any more work there. He must have got another job of some kind and perhaps he was un'appy about it."

"Did he say where he was going abroad?"

31

"Australia, he 'inted. I asked 'im. He didn't seem so sure, though."

"Did he go in a hurry?"

The questions and her anxiety were bewildering the poor woman. She passed her hand across her forehead and swept back her dishevelled hair.

"What was you sayin'?"

"Did he leave in a hurry?"

"Not exackly. Early one mornin'."

"Did he take all his belongings with him?"

"He seemed to have sold a lot of his stuff. He'd just one big suitcase and one of them big knapsacks you carry on your back."

"A rucksack?"

"Eh? No; I think he walked to the station with his luggage."

"I'm sorry to bother you so much, Mrs. Kewley, but this is very important. You see, Mr. Oates has vanished."

"Surely not! 'Ow could 'e? So nice, too, in his better days."

"And there's nothing at all he left but a picture?"

"Nothin' else worth mentionin' .... "

"What do you mean?"

"There was a letter. Somethin' and nothin', you might say. He went without it. You see, the glass on 'is dressin'-table" got loose and he wedged it so's he could shave in it."

Mrs. Kewley didn't need asking to get it. She crossed to an old painted sideboard with two little drawers on top of it at each end, like the hobs of a fireplace. She rummaged in one which seemed to hold her personal odds and ends and produced, at length, a battered envelope folded in a tight wedge, probably just as she had found it.

"There it is .... It's from a woman called Nellie Forty. I once heard Mr. Oates mention her. A letter come and he said, 'It's from dear old Nellie Forty, bless 'er,' or somethin' like that. He told me she'd once been a family servant and she got married and her husband died and left her comfortable-like, and she kept 'ouse after for Mr. Oates's brother, Finloe, till 'e got married himself. Mr. Lysander was very fond of Nellie."

Littlejohn was reading the letter with one ear cocked and listening to Mrs. Kewley.

32 railway terrace,

Norbury. Sunday.

Dear mister Lysander

It was nice to here from you thank you for rembering my birthday and for the nice pressent you sent along. time flys dosnt it now i'm sevty five. i was turning over some things the other days wen i come acrors the broach you and mister finloe boght me when i married Forty. That some time sinse isnt it— well i hope you are in the pink as you use to say and hears hopping you will soon be round at the above adress to see me agen.

hopping you are well as it leaves me at present

your loving old

Nellie.

"May I keep this?"

"No use to me, sir. You might as well."

"Have many people handled it?"

Mrs. Kewley was annoyed.

"No, they 'aven't. I don't pass on my gentlemen's private affairs to all an' sundry. The postman and me and Mr. Oates would be all. I read it, of course. Wondered at the time if it was important. There's nothin' in it, though."

The telephone bell rang and Mrs. Kewley panted off to attend to it. It was for one of the tenants, and she said he wasn't in. Two floors up and you had your own instrument if you wanted it; beyond that, you used the common one in the hall. The caretaker returned crestfallen.

"I can't think what's happened. She said she'd let me know. She's past 'er time already. I'd better go whether or not and see if she's all right."

"Where did you say Lizzie lives?"

"Putney."

"Stay a bit longer and answer a few more questions and I'll see you off in a cab."

"I can't afford sich luxuries, bless you, sir. Never took a taxi in my life. The old bus is good enough for me."

"I'll pay...."

The woman could hardly believe it.

"You will? What else was you wantin' to ask?"

"First of all, you might just give me your fingerprints, Mrs. Kewley."

"Whatever for?"

"I want some for Mr. Lysander Oates's records."

Littlejohn produced his shiny silver cigarette-case which his wife had given him on their silver-wedding anniversary. Solemnly Mrs. Kewley squeezed the surface with the fingers and thumb of each hand. Littlejohn gently wrapped up the case in his silk handkerchief and gingerly put it in his pocket.

"What did Mr. Oates do in his spare time? Had he any friends or relations he visited?"

The woman pondered.

"His brother somewhere in Surrey...."

"Any more? Just think whilst you're getting your things on. I can wait. In fact, I'll get you a taxi."

Mrs. Kewley started to bustle around. She already had two American leather bags bulging with stuff. What it all was, was the old mystery of what such domestic helpers find to fill their bags to overflowing.…

Littlejohn telephoned to the Victoria cab-rank.

Mrs. Kewley returned wearing a shapeless felt hat and a worn sealskin coat given to her by a tenant many years ago and cherished as her best. Her poor swollen ankles showed below it trussed in shapeless but bright old boots. She was drawing a pair of woollen gloves over her hardworking hands.

"I was just thinkin' what you said. He went on holidays with a friend sometimes. I think 'is name was 'Unt…a schoolmaster, he was, somewhere in the north. A bachelor, I do believe, and fussy in 'is ways. The only other I can think of is Mr. Gamaliel, who keeps the book store round the corner in Risk Street. They used to play chess together. Sometimes, Mr. Gamaliel came round 'ere, but most times Mr. Oates went to him. 'Is shop's in a basement on the right, jest round the corner."

"Has he been lately? I mean, did he go right up to leaving here?"

"I wouldn't know, sir. He might 'ave called on his way 'ome late. Hadn't we better be goin', sir? The taxi's just drawn up."

The telephone rang and Mrs. Kewley rushed out to deal with it.

She was annoyed when she returned.

"The baby's come, an' me not there! It's a little girl, born half an hour after the pains come on. I never heard the likes.… They say it looks like me. That's a comfort, an' no mistake. All me son's children—all boys, too—took after the late Kewley.…"

She started to draw off her gloves and remove her hat.

"Aren't you going? I'm sure Lizzie would want to see you."

"Do you think so? Well, she's 'ad it at home. Always 'ave 'em at 'ome, I told 'er when she married Charlie. In these big 'ospitals they've so many babies about, you never know when you're gettin' your own back. Do you, sir?"

No use going into the pros and cons, so Littlejohn took both the bags and helped her down the front steps to the taxi. He paid the driver....

"I'm sure I'm very much obliged, sir. I never..."

"Good-bye, then, *grandma*, and good luck to you...."

And with that, Mrs. Kewley was whipped from sight along the Buckingham Palace Road.

Littlejohn walked back to the Yard and handed his case to the fingerprint department. Then he filled his pipe and sat down to read the report just to hand by special messenger from the Rodley police.

It was all there. The forged bank documents; the strange behaviour of Finloe Oates after his wife's death; the murder of Fishlock.... Montacute's theory that the most recent occupant of the bungalow hadn't been Finloe Oates at all, but somebody else.

"Whoever it was, seems to have worn gloves all the time and we were unable to discover his identity that way..."

Littlejohn took out another ready-filled pipe and lit it. Both brothers had behaved alike. Carrying on queerly at home; then off abroad. But Finloe had been at home all day and Lysander all night. Suppose Lysander had been filling the role of both ... or Finloe for that matter....

There was another enclosure in the covering envelope; a photograph of a set of fingerprints.

Montacute had hastily scribbled a note in his own hand.

Later.

Dragging operations in the pond behind the house resulted in discovery of body of Finloe Oates. Almost unrecognisable, but identified by false teeth by dentist of deceased and by silver plate in left leg from old fracture operation.

Enclosed fingerprints taken from a spade used by someone to dig up body of dead dog in back garden of Finloe Oates's house. May be of use. Murderer of Fishlock may have been unable to dispose of his body in same way as Oates's because neighbouring farmer had after approx. date of Finloe's death and disposal, loosed a savage dog to keep off intruders at night. "Query: Was intruder murderer of OATES disposing of corpse?"

J. D. Montacute.

Cromwell entered smiling. He'd just won thirty-five bob in a sweepstake and believed his luck had turned.

"Fingerprints just gave me that for you, sir."

It was a picture of the prints from Nellie Forty's letter after the superfluous ones had been eliminated. Littlejohn took out a jeweller's glass, screwed it in his eye and compared Montacute's photograph with those just to hand.

"H'm. Lysander dug up the dog's body," he said to himself.

Cromwell's face fell.

"What?"

"Looks as if Lysander dug up the dog, killed Finloe, and then vanished. Tell you later. Just have those two sets officially checked, will you, and then come back? We've got a whale of a case. Double murder, impersonation, disappearance, forgery, embezzlement.... The whole shooting-match.... "

He asked for the Rodley police.

"Yes, they're Lysander Oates's prints. It looks as if you're right, Montacute.... I got a set from a letter in his old rooms.... No, we haven't laid him by the heels; he's vanished. I'd better come to Rodley to dovetail both ends."

Montacute couldn't hide his excitement. He started a long tale. As far as his end went, it all seemed sewed-up and in order.

"...We've even found out why Lysander stayed at the bungalow impersonating his brother. Finloe was sixty two months ago. He'd a three thousand endowment policy matured on his birthday. We found a circular among the accumulated letters... from the Pentagon Insurance people asking if he wanted to buy an annuity with the proceeds. We got the Pentagon people and it all came out. Lysander stayed on to collect. By gad, he took a big risk, too. The local insurance agent is new, and, as is usual, went to deliver the cheque in person. Lysander received the £3,000 posing as Finloe. Dark glasses; said his eyes were bad. You couldn't blame the insurance man. After all, he received him at the house and signed the receipt in a tolerable imitation of Finloe's hand. He must have paid the cheque in at his own bank. If we get Lysander, we're in the clear.... I'll be seeing you, then...."

"If we get Lysander.... If...Don't be silly!" muttered Littlejohn.

The trails were cold and Lysander Oates had gone, with ten thousand pounds of his brother Finloe's money.

# CHAPTER FOUR
# THE SHADY DEALER

M r. Mortimer gamaliel kept a bookshop in a basement in Risk Street, Pimlico, and, judging from the records about him at Scotland Yard, he lived a sordid, hand-to-mouth existence. There had been a number of county court actions gazetted against him for debt and the reason he had attracted the police arose from the sale of a spurious modern master, which an innocent bookworm had bought for a Cézanne and which the experts had at once declared a fake. Somehow Gamaliel had wriggled out of a criminal charge after refunding the money.

Instead of tumbledown poverty, however, Cromwell found the painters decorating the outside of the bookshop. The railings which assured that you walked properly down the steps to the shop instead of falling in it, were receiving a bright coat of black paint with gilt on the wrought-iron spearheads.

"Things bucking up a bit?" said Cromwell to the painter.

The man poised his brush and turned a sad emaciated face to the sergeant. His cheeks were spotted with the black he was using and he looked to be starting with German measles. His walrus moustache turned up at the corner with pleasure. He was glad of a change from work.

"Yuss. This chap's suddenly come into money by the looks of it. One day in the county court and nearly chucked out of his shop for not payin' the rent. Next, he's poshing the place up. Not that it didn't need it."

"Backed a winner?"

"Don't ask me. I made sure of my money before I started this job. Paid a fiver down and the rest as work progresses. I've not started inside yet. What the 'ell we'll do with all them books while I'm at it, Lord alone knows.... "

"Do you know Mr .... Mr ....?"

It was on the window. "Mortimer Gamaliel, Books," in frayed black letters.

"Mr. Gamaliel...? Yes; I know 'im. I live round the back. He's a bit of a mystery...."

From the window below street level a face was watching them. The painter tried to look as if he didn't know Cromwell and went on with his daubing.

"That's 'im lookin' at us," he said from under his moustache.

The face gave the sergeant quite a turn. It reminded you of a mask, a miniature of those strange carnival getups that parade in Nice in their season. A round, livid face; a snub nose; large mouth; and peering, protruding watery eyes. To crown the lot, a thatch of red hair which might have been a wig. Cromwell hurried down the stone steps and into the shop. The odours of old books, damp paper, foul air and greasy cooking met him at the door.

The place itself consisted of a maze of passages formed by shelves on which were packed, so that you couldn't put a penny between them, thousands of books of all shapes and sizes. A large fire burned in an old-fashioned iron grate at the far end of the cellar. Even then, it wasn't too warm below ground level and the stone floor added no comfort to it, either.

It was evidently a place where you came and browsed without any obligation to buy. There were two or three other strange occupants with their noses deep in old volumes. A man in a heavy overcoat, threadbare, down-at-heel, enjoying a free read and making nervous gestures with his free hand in his scraggy beard; a girl, apparently a student, eagerly searching among some medical books, bobbing her head up and down like a drinking hen as she read the titles; and a man, who looked like a bookie, for some queer reason interesting himself in a volume from a set of Calvin's "Institutes".

The surrounding walls were whitewashed and badly needed another coat. Hanging on these at eye level was a string of pictures, some modern and incomprehensible; others, big and little oils in palette-knife and brush work. Mr. Gamaliel still appeared to be dealing in his fake pictures.

"Seeking anything in particular?"

Mr. Gamaliel had spotted the newcomer and seen him talking with the painter. His poached eyes ran up and down Cromwell, trying to size him up. Fortunately the sergeant looked like a student of theology and the bookseller had a large stock of works on the subject which nobody ever bought. He purchased such volumes by weight as a rule, making sure, at least, of their salvage value.

Cromwell didn't beat about the bush.

"I'm from the police … . "

Mr. Gamaliel's livid cheeks grew more purple.

"No need to question the painter, then. What do you want?"

"You were a friend of Mr. Lysander Oates, I believe."

The bookseller looked relieved. His colour improved and his loose, thick-lipped mouth opened in an oily smile. It wasn't a pleasant sight. The cat spotting the mouse! The lips parted and the top one curled back revealing a row of uneven stained teeth. He took out a packet of cigarettes, offered one to Cromwell and lit one himself when the sergeant declined. The man in the beard started to cough.

"Come over in the corner.... "

There were two chairs, a shabby saddleback and a wooden armchair beside the fire. A teapot stood on the hob and the remains of a meal littered a plain table nearby.

"Sit down.... "

Cromwell could see a crude bedroom through a door ajar on one side of the cellar. Mr. Gamaliel seemed to lead a troglodyte existence under Risk Street.

"Where is Mr. Oates, do you know?"

Mortimer Gamaliel emptied the smoke from his mouth in a vicious puff.

"I haven't the least idea. I've not seen him for weeks."

"You were friends, I believe?"

"We played chess together. What is all this about?"

The bookseller's voice was deep and wheezy as though it came from a long way down with great difficulty. He kept coughing loosely as the smoke caught him.

"Mr. Oates has disappeared. We're anxious to find him. I might say there seems to be foul play connected with the affair."

"Well, I've nothing to do with it. We were a couple of rather lonely bachelors living on our own. He came here sometimes for books and we struck up an acquaintance. Then we started playing chess.... "

"When did you last see him?"

"Almost three months ago. He suddenly stopped coming. We were half-way through a game, too, and I thought it strange."

Mr. Gamaliel's eyes were never still. Looking round the shop, unpleasantly watching the girl at the medical section, staring straight at Cromwell trying to fathom his thoughts. The sergeant got the queer feeling that the eyes might be made of glass. They took everything in, but he turned his head instead of rolling them in their sockets, almost like a ventriloquist's dummy.

"So, you don't know what happened to him?"

"Why should I? I wasn't his keeper."

"Did you know anything about him other than he played chess?"

"Not much. He was a commercial artist...."

"Anything else? Were any of those done by him?"

Cromwell turned and waved a hand in the direction of the picture gallery on the walls. As he cast his eyes back on Gamaliel, he found he'd caught the bookseller on a sore spot. The colour of the cheeks had changed almost to black by the light of the fire. The podgy hands with their stumpy fingers and flabby palms were gripping the arms of the chair convulsively.

"Certainly not! Those are worth more than anything Oates ever did."

"I'm sorry. Do you collect pictures...?"

Mr. Gamaliel's glazed eyes fixed themselves on Cromwell's, still trying to fathom what he was getting at.

"No, I don't. I frequently buy collections of books from large houses and I'm interested also in pictures, if they're any good. I get them when I buy the books and deal in them a little. Are you satisfied?"

He relaxed again and the heavy cheeks which had grown round and inflated with rage sank and hung like little bags from his jawbones.

The old man at the shelves took out a flat tin box, extracted a fag-end, lit it and started to cough in paroxysms which shook the shop. Mr. Gamaliel looked annoyed.

"Haven't you found what you wanted, Mr. Cuppleditch? You'd better leave it now and come back...."

The man in the beard looked up with hungry eyes.

"Certainly, Mr. Gamaliel, certainly. No offence, I'm sure...." And with that he bolted, his old coat billowing behind him.

The painter presented himself and asked for some hot water for his mid-morning tea.

"What again!! Take some from the kettle...."

Something had rattled Mr. Gamaliel. Something to do with the pictures. He was definitely uncomfortable. But the walrus of a painter was quite unperturbed. He poured some of the boiling liquid in his can into which he had previously emptied a screw of paper containing his tea and sugar.

"Any milk, sir?"

"No.... It's not come yet."

As if knowing what the conversation was about, a large tomcat emerged from under some shelves and flung itself on Mr. Gamaliel's lap. He stroked its sleek black fur fondly. He had a weakness for cats.

The painter was disposed to chat.

"By the way, that picture..."

He pointed at a beautiful street scene with his can.

"That...what you may call it?...that Yew-tree-lo...You know the one? I dessay I could get you a sale for that. I know a bloke who collects..."

"Nobody said it was an Utrillo. It might be a copy, but it's not a genuine..."

"But you said..."

"I didn't say anything.... And now take your tea and drink it outside. I'm busy and it's private...."

"Oh, all right. Keep your shirt on. Only tryin' to 'elp. You did say it was a Yew-tree-lo..."

He shrugged his shoulders and shuffled off with his tea. "Stupid fool!"

Gamaliel was furious again. The girl had found the book and wanted to buy it. The bookseller could hardly be civil for temper and took the money without a word of thanks.

"That one of Oates's efforts?"

Cromwell said it half in a joke, but Mr. Gamaliel didn't think it funny. He rose and towered over Cromwell.

"Look here. I've had quite enough of this. Leave my pictures out of it. That's not what you came for, is it? Or, am I wrong? Are you snooping...?"

So, that was it! It looked as if Oates had been in the fake masterpiece racket. No wonder Gamaliel looked uncomfortable and jumpy. Perhaps he knew more of Lysander's disappearance than he pretended.

"I'm not concerned with the pictures, but if Oates was connected with them, they interest me. I'm after Lysander Oates, and that's all for the present. Have you any idea where he might be?"

"I've told you. I don't know a thing."

"Did you notice anything peculiar about him before he left?"

"How peculiar...? What do you mean?"

"Did he seem preoccupied? Had his habits changed? Did he talk about anything? Did he seem short or flush with money? That sort of thing...."

Mr. Gamaliel's dead eyes gave no flicker of response. "I didn't notice anything about his behaviour. He mentioned his sister-in-law having died. Seemed fond of her and a bit upset.... His habits were the same. I tell you, I only saw him one or two evenings a week. We went to the theatre once or twice and had dinner out. He didn't seem very different from before. He always had enough money for his needs. I didn't notice him throwing it about any more than usual.... I can't say much about his talk. He wasn't one for talking a lot.... Sociable, but not a big talker...."

To Cromwell, it felt like being in prison; in another world. Not another soul in sight; the distant steps of passers-by in the street, very far away; not a sound except the fire falling now and then, the cat purring and Gamaliel's voice, deep and bubbling bronchially.... And those dead eyes and the malevolent look of the bookseller. His wits felt dim, too. The airless atmosphere of the cellar, the stuffy, hot tobacco-impregnated air, damp, musty books.... Cromwell felt like falling asleep. And then Mr. Gamaliel would...He shook himself.

"Did Lysander Oates ever lend you money, Mr. Gamaliel...?"

The fat man looked as if he couldn't believe his ears. He levered himself to his feet again and stood rocking with rage on his heels.

"Really, sir! My private affairs have nothing to do with you! I protest...I shall complain.... "

"All right, all right. Don't have a fit, sir. I was only..."

"You were only insinuating that I had something to do with Mr. Lysander Oates's disappearance. Let me tell you, sir, I had not! Why should I want him out of the way? As for money...well...he borrowed from me some time ago and just before he went he paid what he owed. Almost a hundred pounds. I am using it now to have my premises improved. Now, are you satisfied?"

Cromwell said he was, but he lied. He remembered the succession of county court judgments against Mr. Gamaliel for debt and wondered where in the world he could raise ten, not to mention a hundred pounds to lend anyone.

There was something fishy about it all. Oates was connected with the fake picture racket in all probability and Gamaliel had taken money from him, too....

"I have to go out...I have a sale to attend. I can't waste any more time with you. So, if you will oblige..."

How did Gamaliel make his money? Selling odd books for a few coppers a time, poked away all day in a cellar, hawking faked pictures, being sued for debts he couldn't pay....

"Do you hear me?"

"Yes. I must be going. Did you know Lysander Oates's brother, Finloe? Did he ever mention him?"

"No...I didn't even know he had..."

"Come, come. You mentioned his sister-in-law. Surely he needed a brother for that!"

"I was just going to say, if you'll allow me to go on, I didn't even know he had a brother till he said his brother's wife was dead...."

"He hasn't a brother any more.... Finloe Oates is dead. He was murdered...."

"So that's what you're after? Why didn't you say so at first? I suppose you think I did it...Or, at least, one would assume you did, the way you've been questioning me. I never saw Finloe Oates; never wanted to see him. For that matter, I wish I'd never seen Lysander, either...."

The bookseller was in a rage again. Strange, whenever you got him on a raw spot, he flew off the handle. Cromwell wondered what was stinging him now.

"Why? I thought Lysander Oates was a good friend of yours. You said so. Did he nearly land you in gaol by his bad faking of pictures, or something, and did you hate him for that?"

The eyes flickered but otherwise still showed no sign of life. But Mr. Gamaliel was again swollen like an angry frog.

"Say that before witnesses; say it before witnesses, I say, if you dare. I'll have you broken for that.... I ..."

"Now, now. You know you just missed trouble with your pictures, Mr. Gamaliel. We know all about it.... "

"That's over and done with. It was a mistake and you know it. I willingly repaid the money and the case was dropped. It had to be. I acted strictly bona fide...."

"All right. I'm not saying you didn't. But you seem to hate Lysander Oates for something, Mr. Gamaliel."

"Nothing of the kind. I only said I was sick of all this inquisition about him. Why should I be pestered? Now, go away and leave me in peace. My heart isn't good and this sort of thing upsets me."

"I'm sorry. But we must find Oates, you know. We can't leave a stone unturned. We want to question him about his brother's death...."

"Surely, you don't suspect...?"

"I said we wanted to question him. Do you know where he might have gone?"

"I don't know and I don't want to know. And now, good-day. I must be going myself."

"Just one more question, sir. Had Oates any other friends in the neighbourhood; someone who knows a little more about him than you are prepared to say...?"

"What the hell do you mean by that?"

Gamaliel, who had been putting on his raincoat in a frantic pantomime of hurrying off, turned, his movements cramped by the fact that he had both sleeves half-on. His paunch protruded hideously from between the two edges of the garment.

"You haven't been very helpful, you know. Lysander Oates spent a lot of time with you; yet you say you never talked, you know little or nothing about him, and have no further interest in him. He also, I believe, indulged in a little forging, or faking of modern masters; yet you say you know nothing of his financial affairs.... "

Gamaliel struggled with his raincoat. He had thoroughly entangled himself in the sleeves and folds of it and this added to his fury. Finally, with a rending sound, the seam gave way and left him with two parts dangling from his shoulders. Cromwell reached out a hand and sorted him out.

Mortimer Gamaliel sat down and put his head between his hands. Then, slowly, he raised his face and his dull eyes fixed themselves on Cromwell's face.

"You want to pin this on me, don't you? You want to bully me into confessing I killed him. Well, you'll have to try again. I'm going straight to my lawyer...."

"I thought you had a sale to attend...."

Outside, the painter was busy on the railings again. Up and down, up and down. He kept casting his eyes in the direction of the two men silhouetted by the flames of the fire at the far end of the cellar. He watched what he thought was Cromwell struggling with Gamaliel, saw the bookseller raise his hands to heaven as he cursed the detective, saw him thrust his face close to that of Cromwell. And then the painter seemed to make up his mind. He carefully placed his brush in his paint-can, wiped his hands on his trousers, and descended to the cellar. Gamaliel was shaking his fist in Cromwell's face and threatening to have the law on him.

"You'd better be careful," said the painter to Cromwell, as though he were calmly passing the time of day. "That fellah's got a loaded revolver in his pocket. I see him looking at it to see it was all right this mornin'. I see it all through the winder, like...."

Quickly, Cromwell's long arms shot out. He seized Gamaliel in a firm embrace with one arm and with his free hand sought the bookseller's pockets.

"'Ere, 'ere, 'ere," said the painter and with measured tread approached the struggling men, grasped Gamaliel's jacket by the collar and drew it half-way down his back, locking his arms at the biceps. Then he sought one pocket with the familiarity of experience and tugged forth a large, old-fashioned revolver. Cromwell released the bookseller and took the weapon from the workman before he realised that it had gone.

"'Ere, 'ere...."

"Police."

"I thought so.... Good job I got paid in advance. Expect he's in for a stretch now."

Gamaliel had flung himself exhausted in his armchair. He'd had an awful morning and didn't feel well.

"I haven't done any harm.... "

"What have you got this for? People don't go about with loaded revolvers if they don't mean harm."

"That they don't," said the painter. "I thought that when I see 'im with it...."

Mr. Gamaliel raised a livid face.

"You get out! Go and get on with your painting."

The painter patiently shrugged his shoulders.

"No business o' mine, except I want pay in advance for my work...."

"Clear out...."

"Well, Mr. Gamaliel; I'm waiting for what you've got to say. What's this gun for?"

"My own protection.... I'm afraid. I'm in terror for my life."

"You'll have to do better than that, sir, if I'm not to take you along with me for illegally carrying arms."

"It's not illegal. I've got a permit. I carry large sums after sales sometimes. It's true. I'm afraid of Lysander Oates. He said he'd kill me.... He's out to get me, I know he is."

The bookseller was almost on his knees begging to be believed.

"Why should he want to kill you?"

Cromwell couldn't keep the contempt from his voice. The fat man was beside himself with cowardly fear. His words wouldn't flow. He opened his mouth but nothing came.

Cromwell bent, seized him by the lapels of his coat and shook him.

"What were you blackmailing him about?"

"I wasn't...I didn't.... "

"Come on; let's have it."

"I didn't blackmail him. He owed me money. I asked him for it. He said he'd see I got it and then he never came near for weeks. I went to inquire at his rooms. His landlady told me he never showed up till late at night and went off good and early in the morning. I got up early myself one day, anxious to catch him and get my money. Then I got curious what he was doing so mysteriously and I followed him. He booked a ticket to Netherby. I was just behind him, next but one in the workmen's queue at the ticket office, with a man between him and me. I gave it up there. Two nights later he came with the money. I just casually asked if he'd been to his brother's for it.... My God!..."

Gamaliel was shuddering at the thought of it. He took a bottle from the shelf over the fireplace and drank from it. The air grew heavy with brandy fumes.

"Well?"

"He went mad.... Tried to choke me. 'I'll kill you for this,' he said. 'You've followed me. What do you know?' I said, 'Nothing; I only happened to be on the station at the booking office...!' What *could* I say? Luckily for me, the policeman on the beat here tries the door about eleven each night and just then he called and found it loose. He put his head in. I made an excuse to get him to stay. I said I had a book which would interest him about the police. Oates cleared off and so did I as the officer left. I stayed in an hotel near St. James's that night. I was terrified.... Next day I kept away. Then, I rang up Oates's landlady. She said he'd gone abroad. With that I came back, but I got a revolver.... A friend of mine lent it me...."

"I guess you were blackmailing him about something, though..."

But Mr. Gamaliel wasn't listening. Overcome by fear and emotion he had collapsed.

# Chapter Five
# Branch Bank in Pimlico

The Home Counties Bank branch in Pimlico hadn't been open very long and the young, alert manager greeted Littlejohn eagerly. He thought he'd called to open an account. His smile assumed an air of bitter resignation when he heard the Inspector had called on police business.

"We've only been open three years and naturally we get a lot of ragtag and bobtail until we get used to the locality. Is it about another dud cheque?"

"Not exactly. I understand that Lysander Oates banks with you, sir.... "

The manager was a bright young fellow of about forty with a fresh complexion, blue eyes and a small moustache. The eyes lit up. Here was something big! He told his second in command, a stocky youth with a heavy handlebar moustache, that he wasn't to be disturbed and led Littlejohn into his private room, the furniture and light green carpet of which had not yet lost their bloom of newness.

"I'm glad you've called. It seems Mr. Oates has disappeared. The police and Silvesters' Bank at Rodley have been interested in him, too. What can I do to help...?"

A callow junior tapped on the door and entered with two cups of tea.

"First of all, sir, what kind of an account did he keep?"

The young manager looked cautiously over the rim of his teacup.

"I know your dealings with customers are very secret, but this is important. Finloe Oates, Lysander's brother, has been murdered and Lysander has vanished. There's a question of the spiriting away of Finloe's funds—quite a small fortune—and we want to know if Lysander had any hand in it."

The manager, Mr. Donald Macgreggor, carefully laid his empty cup in his saucer. He came from a line of cautious Scots and you could see his mind working as he carefully pondered what was the right thing to do.

"Yes," he said quickly, at last. "Yes; I think he did have a hand in it. But let this be understood, sir, if you please: anything I tell you will be kept strictly confidential by you, personally, and if you want to make it public, you'll give me the proper legal protection of the courts...."

A bright young chap, thought Littlejohn. He'll go far. He was right... but that doesn't concern us here.

"I agree, sir. First, did Lysander Oates pay in to his credit, at intervals, three drafts drawn by Silvesters' Bank on their London office?"

"Yes, he did. They were payable to his brother. I remember them well. Naturally, I asked him what it was all about. We need to be careful.... The drafts were payable to Finloe Oates, endorsed by him, and thus, technically, payable to bearer, which enabled us to credit them to Lysander's account. He was a decent client, you know. Perfectly straight and above board, with a good balance of his own always here. We took the drafts for his credit."

"What was the amount in all, sir?"

"Just a minute...."

The manager went to get the ledger himself.

"Let me see…. Seven thousand in all… paid in in three instalments. Then, there was another credit for three thousand pounds later. That was paid in by post…."

"Ten thousand in all…."

"Yes; and all withdrawn in one pound notes, in four batches."

"Didn't he leave any balance?"

"Three pounds…."

Mr. Macgreggor's face drooped. At one time it had looked like being a very nice account. Now…

"Since then, there haven't been any transactions in the account."

"Did he explain what it was all about?"

"Yes. Naturally, when he called for three thousand in cash, O'Brien, the cashier, referred to me. Mr. Oates said he was buying property and wanted cash for the settlements. He got quite huffy when I suggested a bank draft. He said that at present, the economic situation was such that the pound wouldn't be worth much if prices kept rising, so he was putting his resources in land and buildings. During the next week he had two more withdrawals which cleaned him out except for a pound or two."

"I'm sorry to say that it was his brother's money he was handling. The drafts were from sales of securities; the cheque for three thousand pounds from proceeds of a policy on Finloe's life…."

"Good Lord! You don't mean he killed his brother! What about the endorsements on the drafts and the cheque for three thousand pounds…?"

Poor Macgreggor knew the answer before it came. He turned as pale as death.

"Forged, I'm sorry to say."

"By Lysander?"

"Yes, or so it seems."

"But... Well, he was always such a straight chap. I know one has to be cautious about endorsements, but I never thought of him as a rogue."

"Neither did any of us. He seems to have gone completely off his head."

"But whatever am I going to do? The bank is liable for the forgeries.... We'll have to make it all good."

"Silvesters' are faced with the same problem. The point now is for us to find whoever has the money. They can't have spent it all. If we can recover it, well and good. So, you'll help us all you can?"

"Of course.... I'll have to report this, though. I'll get sacked.... "

"Not if I can help it. Older and more experienced men than you have been taken in here, sir. We'll do what we can."

Macgreggor was so distressed he could hardly bring his thoughts back to the problem in hand.

"I'd better go up to Head Office and make a clean breast of it right away.... "

"You say it was taken in pound notes?"

"Yes.... "

"Clean or soiled?"

"Soiled. We hadn't all those clean available. He took twenty soiled bundles of five hundred, all told. I paid him myself.... I must be a fool!"

"Rubbish! Everybody seems to have thought well of Oates. How long has he been out of touch with you? I mean, when did he make his last withdrawal?"

The manager looked wanly at the ledger.

"April 27th saw the last withdrawal, sir."

"Don't take it so badly. You're not alone in this, you know. There's murder involved and besides, the drafts you took for credit had been issued by the bank in Rodley against forged cheques...."

Mr. Macgreggor raised his eyes to heaven.

"What a hell of a mess.... And just as I was getting along nicely in my job. Anything else you want to know?"

"Do you know a man named Gamaliel?"

"The bookseller, you mean? Yes. I hope he's not another, because I could understand it if he went the wrong way."

"Why?"

"Fishy. Decidedly fishy."

"In what way?"

"He nearly got gaol for a phoney picture deal. Passed a fake off as a modern master. He got a smart lawyer and they brought it off as a mistake. But he was lucky."

"He keeps an account here?"

"Yes."

The manager started to look cautious again.

"A good one?"

"On and off. He was in very low water at one time. Then he got friendly with Lysander Oates. In fact, Oates introduced him here. I guess his previous bankers turned him out. I'd a bit of trouble with him at the start. Drawing cheques when he wasn't in funds."

"And then?"

"He borrowed from Oates, or I assumed he did."

"Tell me about it."

"Might as well be hanged for a sheep as a lamb. Oates drew out several sums of money and, later, Gamaliel paid part of it back in his own account. I recognised the notes. Looks as if he'd been borrowing."

"Or something else."

"What do you mean?"

"Blackmail, perhaps. Or, more likely still, Oates was in the phoney modern masters racket. He painted them and Gamaliel sold them and they shared the spoils. Oates must have insisted on doing the share-out himself."

"Wait a minute; perhaps the ledger..."

Macgreggor turned over the pages and then went in the office for the previous ledger.

"Yes. There's a cheque paid in to Oates's credit for three hundred. Then, two days later, Gamaliel got a hundred from Oates and paid it to his own credit. Six months later, there's a similar set of deals.... Looks as if you're right, Inspector."

"Now, can you tell me, in confidence, if Gamaliel has paid in any large sums lately...sums which might have been parts of Finloe Oates's money?"

"No. Last April he drew three hundred from somewhere in cash and paid it in. Since then, he's been drawing out. This lot won't last much longer now that Lysander's gone."

"Had you any reason for thinking Lysander Oates was going abroad, sir?"

"Bolting? I haven't a clue."

"He didn't ask you to get permission for him to move funds abroad or even obtain an allocation of currency for foreign travel?"

"No. Let's confirm that with O'Brien."

Mr. Macgreggor went to the door and called his subordinate, who arrived with great speed and glanced closely at his chief. It was evident he'd noticed how disturbed the manager looked and he began to be distressed himself, for he was fond of Macgreggor.

"Anything wrong?"

"No, Len. This is Inspector Littlejohn from Scotland Yard. He's called about Lysander Oates, who seems to have vanished into thin air, taking with him ten thousand pounds of his brother's money which he paid to credit on forged endorsements...."

"Crikey! I beg pardon... dear me!"

"We're trying to lay him by the heels as quickly as possible, Mr. O'Brien, and recover the funds. Mr. Macgreggor wants to ask you if you dealt with Oates about some foreign currency before he left."

"You mean, he bolted abroad? No; he didn't come to us for funds."

"Thanks. We won't keep you, Len...."

"Cheer up, Mr. Macgreggor. Things'll turn out all right...."

"I hope so, Len...."

O'Brien gave his manager a comforting, affectionate pat on the shoulder and left them.

"I think that's all for the time being, sir. It looks as if Mr. Lysander Oates won't be doing much banking with you again. He's hardly likely to call to draw his balance now."

"No; nor to claim his Will, as far as I can see...."

"His Will?"

"Yes; we hold a sealed envelope here in safe custody for him. It's marked 'Will' on the cover."

"That would be interesting. I don't suppose I could borrow it?"

Littlejohn smiled a wry smile; Macgreggor smiled back.

"Hardly. Our authority doesn't extend to that, even for the police. Mind you, I think in his hurry he forgot all about his Will and it's likely to stay here till it rots away. But that doesn't make much difference; I can't help you there."

"What had I better do about it, then? It's vital that we see that Will. It may give us a valuable clue."

"I can only suggest one thing; there's the name of a solicitor on the outside of the envelope, I'm sure. It looks as if it was done in a lawyer's office, sealed there and brought straight here. Just a minute, I'll get it up."

Macgreggor hurried out, leaving Littlejohn alone in the room. If only for the young banker's sake, he felt he must do something about tracking down Lysander Oates and recovering as much of the stolen funds as possible. He felt he would like to write a letter to the Home Counties head office and tell them how useful their Pimlico manager had been and to suspend judgment until later. But they didn't need a Scotland Yard Inspector to tell them that; they were wise enough to know it without. Littlejohn was looking at a framed photograph on the mantelpiece when Macgreggor returned.

"My wife and two boys," he said, indicating a pleasant smiling woman with a boy of about five on one side and a three-year-old on the other. "I'm worried, Inspector...."

"Keep your chin up. We'll soon have whoever did it."

"The package, sir. Here it is."

A blue, foolscap envelope, endorsed "Lysander Oates. WILL." On the flap of the cover: "Mathieson, Curtiss, Leader and Mathieson, Gedge Court, S.W.1."

"They're sure to have a copy, sir. I'd call there, if I were you. Quite decent people. Mention my name if you like."

"Thanks, Mr. Macgreggor. You've been very helpful and remember, if I can be of any help, let me know at once. I'm even prepared to call on your General Manager and put your case in its proper perspective, if you need me! It's one big mistake, not just an isolated episode at the Home Counties Bank, Pimlico, and when the whole is solved, you'll be all right, I'm sure...."

Macgreggor's voice was quite husky when he spoke again.

"Awfully decent of you. I'll not fail to let you know if I need your help. Meanwhile, anything more I can do?"

"Just one thing. Have you any specimens of Lysander Oates's writing, sir. And, come to think of it, of Gamaliel's as well. This is a forgery case, you see, and if we can get samples of the writing of all concerned ... Not just signatures, I mean, but a fair and varied sample."

"I think I can help. Gamaliel travels about a bit and writes now and then for money to be sent by post. And we'll have the letters Mr. Oates sent with the drafts he paid in. Excuse me."

The manager went off again and returned after a minute or two with two sheets of paper; one bearing a sample of Oates's hand and the other of Gamaliel's. The first was done in a neat, educated hand, almost that of a scholar whose studies have turned his style to Greek lettering. Gamaliel's was aslant and sprawling, as if he'd written it with his head resting on his left arm and driven the pen along without much care about how or what he was writing.

"Gamaliel's a shocking fist, hasn't he?"

"Dreadful ... ."

Littlejohn pocketed the specimens and the banker saw him to the door.

"Good-bye and thanks. And don't forget, Mr. Macgreggor. If you need me ..."

"I won't forget. If I can do anything, let me know ... . "

Gedge Court was one of those amazing little jewels tucked away in the heart of Pimlico among tall, ugly houses. A passage and then a courtyard surrounded by plane trees, a garden in the centre, and a fishpond and sundial to round it all off. Golden carp were lying idly in the water. They looked hundreds of years old and, together with Gedge Court, had survived bombs, V.1s and V.2s and the rest of Nazi devilry throughout the war. Littlejohn found the plate of the firm of lawyers who had been there in practice as family solicitors since the days when Pimlico with its wealth kept a multitude of prosperous partners busy every day.

There wasn't a single remaining Mathieson, Curtiss, Leader or other Mathieson in the firm. Instead, Mr. Wilmott Hazlett bore on his narrow, humped shoulders the burden of the lot. He looked busy when the inky junior ushered Littlejohn in the lawyer's office. Japanned boxes, filing cabinets and stacks of old documents littered the place. The table, which was large enough to hold a whole board of directors, was stacked high with parchments and conveyances of all kinds; they even hung over the edges like laundry out to dry. One wall was full of law books and in odd patches on the dirty walls hung framed and flyblown pictures of dead and gone lawyers and painted caricatures of men in legal wigs and gowns. Frowning down on the lot, a lithograph of Blackstone. In the midst of all this mess sat Mr. Hazlett, a small space cleared before him to enable him to manipulate a pen or fumble with a document. A few chairs, leaking horsehair, scattered here and there, reminded you that the many partners, gone, but not forgotten on the doorplate and stationery, must surely have risen from them for the last time æons ago, and since then they had not been sat upon....

"Good morning.... Whatissit?"

Mr. Hazlett was small, slightly humpbacked from bending myopically over deeds and briefs, and he had the complexion of a corpse. His bony body looked like a skeleton clad in black, his stiff white hair reared from his pate like a shaving brush, and he wore white spats.

"Whatissit?"

Like the hiss of a cobra.

But Mr. Hazlett wasn't all that bad. Although nearly sixty, he still liked a game of tennis; the rattle of his bones on such occasions must have been terrifying. He was unmarried and the favourite uncle of a large number of pretty nieces. He also wrote theatrical criticisms under another name for a prominent daily and he had broadcast under his pseudonym in a Brains Trust and put the rest of his team to shame by his erudition.

Littlejohn told the lawyer why he had called.

"Oh ...."

It was a cry of wonder and relish.

"He! So Lysander's vanished, has he? I knew that one day he'd do something very adventurous. Did you ever meet him? No? Pity. Would have made a good sea captain. Short, stocky, good chin and blue eyes that seemed to be scanning far horizons. Do I sound melodramatic? Forgive me, Inspector. I mustn't waste your time."

"You're not, sir. Please go on .... "

Lysander Oates was taking shape at last.

"Had a brother. Seen from behind, they were as like as two peas in a pod. Front view, however, much better in Lysander. I knew them in the old days. Did their bits of legal work. Finloe was mean-faced. Eyes too close set .... What do you want?"

"Did you make a Will for Lysander, sir?"

"I drew one up, yes. Why?"

"The original's in the Home Counties Bank and, therefore, inaccessible. I'd like to know how the Will runs. It may prove a valuable help in tracing Mr. Lysander."

"In what way?"

"We might have a word with any beneficiaries, sir. Those to whom he left his money may have been close to him, you know."

"H'm. Ahem. Bit irregular. All the same, I'm an officer of the Court and I must help all I can. I'll tell you the contents, although you can't see the copy. That would be going too far. The contents run roughly like this...."

Mr. Hazlett reeled them off from his marvellous storehouse of memories. It had been his undoing as a broadcaster, because, after all, he'd been supposed to be a member of a team, but had proved a talking encyclopædia, which made his fellow-brains-trusters very peevish.

"...First of all, five hundred pounds to his old friend, Nellie Forty. Know who she is?"

"Yes; I heard all about her yesterday. An old family servant."

"That's right. Nellie was seventy-five last October and married Forty in 1914. She...But there, this is getting us nowhere.... Next: One hundred pounds to a certain Mortimer Gamaliel, bookseller, of Risk Street, Pimlico.... To enable him to buy himself a Chinese set of chessmen in ivory in memory of their games of chess together. In May, 1948, Gamaliel became involved in a risky business of selling fake masters, Cezanne and Van Gogh, and narrowly escaped prison.... But that's irrelevant...."

A young lady entered in response to a hidden bell.

"Bring in the sherry, please, Miss Minter. You must have a taste of my sherry, Inspector. Excellent. Stop me if I start to talk wines. I'm a terrible old gasbag.... Where were we? Next, five hundred pounds to my lifelong friend, Theodore Hunt, schoolmaster and bachelor of science, of Bishop's Walton, Yorkshire. They were contemporaries at school. I remember Oates telling me when we drew up the Will, that they often spent holidays together. Hunt is not only a bachelor of science, but also a bachelor in the matrimonial sense, shall we say. He lives with an epileptic sister who has, I believe, been a great trouble to him. It has prevented him from marrying and kept him out of the world in a quiet school ... a preparatory institution. He not only teaches and claims a good share of scholarships for his boys, but writes sermons for illiterate clergy and essays for the loftier reviews. He has also made several unsuccessful attempts at novel writing. I gather his masterpieces were too erudite for the vulgar reader. But there I go again. I would see Mr. Hunt, if I were you. No need to fear his sister. She is afflicted by what is called *petit mal,* not *grand mal.* Which means she does not suffer from the more dreadful forms of fits, but from black-outs during which times she is unaware of what she is doing and when she recovers, doesn't know she's had 'em. A terrible tie for Hunt. And again ..."

Here Mr. Hazlett lowered his voice and had the air of imparting a mysterious secret to Littlejohn.

"And again ... such blackouts are sometimes the features of homicidal mania! Crimes are committed, crimes of the most horrible, crafty and violent kind ... all with the perpetrator unaware of what he or she is doing .... Terrible!"

Mr. Hazlett pulled himself together and his eyes sparkled again. There was an excited, malevolent look in them, like that of a vindictive old gossip.

"Lastly: Residue ... not to his brother as you'd expect, but to his sister-in-law, Marion Mankelow Oates; failing her, to his brother, and failing the pair of them, to endow a bed in the Pimlico Hospital in memory of Marion Mankelow Oates. And as he said that, Lysander whimsically remarked, that he wished she'd taken the Oates from him, instead of from Finloe .... "

He cackled and then grew solemn.

"Lysander Oates loved his brother's wife, you see. They both wanted her but that narrow-eyed Finloe got her. No accounting for women's tastes, is there? Never married myself. I'm scared to death of women!"

They sipped their sherry and Littlejohn praised the wine.

"Knew you'd like it. Don't let me get talking about it or you'll be here all day. If I've told you all you need, you'd better go. I've work to do and with a kindred spirit at my elbow, I'll never finish."

He caught Littlejohn glancing down into the courtyard from the tall, narrow window of the room.

"Nice spot, isn't it? Wonder to me how it missed the bombing. Narrow escape once or twice. I remember one night when I was fire-watching I thought we'd have boiled-fish from the pond there next morning. Incendiaries.... Better go. I can't stop my flow of reminiscences if there's anybody here to listen. Good day, Inspector. I'll know all about you now whenever I read of your cases in the newspapers. You're fifty, live in Hampstead, near the Heath, married, no children, born near the Lakes, in Lancashire, educated local grammar school and Manchester Police Force, very highly thought of by the Commissioner at Scotland Yard and, I may say in confidence, by the Home Secretary. Likely to go far.... "

"Really...."

"Ever read Sherlock Holmes?"

"Yes, sir...."

"So do I. But I didn't deduce all that. I was interested in your handling of the Blow case at Nesbury and looked you up. I have my ways of finding out.... "

"So I gather...."

"And now, be off. I'm taking my niece to the Haymarket later to a first night and I've no time to waste on trifles. Good day, Inspector."

And before Littlejohn was half-way down the stairs, Mr. Hazlett was totally immersed in trying to prevent a butcher of Devonshire from suing a bishop for slander.

# Chapter Six
# The Barmaid at the
# Naked Man

The Rodley police were obviously relieved when Littlejohn and Cromwell arrived there to take over the case. Montacute wrung their hands until they both winced.

"I'm glad to see you both. This is a pretty kettle of fish and no mistake. The thing's boiled over properly since I wrote to you. I've just got the post-mortem on Finloe Oates and, believe it or not, the odds are he died a natural death. What do you think of that?"

Although it was a hot day, the private office was dark and cool and all the bluebottles in Rodley seemed to have sought refuge in it. They kept buzzing round and beating themselves against the window-panes. Now and then, Montacute raised a large hand and flailed it round his head uselessly to drive them off.

"You can always tell when there's a body in the mortuary, next door," he said cheerfully.

Across the square you could see the fine town hall set in an avenue of trees and green lawns, with Silvesters' Bank right opposite on an ideal site. Mr. de Lacy was looking through the window wondering when he might receive another attack from the police. He regarded their present quiet as ominous.

"Will the pair of you be staying here, because, if so, I'd better...?"

"I don't think so, sir. This case doesn't seem centralised in Rodley and there's a quick service to London and plenty of trains."

"That's right. And now that's settled, I'll tell you what's happened since I reported to you. As I said, the doctors think Finloe Oates died of a heart attack. His corpse was a pretty mess when they got at it, after being in a sort of old tanpit for months, but they say there didn't seem to be much superficial damage. His heart, however, was in fearful shape and it's as likely as not, he received some shock or other and died. It looks as though, let's say, Lysander and he had a struggle and Finloe's heart gave out. Then, Lysander got wind-up and hid the body."

"Or else, if he knew of Finloe's money, he hid the body, rather than report it, and set about obtaining his brother's little nest-egg for himself. Finloe mustn't have remembered Lysander in his Will, Montacute, so Lysander wouldn't report his brother's death and let the law dispense the legacies.... By the way, did Finloe leave a Will?"

"He made one, but wrote to the bank for it, or rather, Lysander wrote for it. The letter went to the bank asking for it to be posted to Netherby, which it was, before Lysander started liquidating Finloe's fortune. So, what you say is right. Lysander first found out where the money was going, must have seen he didn't inherit, so started to help himself."

"Wasn't there a copy of the Will anywhere? Say in the house, or in some local solicitor's office?"

"We've combed the town. No solicitor in Rodley drew it up. We can't think where to look now."

"I may be able to help. May I use your phone?"

"Whatissit?"

Mr. Hazlett was in his office in Gedge Court when Littlejohn got the call. The Inspector could imagine him, with his shock of shaving-brush hair, fumbling and rooting among the tremendous mass of papers on the large table.

"Oh, hello, Inspector. What are you after again?"

Yes; Mathieson & Co. had been Finloe's solicitors, too. In fact, the lawyers for the Oates brood for generations. Mr. Hazlett hadn't thought to mention it at the time.

"...That will be simpler than Lysander's behest. Quite simple. I have a copy here and we added a codicil about eighteen months ago. Where's the original?"

"That's been withdrawn from the bank, and presumably burned. Whoever occupied the bungalow after Mr. Finloe's death seems to have burned everything, family photographs, too...."

"At first, Finloe left all he had to his wife, with one exception. He added a codicil bequeathing one thousand pounds to a certain Florence Judson of Netherby. After his wife's death, he almost at once added another codicil, pending his call to check a new draft I was preparing. This time he left ALL to sweet Florence, whoever she may be."

"Is that all, sir?"

"I hope so...I hope so...."

Florence, or rather Florrie Judson! Montacute almost fainted! He took a drink of water from a carafe on the table and then announced that Florrie was the barmaid at the Naked Man, the village inn at Netherby.

"We'd better have a word with Florrie," said Montacute. "But first, let me tell you something else. It's about the forgeries. You'd left the Yard after the report came through.

From the specimens of Lysander Oates's writing you got, they say that the three drafts on London and the insurance cheque were endorsed, they think, by Lysander."

"What did they say about the specimen of Gamaliel's writing?"

"Drew a blank. It seems he wasn't in it at all."

"And the letters to the bank, the ones about the sales of securities and the like, and the one asking for the Will? You sent them to the Yard?"

"Yes. They weren't written by Lysander. It just beats me. How many of them were buzzing round Finloe's fortune? There must have been a whole gang of them."

"Certainly Lysander must have had a partner, if there are two lots of handwriting involved. It looks as if Lysander could just manage a rather successful copy of his brother's name, but fought shy of a full letter and had to get somebody more skilled at forgery to do it for him. Now if Gamaliel...But you say he wasn't in it?"

"That's right."

"Funny; damned funny. I'd better make a note of this."

Cromwell, ever on the alert with his little black book, did it for Littlejohn.

Bank drafts: Endorsements forged by Lysander Oates.
Cheque: Also forged by Lysander.
Letters: Written by somebody who wrote Finloe's hand well, but not by Lysander.

"What about the postal receipts the postman said were signed for registered packets?"

"They're finding them. Lord knows how long they'll take."

"Any luck with Lysander yet?" asked Montacute.

"Not a thing. He seems to have disappeared completely. He said he was going abroad, but the ports, airports, shipping offices have been combed without result. The Passport Office says he doesn't hold a current passport in his own name and the banks haven't arranged any currency permits for him. He's somewhere in the country, alive or dead.…"

"Dead! You think…?"

"Well, he had a confederate, judging from the forgeries; so anything might have happened. Shall we see what Florrie Judson has to say?"

Cromwell and Littlejohn strolled into the Naked Man at Netherby and asked for a pint of ale each. No doubt about it, the barmaid who served them was very attractive for those who liked them that way. Tall, well-built, full-bosomed, self-possessed, with painted nails and fair hair, assisted by peroxide. She looked a bit down in the mouth, probably because the papers had, that day, given an account of what they called "The Horror at Shenandoah."

The landlord, a little chap like a jockey and dressed to match, kept a wary eye on the two strangers. He'd been killing a few pigs on the sly in the outbuildings and his conscience pricked him at the sight of anybody who might be from the police or the Ministry of Food.

"Miss Judson?"

The barmaid started as Littlejohn addressed her. It was a long time since anyone had addressed her by her Sunday name. It was either Florrie, Ducks or Lovely. She patted her bright hair waves.

"Yes. What do you want?"

She looked on tenterhooks and evidently expected something or someone to call about recent events.

"Police. May we have a quiet word with you somewhere?"

Mr. Chubleigh, the landlord, almost rushed forward and said "Isn't it me you want?" but stopped himself just in time. His bloodshot eyes rolled up and down the two detectives.

"Go in the office with 'em, Flo. I'll take over."

Not that there was much to take over; the place was deserted. Florrie led them into a small room behind the bar, where a rickety roll-top desk, a stack of papers, some betting dailies and a lot of racing pictures fastened on the walls with drawing-pins, indicated that Mr. Chubleigh was in the habit of retiring to balance his accounts, pick winners and meditate, and asked them to "be seated, please". She reserved a special form of affected speech for callers above the average.

Florrie closed the door, greatly to the annoyance of Mr. Chubleigh, who was anxious to know what it was all about and was hanging round within earshot, breathing on glasses and polishing them with a dirty cloth. She eyed them up and down without speaking.

"I'm sorry to bother you, Miss Judson, but it's about the late Mr. Finloe Oates. You knew him?"

In answer, Florrie began to cry. It started with dry undulations of her unctuous bosom, rippled along her firm white throat, and flowed from her mouth in a long howl. At the same time, large tears like minute glass marbles formed and rolled one after another down her plump cheeks and off the end of her shapely chin. She seemed to be having it all to herself, too, as though nobody were there. Hugging a little sad secret and weeping over it.

"Yes, I knew him," she gulped at length. "He was a friend of mine and very good to me. What I'll do now, I don't know.... "

She hadn't yet reached the handkerchief stage. Her face was wet all over as if she'd just raised it from a washbowl.

"Excuse me.... "

She fished in the pocket of the smart and remarkably becoming scarlet jacket she was wearing over her dark blue silk frock and took out a ridiculously small handkerchief, which she applied dexterously and to good purpose.

"What were you wantin'?"

"Just this, Miss Judson: what were the relations between you and Mr. Oates...?"

Florrie had forgotten her grief. She was just working herself up into a state of passionate indignation.

"Now don't misunderstand me, Miss Judson.... "

"I should think not, indeed! I may be a barmaid, but I'm respectable. And I'd rather stop a barmaid than do what some do I could mention. Not that I haven't had the chance.... "

They didn't know what to say to all this rigmarole. Whatever they replied would probably be wrong. They let her go on.

"Mr. Oates and me was just good friends. Not that we couldn't 'ave been more. He was very fond of me, I'll admit it, and not ashamed of it. But 'let's keep it straight and above board, Finloe,' I told him, and he respected me for it."

"He must have done, because he left you sole heir by his Will."

Instead of lifting her up, the news cast her down. She didn't want to know how much or why; she was just overcome by the idea that somebody thought so much of her. She wept again.

"I didn't want his money. I swear it. Oh, you can have plenty of men of a sort, out for all they can get. But you're lucky when you find somebody who loves and respects you for what you are. He wanted to marry me.... "

She said it with pride, quite forgetting all else, and then realised what she'd said.

"When was that?"

"After the first Mrs. Finloe died. When else? What do you think I am...?"

"He was in love with you before his wife died?"

"Yes. She was an invalid, he said, and nagged and bullied and didn't understand him...."

The old, old story!

"And he fell in love with you and wanted to marry you?"

"He told me I was the only one he'd ever loved, but he didn't propose till his wife died. Look here, what do you take us for? We wasn't all that bad. We just loved one another, that's all, and I'm proud we did. Now he's dead...."

It trailed off like a melodrama.

"And he remembered me in his Will. That's wonderful of him. Though it won't be much. He said he only just managed to make ends meet...."

Littlejohn thought of the ten thousand pounds which had been spirited away and which would come to Florrie if he recovered it. It might come to far worse people than her, but he couldn't tell her any more than she already knew, except...

"I ought to tell you, someone embezzled all Mr. Finloe's money and we're out to find it and who did it. Can you help?"

"What! They stole his money and him hardly cold...?"

She still thought of it as Oates's, not as her own, it seemed.

"The dirty rotters. If I could only lay my hands..."

But she shrugged them helplessly. She didn't know a thing, she said.

"I never went to his 'ouse. It wouldn't have been right and him with a wife there. He asked me to marry him after she died, but we kept it a secret till a respectable time after and I never went up to see the home he said would be mine. It wouldn't 'ave been right to the dead, so soon after...."

"And then, shortly after his wife's burial, Finloe Oates disappeared...went out of circulation. He made no effort to see you, did he?"

"I 'aven't seen him since the end of March."

"Tell me what happened between his wife's death and the last time you saw him."

"We'd been in the habit of meetin' just after dark in the little wood behind his house. Nobody ever saw us, as far as we knew. Nobody talked about us and you may be sure they would 'ave if they'd known. After Mrs. O. died, we met as usual, twice a week till the end of March, when suddenly, Finloe stopped comin'. I didn't know what to think. I went a time or two and still he didn't come to the old place."

"Then what?"

"I made some inquiries, discreet, you know, but nobody'd seen him. All I got to know was from the postman that Finloe 'ad shut 'imself up and wasn't comin' out. I went up to the bungalow after dark two or three times. Then, I plucked up courage and rang the bell, though there was no light showin'. They said he was indoors in the day, but I wouldn't dare go in daylight, with the women on the road always peepin' round the curtains. I'm sure there was nobody in the bungalow when I went. No wonder. 'E was dead...."

She wept bitterly again.

Florrie was an amazingly ingenuous girl. She seemed to think it right to tell the police all her private affairs with Finloe Oates. As though they'd already been husband and wife at the time he vanished.

"Did Finloe Oates ever tell you he was interested in going abroad?"

"No. He'd made his money abroad, but said he never wanted to leave the old country again. He'd be content if he got me."

"You mean, if his wife died…. Did he say he wished she were dead?"

Florrie was up in arms at once. A real burst of maternal pugnacity.

"Don't you DARE! He *never* said such a thing. He said he wished he'd waited till he found me, but never once did he so much as hint…"

"All right, Miss Judson…."

To address her by her Sunday name seemed like pouring oil on troubled waters; it reminded Florrie that she ought to behave appropriately, like a lady.

"After Finloe Oates ceased seeing you, did you ever see him at all…in the distance…any message?"

"Not a thing. He just vanished without a word. I thought he'd tired of me. But it seems he didn't…."

Littlejohn stepped in before there were more tears.

"How did you first meet?"

"Here. He used to come down every night just before supper for a pint of beer. We got friendly. He seemed lonely and in need of a friend…."

There was nothing much more to do at the Naked Man. The landlord bustled up to them as they entered the bar again, eager to know what had been going on. They just bade him good-day.

"They're just buryin' poor Jack Fishlock…. "

There was a chapel opposite the inn, a small place, gaunt and cheerless, with a lot of tumbledown old gravestones in the ground which surrounded it. Fishlock had been declared murdered by person or persons unknown, and now they were putting him to rest. A thin knot of mourners, all stiff and self-conscious in their best black, gathered round a grave under the warty poplars. The widow, supported by two men, was with them. The weather was now sultry with a threat of thunder in the air. A sense of foreboding ….

"Man that is born of woman hath but a short time to live … and is full of misery. He cometh up and is cut down like a flower; he fleeth as it were a shadow …. In the midst of life we are in death …. "

The dry, shrill voice of the thin, starved-looking clergyman in white tie, frock coat and with white whiskers, rang round the centre of the village. Everything grew silent.

" … For now I shall sleep in the dust; and thou shalt seek me in the morning, but I shall not be …."

Finloe Oates might not have been murdered, but Jack Fishlock … well … there was no doubt about his fate. Poor Fishlock, who had called to read the meter at the wrong time.

# CHAPTER SEVEN
# NELLIE FORTY

Railway terrace, Norbury, was, as its name indicated, a row of cottages facing the main line. Half the row was in ruins after a German bomb hit it. The remainder was as neat as a new pin, with little squares of garden, peculiarly cultivated, in front. There was keen rivalry among the tenants in the way of gardening. A greenhouse occupied practically the whole patch which fronted one cottage; another raised vegetables of agricultural-show proportions; a third was set out in neat flower-beds and quaint rustic erections, whilst next door, the man grew roses on every scrap of ground and in as much of the air above the earth as he could conveniently reach. The late Mr. Forty had gone one better and built a tortuous rock-garden of whitewashed clinkers, old drain-pipes and carved paving-stones. Mrs. Forty carried on the good work in spite of failing health, and it was among a lot of nasturtiums sprouting from the tops of drain-pipes full of soil that Littlejohn found her.

"Let me get rid of this lot first and then tell me what you want..." she said, and she indicated a basinful of nasturtium seeds.

"I always raise me own seed. Believe it or not, these seeds come from those as Mr. Forty planted with his own hands when he brought me here years and years ago. It cheers me up to think of 'em still being here...."

A buxom, healthy-looking old lady was Nellie, on the small side, with shrivelled apple cheeks and brown eyes. She wore her white hair in a bun and was dressed in a black bodice and old-fashioned long skirt. She was bad on her feet.

The front door of the cottage was open, and Nellie invited Littlejohn to come inside. It was a two-up and two-down place at the very end of the row. Along the side was a railed enclosure wherein the late Forty had, in his day, erected a stable and cart-shed, for he was a carrier. His widow now let these appendages to a rag-and-bone dealer and all the time Littlejohn was there, you could hear the tenant talking loudly and amicably to his donkey.

"That's my girl..." as though the ass needed reassuring.

The living-room was full of old-fashioned furniture, bought second-hand even when Forty brought home his bride. Nellie must have spent a lot of time with dusters and furniture cream, for you could see your face in the sideboard, the cushions slid uncomfortably about on the polished wood and leather of the chairs, and the linoleum was so highly glazed that it paid you best to hop from one to another of the home-made rugs which dotted the floor. Nellie sat down heavily and invited Littlejohn to make himself comfortable in a chair opposite her own.

"I'm all right, except for my bunions," she said, apropos of nothing much. "And they'll be the death of me. I can't walk far because of 'em. Result is, I'm gettin' fat and the doctor says that's not good for me heart and chest. Yes, it's me bunions as'll carry me off."

She laughed a hearty, wheezy laugh.

"I never asked you what you wanted. I'm gettin' that way. Forgetful.... What was you wantin'?"

Littlejohn told her who he was and why he had called. She confessed she'd thought he was somebody trying to sell something. They often called and she always asked them in for a bit of company.

"It's about Finloe, isn't it? I read about it in the papers. Had a right good cry about it, I did, and then got over it. I suppose he died of heartbreak after he lost Marion."

"Perhaps he did, Mrs. Forty, but they found his body in a pond behind the bungalow, you know."

"I saw it. They said somebody must have murdered him and thrown in the body. Now why would they want to do that?"

"For his money, no doubt."

"Did they now…. "

In her young days, Nellie had been a masterful, high-spirited girl. Many a man would have given his eyes to possess her before Forty arrived with his horse and trap and carried her off. He had treated her well, too, but his death from a long and dreadful complaint had taught his patient wife that nothing thereafter was too terrible for life to offer or for humans to bear with fortitude and now, all passion spent, she accepted whatever came with calm fatalism.

"Lysander's missing, too. We want to find him."

"I haven't seen either of 'em for many a long time. They wrote to me at Christmas and on my birthday. I nursed them both as babies and stayed with the family till I wed Mr. Forty. After Forty was took, I did a bit for them both now and then, till I guess they didn't want their old Nellie any more."

"I'm sorry to say that everything points to Lysander having robbed his dead brother's estate. Then he disappeared and hasn't been seen or heard of since."

"He wouldn't rob his brother unless there was good reasons. Finloe must have left his money to some silly or other.

He always was the most foolish of the two. They was both good boys, though. A nice family, if you ask me. Mr. and Mrs. Oates, the father and mother of the two boys, brought me up. Took me from an orphanage and was wonderful kind to me. I might have been one of their own. Then, I looked after the children when they came. Those boys wouldn't have harmed one another for the world."

"They were on good terms, then?"

"Always. They had a fight about Marion, I remember. Both wanted her. She lived a few doors away from the family. Balham, we lived in then. All the boys of the neighbourhood wanted Marion. Pretty as a picture, with blue eyes and long fair hair. And she chose Finloe of them all. Might have done better.... A doctor called Malone was after her and young Will Hazlett, the lawyer, but she chose Finloe...."

"Hazlett?"

"Yes. His father was the family solicitor and Will followed him. Will never married when Marion turned him down."

"You mean Mr. Hazlett in Pimlico?"

"The same...."

Marion had chosen Finloe, then. And when she grew older and her looks faded, Finloe turned to Florrie Judson. Well, well.

"He made all our Wills, my own included. Not that I've much, but I've no intentions of it goin' to my goodfor-nothin' next-of-kin who'll drink it all away and are waiting for me to pass on and let them..."

"There was murder connected with Mr. Finloe's death, too. An electricity meter-man was found killed in the house...."

"Was he now? God rest 'im. But neither of my boys would do that. No. Kind to animals, kind to 'umans, I always say, and those boys was always fond of animals."

That was one way of looking at it. Littlejohn couldn't help comparing in his mind the different ways various people looked at the Oates brothers. To Nellie they were little heroes, kindness itself. To Flo Judson, Finloe was a sort of knight errant; to Hazlett, he was mean. Lysander was a nice man to Mrs. Kewley at the flats; Gamaliel saw him as a killer and was scared to death of him. His bank manager considered him respectable!

Littlejohn felt handicapped in the interview. Mrs. Forty was old and living in the past. To talk about one brother robbing the other seemed almost profane in the face of her belief in them and her memories of the days when the Oateses were all together and she was happy to serve them. Her old face looked like one of those figures carved in wood, immobile, serene, patient. She sat facing Littlejohn, happy to talk about the boys she had reared, resolute in her faith that they could do no wrong.

"I'll make us some tea."

Nellie had taken to Littlejohn and wanted to please him. She waved aside his protests, levered herself from her chair, and toddled into the lean-to kitchen. The kettle must have been on the boil, for in record time she was back with a teapot, tea-things and some homemade cake, all nicely arranged on a tray. She had been brought up in the true below-stairs fashion of other days. Neat, courteous, knowing her place.

"Like it strong?"

"There was another chap, too, who was sweet on Marion...."

Over the teacups, Nellie expanded. She seemed to take up the tale from a string of reminiscences silently running through her mind.

"His name was Hunt. A special friend of Mr. Lysander's. He taught at a school near where we lived. Used to come to the house. Marion was always in and out and Mr. Hunt—Theo, they called him—was crazy about her. Used to eat her up with his eyes, if you know what I mean … ."

Another of them! Gamaliel would be in it next! All the characters in this sorry tale seemed to have been ex-admirers of the late Mrs. Finloe.

Outside in the shed, the rag-and-bone man kept comforting his donkey. "That's my girl … ."

"That's Mr. Jealous, the ragman, sorting out his rags and bones and old iron. He rents the stables my husband once had. Talks to that donkey of his for hours on end as he works. Not that Violet isn't almost 'uman, but it sounds that funny … . "

"What was I saying? Oh yes … Theo Hunt. He hadn't a chance, even if Marion 'ad liked 'im. Such a poor lot, his family. Father died and left Theo to support his mother and a sister who was a bit queer. Then, when his mother died, he was left with his sister to do for. Terrible time, he had. If she didn't get her own way, she had hysterics and threatened to do away with herself. Proper burden to him. He left with her and took a place in a quiet spot up north and we never saw him again. I never liked him, though. Sarcastic spoken, bitter, as you might say. Not without good reasons, I've no doubt, but I never liked the way he looked down his nose at me as though I was a common servant, instead of nearly one of the family … . "

Littlejohn sipped his second cup of tea and ate his second slab of Nellie's home-made cake. He let her talk on, giving him more background of the Oateses and their circle.

"Did Lysander do well, Mrs. Forty?"

"Not bad, as far as I could gather. He used to tell me quite open in his letters how things was with him. He was makin' quite a passable livin' from paintin' posters, I think it was. Finloe, of course, made his money somewhere abroad. They neither of them wanted much."

"Did Marion go abroad with Finloe?"

"No…. Oh, didn't I tell you? My memory's that bad. Finloe and her was engaged, but Finloe, who was in business in the city, went bankrupt in the slump and they couldn't get married. Or, at least, Finloe wouldn't. It was broken off and Finloe went abroad. Marion waited for 'im, in spite of all the offers she got, and they married after he got back. Made 'is money pretty quick, I believe. Land buyin' some-where…. I told Finloe what I thought of him, goin' off like that and leaving Marion. As I got older, I sort of became a second mother to the boys. I told them what I liked and they came to me for advice."

"And very wise, too, I would think."

"Well, I was the only woman they could talk to. A man needs a woman's advice sometimes. Other men aren't half as good as a woman with experience, and I say it without boasting, I've had plenty of that. What with Forty nearly goin' broke himself and me havin' to turn-to and be a sort of stable-boy because we couldn't afford to pay one, and drivin' the carts around. And then, poor Forty got cancer and lingered on for nearly two years with me nursing him night and day. I know a bit about life by this, Mr. Littlejohn."

"I'm sure you do, Mrs. Forty."

She collected the tea-things and removed the tray to the lean-to again. Outside, the rag-and-bone man was leading off his little fat donkey hitched to a little cart on another round of collecting. "Come on, Vi'let, come on. That's my girl, that's my Vi'let."

"He's lost his wife and his son's missin' in Korea. All he's got left is Violet. Without 'er, he'd go mad, I'm sure."

"Have you had anyone around lately inquiring about Finloe and Lysander, Mrs. Forty?"

"Nobody particular…. There was a sloppy sort of fat man round the other week, though. Looked ready to drop dead of a heart attack. He asked if I knew where Lysander was. He wanted to send him some money and Lysander had left his old address. He looked more like a broker's-man to me, so I said I didn't. Which was true."

"That sounds like Mr. Gamaliel. I wonder what he was after."

"What name did you say?"

"Gamaliel…."

"That's it. He left his card. Asked if I'd let him know if I heard from Lysander. I forgot it…."

Nellie thrust two fingers inside a toby jug on the mantelpiece and drew out a piece of pasteboard.

M. Gamaliel,
Bookseller.
9b. Risk Street, S.W.1.

So, Gamaliel was on Lysander's track, too.

"I didn't like his looks at all…. Slimy…."

"I've heard of him…."

As Littlejohn was thanking Nellie Forty for the nice tea and bidding her good-bye, Cromwell was sick visiting at Pimlico Hospital. They'd taken Mr. Gamaliel there after his collapse and the doctors said his heart was so bad he'd be detained for some time at the government's expense. This, it appeared, suited the bookseller, who, for some reason, was scared for his life.

"He'll get over it in time, but it's obvious he's been under severe strain for a considerable period," the matron told Cromwell. "You can see him for five minutes, but don't get him excited."

Gamaliel was in the public ward, which was a great relief to him. All he wanted was plenty of people about him. His nerve had completely given way. There were screens around the next bed and a parson furtively passed behind them.

Everybody else among the visitors was carrying flowers and presents for the sick in the ward. Cromwell smiled grimly to himself as he followed the nurse to Gamaliel's bedside. The thought of taking a bunch of carnations to the bookseller was very funny indeed!

"Well?" he said to the bookseller. "How do you feel?"

Gamaliel groaned.

"I'm awful…. I shan't be out of here for some time, they tell me. Suits me. The boy next door is looking after the shop. I've worked hard all my life and I've earned a rest, especially now it's free…. "

He tried to smile, but failed miserably.

"You're scared, Gamaliel, aren't you? What about? Lysander Oates surely doesn't hate you that much. Besides, he's vanished. Nothing to fear there now."

Gamaliel was too weak to argue.

"I don't know where he is, but he's out for me, I know. I didn't tell you, but two days ago, a brick fell off the top of my building within six inches of my head. I'd have been killed if it had hit me. You might say it was an accident… but after I told the landlord the roof was dangerous and he'd straight away had it examined, another brick fell and just missed me. I got coming and going through the back window. It wasn't safe through the door…. "

Cromwell smiled. The vision of the flabby man in the bed scrambling over the sash every time he wanted to leave or enter his shop struck him as comic.

"Oh, you can laugh.... But I'm staying here as long as I can...I've had enough of Risk Street for a bit. I couldn't sleep at night for it...."

An evangelical sick-visitor was travelling from bed to bed dropping a cheery word on his way.

"How are you to-day, friend?" he said to Gamaliel.

"I'm bad," said the bookseller, apparently anxious to convince everybody that he'd better remain there indefinitely.

"Cheer up.... We'll soon have you well and out again. You'll be seeing quite a lot of me and if there's anything I can do...Any friend you'd like to visit you...?"

Mr. Gamaliel groaned. Cromwell, who seemed in quite a merry mood among all the cheerful patients and nurses, almost asked the reverend to send Lysander Oates to visit Mr. Gamaliel, but thought perhaps the joke would be out of place or produce a relapse.

"Well...I'm glad to find you better...."

"I feel bad...."

"Anything you'd like?"

"Yes; tell that blasted painter he's fired. Spying on me all the time and blew the gaff about the revolver. I'll get even with him for that.... "

"I thought you were bad. Better not get excited."

Mr. Gamaliel closed his eyes and pretended to be exhausted.

"Keep an eye on him," Cromwell told the nurse. "He's scared stiff of something. I'll call again."

"I'm going north to see Hunt," Littlejohn told Cromwell when they met again at the Yard. "I'm getting tired of all these red-herrings. Forgery, bank swindles, bricks falling on people, family secrets, Lysander out gunning for Gamaliel. We're just wasting time. What we want is to find Lysander

Oates and get his story. I've a queer feeling that he's dead, though...."

"Why?"

"He had a partner in this business and ten thousand pounds is a lot of money. Very tempting bait. It might have ended as a huge swindle and little else if only Fish-lock hadn't poked his nose in the house just as the criminal was there and busy. He had to be silenced, and now, it's murder...Lysander has either gone very successfully to ground or else he's dead."

"What about the bricks somebody tried to throw at Gamaliel?"

"Gamaliel either knows something he won't talk about, or else he's unwittingly stumbled across something the murderer thinks will betray him. On the other hand, the bricks might have fallen through decayed mortar and force of gravity...."

"When are you going to see Hunt?"

"Now. And whilst I'm away, you might go back to Netherby and just knock around the place and see what you can gather. Try the station and the local bobby. P.C. Mee...that's his name, and don't make jokes on it. He resents it strongly...."

# CHAPTER EIGHT
# DALBAY HALL SCHOOL

Littlejohn took the main-line train to York, changed there to the local branch and, after about two hours of slow, ever-stopping travel, arrived at Bishop's Walton. There was a small station at Dalbay Hall which would have been more convenient for his purpose, but it opened only at the beginning and end of school term when boys and their boxes made up the traffic to Dalbay Hall School.

Bishop's Walton was a small compact market town with a single High Street of respectable shops and behind them a mass of small tidy workers' cottages. A fine church, a few gaunt barren dissenting chapels, a basket works, and a factory which processed for the hat trade the skins of rabbits caught on the local heath and moors. The country was wide sweeping and undulating, the houses were of stone, the town was in a saucer of hills and heath, and rheumatism was prevalent.

Dalbay Hall, the famous preparatory school, was two miles from Bishop's Walton, but the town was not out of bounds. The number of tuckshops and outfitters testified that the tradesmen thrived on the scholastic industry. There were a lot of boys about when Littlejohn left the station. Some had purple caps with yellow stripes; others, presumably the *élite*, were either without hats, which was forbidden, wearing sporting scarlet caps, which denoted a prefecture, or flaunting boaters of straw, the sign of the senior. The boaters regarded the caps with contempt and ate in special tuckshops whence the small fry were excluded. The purple tie of the school was the law, but certain blades removed these and replaced them by flamboyant articles of the prevailing American fashion when they came to town. They also ogled and flirted with the girls of a feminine counterpart of Dalbay Hall, although fraternising with the opposite sex was strictly proscribed by each establishment.

It had not been very hard to find out where Theodore Hunt was employed. A scholastic agency had done the trick and now Littlejohn was on his trail. Presumably Hunt lived out of school with his eccentric sister. The Inspector took a taxi and set off in search of him.

The well-known headmaster, "C. K. B."—Charles Kingsley Bompass—frowned hard at Littlejohn's card. The Head was only forty-five but he looked sixty. His hair was white, he stooped scholastically, he was tall and thin, his eyes were like cold steel and his lips thin and mobile. He believed in discipline, self-discipline, if possible; otherwise forced medicine. He disliked the police because he regarded them as meddlers in what did not concern them. He had been prosecuted twice for flogging. Mr. Bompass, therefore, looked down his nose at Littlejohn's name, tightened his lips, prepared to do battle in the cause of discipline and the birch, and said he would see him.

Mr. Bompass was a bit put-out when Littlejohn entered. He expected a man in a bowler hat which he would not remove and here, if you please, was a gentleman who looked like the parent of a prospective student of Dalbay Hall. He met Littlejohn half-way between the door and his large magisterial desk, as though eager to sweep him out into the passage as soon as he entered.

"Good afternoon. You wanted to see me, Inspector. I'm a busy man. Term-end, you know...."

"I won't keep you then, sir. I wanted to ask you about a member of your staff, Mr. Hunt."

"Ah, Hunt.... What of him? He hasn't been criminally misbehaving, I hope."

Mr. Bompass whinnied at his own joke. As a rule, when Bompass whinnied, they all whinnied. He put down Littlejohn as quite devoid of sense of humour from the start.

"Hunt has been at the *school* quite a long time. In fact, he served under my late father, my predecessor as *Head*. Absolutely reliable, undoubted integrity, a good fellow; I can assure you on that point."

Littlejohn might have been asking for a scholastic testimonial.

"I wanted to see you on rather a delicate matter, sir. I would ask your discretion and co-operation."

Mr. Bompass looked alarmed this time. All kinds of heinous thoughts crossed his mind. Deception, crime, vice, they all passed through his brain in a kind of pictorial procession.

"Good heavens! Not... Not..."

Littlejohn had no idea what the Head was fending-off from his school, but he denied it.

"No, sir. Not that!"

"Good. Good. Pray sit down."

As a sign of his relief, Mr. Bompass was going to be polite and co-operative.

"Tell me all about it, Inspector."

91

Mr. Bompass used the tone he employed to little trans-gressing boys. Any one of them could have told Littlejohn to beware. You told all; then you got a licking.

Littlejohn looked Bompass in the eyes. The man was scared of him! Why? And then, in a flash of intuition, he saw it all. The school was famous for its successes. The man before him might be a good organiser, with his thin lips and steely eyes, now flickering with doubt and fear, but he was no scholar, certainly no schoolmaster. He depended on others for that. Hunt was Bompass's trump card. Forced to live in retreat because of his sister's infirmity, yet reputed to be a first-class pedagogue. Just the man for the *school*. Bompass was scared lest the police should deprive him of his good investment, his Hunt.

"An old friend of Mr. Hunt's is missing. I would like to see him and ask if he knows anything about him, sir."

"Is that *all*...?"

The headmaster uttered it on the breath of a great sigh of relief. He strolled to his desk and sat down there, sur-rounded by what appeared to be reports, account-books, sample text-books and, strangest of all, an assorted pile of cheap, soft-backed novels and strip-cartoon magazines. Every now and then, Mr. Bompass made a raid on the boys' quarters and gathered together their favourite, yet banned, reading matter. Here were Westerns, school tales, Sexton Blakes, Deadwood Dicks and Buffalo Bills, gangsters, and—horrible to contemplate—certain spicy paper-backs with pictures of seductive, half-naked adventuresses, molls and innocents, stark on their covers. Each piece of loot was endorsed with the name of its owner.... Johnson, minor; Smith, J. B., Curtiss ii; and, on the naked bosom of the most unctuous blonde, tied to a chair in panties and brassiere, was written the name: Goodfellow, minor....

"Is that all ...?"

"Not quite ...."

The Head's face jerked with more apprehension.

"We want to know where all the missing man's friends were at certain vital periods in a case we are investigating. A case of murder...."

"What? Surely not Hunt! A mild, one might say, innocuous man."

"Most murderers start by being that. All the same, it's merely routine, sir."

"Very well. What do you wish to know?"

"I'd like to see Mr. Hunt, if I may."

Mr. Bompass swam the breast-stroke in thin air with his arms.

"Not here. Not here, *please*. Call to see him at home. Hunt's domestic arrangements don't permit his living in the school or acting as housemaster. He lives in the town. You'll find him after school, say after seven-thirty, at his house in Abbott's Walk ... Number five ...."

"Thank you. That will suit me, sir. Now, as regards the movements of Mr. Hunt, perhaps you can help me."

"I'll do all I can. I'm sure they were quite harmless. He's a very good fellow.... A bit hamstrung by his sick sister, but an excellent master. A very clever man, but, as I said, frustrated by family troubles. Need I say more?"

"About the dates, sir. Was Mr. Hunt at school all the Easter term?"

"Certainly. Had he been absent, I would have known. In fact, he even stayed on during half-term break to take charge of boys who didn't go home. The boys returned on January 15th for Easter term, which ended, this year, on April 15th."

"That released Hunt from duty, sir?"

"Of course...."

"Did he go away, do you know?"

"Not to my knowledge. I was absent in London for a fort-night. I returned on April 30th. Hunt was at home then, because I asked him to call here to see me and he came at once. I find him very useful in many things and as he rarely leaves home, he is easily available, even out of term."

"You can vouch, then, for his being in Bishop's Walton without a day's absence until April 15th from the start of Easter term and still here on April 30th. In other words, you can assure me there is only the period of your absence in London unaccounted for?"

"That is right. But, surely, you are not seeking an alibi for a man like Hunt. He's not a murderer, you know."

"I didn't say he was, sir...."

This icy, calculating pedagogue was busy counting the cost already of Hunt's possible arrest and disappearance from the life of the school.

"Is Mr. Hunt a wealthy man, sir?"

Mr. Bompass blinked. He knew all about it and was sort-ing out words in his mind to express it diplomatically. It was a habit of his when interviewing parents.

Outside, a clock struck five. It was as if a wind were gen-tly blowing across the tree-lined quadrangle which the win-dows of Bompass's study surveyed like a watch-tower. Classes were breaking up. The rustle spread and grew to a wild roar of closing desks, shuffling feet, banging doors, and then the boys began to file out on their way to the chapel. Another day of cramming almost ended.

"No, he's not wealthy. I have friends who knew his back-ground. Family sickness has always hampered him. I would say he has little more than what he earns here. I have been told he does some free-lance writing, but he is too austere, too fastidious for the present taste of the average reader. A kind of modern Barbey d'Aurevilly, if you understand what I mean.... "

Littlejohn had never heard of Barbey, but he let it pass. He made a mental note of the name to ask his wife. She'd know.

"... So he has made very little. One of his colleagues told me of novels he had written, very good ones, too, as monuments of style, but as breadwinners... well... They were never published."

Bompass rose and walked to the window, anxious to see what was going on in his little kingdom.

"There's Hunt, now. He's taking chapel.... "

Walking alone in the rear of the stragglers, was a medium-built man, inclined to fatness, his gown billowing round him, his cap in his hand. He had books under his arm and his fine head, long and large for the size and shape of his body, was sunk on his chest. He looked like a tracker with his eye on a trail. From where he stood, Littlejohn could make out the sardonic profile, the white hands, the cultivated long hair of the fastidious man, one to whom routine was torture. The dress beneath the gown, too... loose, heavy grey tweed, with an easy-fitting cream shirt and collar and a silk bow-tie.... Hunt slowly vanished in the chapel of new red brick. The whole place sprouted with appendages of brick and concrete, or even timber sheds here and there. The old house had grown far too small for the teeming mass of *élan vitale* which it accommodated for winning scholarships and passing examinations.

"Will that be all, Inspector?"

Mr. Bompass was now very amiable. He was anxious that Littlejohn should leave Hunt for the *school*.

"I think so, sir. I may be back if I find any point on which you may be able to enlighten me."

"Of course. Most pleased. And now, if you'll excuse me. I have my work...ahem...."

He extended a bony hand for a valedictory shake and let it hang limp like a dead fish in Littlejohn's palm for a second.... Across the quadrangle and in at the open window floated the noise of Hunt's ministrations.... The pleasant sound of boys' voices singing in unison:

Lord, dismiss us with Thy blessing
Thanks for mercies past receive....

Mr. Bompass dismissed Littlejohn and turned his attention to the lurid collection of literature which he had gathered from pockets, desks and lockers....

Number 5, Abbott's Walk was a fine old Georgian building with a pillared front, a semi-circular doorstep, and a similar canopy of stone to match it balanced on top of the columns. On each side of the doorway someone had buried an ancient piece of artillery, a small iron field-gun, muzzle downwards, to form a second diminutive pair of pillars. Littlejohn tugged the doorbell, and as he waited, he wondered who, in this small, tidy community, had erected such a gem of a dwelling. It had been the home of a wealthy merchant who had bought the wool from the neighbouring sheep-farmers, distributed it in cottages for miles around to be carded and spun, and then, after collecting it, made it into cloth in a small mill driven by water-power.

"Did you want to see the master?"

A girl of about fifteen opened the door. She wore cap and apron and her hair and clothing marked her, as yet, as a learner in the arts of attire and attractiveness. She was an orphan from a nearby home. Servants never stayed with the Hunts for long; older ones shunned their employ and they were reduced to taking and training girls from the orphanage who, when they had equipped themselves for better jobs, gave notice and left.

Littlejohn handed the maid his card, but before she could take it indoors a head was thrust into the hall and a voice called: "Who is it, Nancy?"

The newcomer couldn't wait for the Inspector to be properly announced and brought in. She snatched the card from Nancy's fingers, read it, and came straight to the door and greeted Littlejohn.

"Good evening. Do come in. I'm not a bit scared of policemen. I've dealt with *hundreds* of them in my life. When we lived in London, I used to get lost *every day* and they always brought me home.... "

She spoke in shrill, excited tones, as if every experience were a great adventure. She had a habit of underlining words and this marked them out, all unknown to her, as gross exaggerations.

"Come in.... What do you want, Inspector? Is it the dog licence? It's *always* summer before I remember to pay it...."

Littlejohn followed her down the long hall, with its lovely soaring staircase, into a drawing-room of fine dimensions. Two spacious windows, with folded shutters, overlooked a tree-lined side-street. A large, marble Adam fireplace at one end of the room. The furniture was gracious and antique; Venetian mirrors on the walls and, here and there, a good picture. It gave you the impression of the home of a patrician instead of a poor schoolmaster and his cranky sister. Here was all the furniture and remaining finery of the old Hunt home in London, all that was left of their father's ruin....

".... He has *several* baths a day, you know.... "

Littlejohn turned to face Constance Hunt. She was small, daintily built, and well-preserved for her age, which must have been around sixty. Her long hair, gathered back from her low forehead, was fixed in a bun at the nape of the neck and was of an even whiteness so bright that it was difficult to make out whether it was white or blonde. That and her firm, pink complexion gave her an appearance of agelessness. She wore a gingham gown, twenty or more years too young for her. Her hazel eyes were wide-set and had an expression of perpetual, innocent surprise. Their lids were heavy and red-rimmed, the cheek-bones high, the chin tapering.... An obvious hysteric, one who sought refuge from the world in an endless childhood; a Peter Pan, refusing to grow up. Littlejohn had met them before; unable to discriminate between truth and fantasy; unreliable witnesses; constitutional liars....

"I'll wait, if you don't mind, Miss Hunt."

"I don't mind at all. I *often* entertain my brother's friends whilst he's in his bath. What were you wanting of him? Not more trouble at the school, I hope. They are *always* having trouble at the school. And my brother *always* gets them out of it...."

Littlejohn was interested in the pictures on the walls; particularly in one to the right of the fireplace. It was the finished article, the real masterpiece, the rough water-colour sketch of which hung over the fireplace in Lysander Oates's old room in Pimlico. Mrs. Kewley had said it was of somewhere in the Isle of Man. Oates must have been an artist when he really tried. Here, in oil, was a sweep of lovely blue hills, decked in gorse, and descending to a wild valley through which ran a white ribbon of road. By the roadside a tiny chapel and, strange in such surroundings, a stumpy chimney of some old factory or mine.... .

"You like pictures.... . Before we came into the country, we had many distinguished artists as friends. They gave us *endless* masterpieces. Our home was like one of the old *salons* where the famous gathered.... . You like this...? My brother did it for my last birthday.... . "

She pointed her index finger, which held a large ring with a heavy intaglio, at an illuminated manuscript in a black frame, hanging by the window. Exquisite work, in bright colours and gold.

> But leave the Wise to wrangle and with me
> The Quarrel of the Universe let be,
> And in some quiet Corner of the Hubbub couch't,
> Make Game of that which makes as much of thee.
> "Very beautiful work, Miss Hunt.
> Very lovely indeed."

And so it was, and filled with the bitterness of Theodore Hunt.

"That is a verse from Omar Khayyám, Inspector. My brother can recite it from *beginning* to *end*. He needs only to read a poem to *remember* it by heart.... . "

A door closed behind them and Littlejohn turned to find himself facing Theodore Hunt, who had entered silently, clad in a foulard dressing-gown, a scarf to match round his neck, and cream, heel-less suède shoes on his feet. He looked rather surprised to find Littlejohn there.

"Good evening. I didn't know we had visitors.... ."

The lips were heavy and turned-down at the corners in ever-present sardonic disappointment; the nose high bridged, aquiline, and with finely chiselled nostrils; the brow broad; the eyes dark and deep-set in tired sockets. The face was colourless, like parchment; the cheeks wore a look of slight inflation as though he were gently blowing them out from the inside ....

Constance ran to greet him. He patted her arm with infinite tenderness as though she were all he had to love and to care for him, and he smiled indulgently as on a child. For a brief moment, as he looked questioningly at her, he was gentle and charming.

"Well, my dear, won't you introduce me to your visitor?"

She was pleased at his mistake.

"Oh, but he's not *my* visitor. As a rule, I get *all* the callers, but this one is for you. He is Inspector ... what is it? ... I can never remember strange names .... However, he has come all the way from London to see you, Theo .... "

Hunt's face was a sarcastic mask. He looked across at Littlejohn who nodded pleasantly, and, for a moment, his face jerked with fear .... Then he was himself again.

"Well ... And to what do we owe this unexpected honour, Inspector, this arrival of Mahomet at the mountain, this coming of town to the country ...? Nothing sensational, I hope ...."

He turned gently to his sister.

"Connie, dear, make us a cup of coffee, will you? I feel like one and I'm sure the Inspector would like to join us."

"But, we haven't *dined* yet, Theo .... We will have it served after dinner. Invite the Inspector to stay, *please* .... "

"I've already dined, thank you, Miss Hunt ...."

So had the Hunts, on corned beef and salad, but Constance was living in cloud-cuckoo land, with flunkeys waiting to serve the courses.

"There, you see. Go and get it, dear, just to please me ... .

Littlejohn felt a surge of compassion for Hunt, so kindly and patient to this poor nitwit, covering up for her, smoothing over her fancies and lies, coaxing her, helping her along the knife-edge of rational conduct, protecting her from trouble.... She smiled archly at Littlejohn as though off to concoct a surprise, and left them. Hunt was himself again.

"Now. What is all this? My sister is not well and must not be excited. As you see, I've coaxed her to leave us for a while. Hurry through your business and then please go."

"Thank you, sir. It's about your friend Mr. Lysander Oates."

Hunt's hands had been hanging by his sides. He clenched their palms and his right forearm slowly rose from the perpendicular to a right angle, with the heavy ring on the little finger biting into the flesh from the pressure he exerted. That was the only sign that the name had gone deep. He relaxed quickly.

"Well? What of him, Inspector?"

"He has disappeared ... . "

Hunt smiled a thin, tolerant smile and he gently flapped his white hands.

"Come, come, come, Inspector. Don't be melodramatic. Surely a man can go away and seek a little peace in these uncivilised and degraded times. That is why my sister and I are here in this forsaken place. We want a bit of peace ... ."

"In some quiet corner of the hubbub couch'd, sir?"

"Ah, I see you've been looking at my illuminations. It pleases my sister and provides a little relaxation for me after pumping ... er knowledge, shall we call it ...? into little boys day after day."

"Yes, I've been admiring it ... and the pictures. Particularly the one by the fireplace there."

You could have heard a pin drop for a second. Hunt had been caught off his guard. Why? Then, he quickly recovered.

"Oh, the one of Wales.... "

Littlejohn felt for the first time that unfailing queer sense of elation which always took him when the first real scent, the faint signs of the trail, came to him, never to be left until the case was ended.

"Wales, is it, sir? Some of Mr. Oates's work?"

Hunt stared at him.

"How did you guess that?"

"It has L.O. in the bottom right corner."

"So it has. Well... It looks as if you've come on a wild-goose chase, Inspector. I'm sorry I can't help you. I haven't seen Oates for nearly two years.... Haven't even heard from him."

"I hoped you might give us some clue as to his whereabouts with being his best friend.... "

"You're mistaken, Inspector. I'm not his best friend. We used to be intimate, but that has declined, till now, well... mere acquaintances... mere acquaintances...."

Hunt seemed eager to convince Littlejohn that Oates meant nothing to him. Too eager....

"Did you know his brother, sir?"

"Finloe, you mean? Yes, long ago. I read in the paper that he died."

"Yes, rather mysteriously, sir...."

"I did read about it, but I can't say the details interest me. I'm busy. I have my work, and the accounts of sordid crime leave me quite cold."

"Sordid crime, sir? He died naturally, I believe, but his body was hidden...."

"I know, I know. I'm not interested, I tell you."

He was annoyed; almost in a rage. Another ostrich, maybe, not quite so bad as his sister, but angry when the unsavoury elements of life disturbed his peace of mind or body.

"Here we are at last…. Well, what are you waiting for, Nancy? Bring it in…. "

Constance was back again and Nancy followed on her heels, trundling in ungainly fashion a tea-waggon decked out for afternoon tea. Silver teapots and other equipment, little cakes, toasted scones…. Afternoon tea at eight in the evening and just after dinner!

"We couldn't find the coffee, so …"

They couldn't find anything, as a rule, unless Theodore personally attended to it. Constance had no memory for little details. They ran out of sugar, salt, tea, coffee and even the staples of diet several times every week. Theo smiled gently.

"Serve it, then, my dear. Thank you, Nancy. That will do."

Nancy made her exit as from a royal levee…backed to the door, her eyes glued on her master, and then fled.

Littlejohn sipped the tea out of Crown Derby china. He shuddered to think of such treasures handled by Nancy or forgotten by Constance. Yet, somehow, here it was, intact. Probably Theo …

There was no sugar in the tea and the brew was heavy. They'd even forgotten how many spoonfuls went into the pot.

"Sugar…? One or two…?"

Hunt was patiently filling the gaps.

"What did the Inspector and you talk about, Theo? Not of me, behind my back, did you?"

"No, no, dear. He was admiring the pictures and your little illuminated Rubai from Omar…."

"But surely he didn't come all the way…?"

"Now, now, Connie. Not before our guest. I'll tell you when he's gone.... "

And shortly afterwards, Littlejohn left them. They saw him off from the doorstep under the stone canopy and Constance waved a tiny handkerchief at him over her head, until he turned the corner and vanished from sight.

# Chapter Nine
# The Chapel at Snuff
# the Wind

Mrs. Kewley was on her knees cleaning the hall when Littlejohn called at Lysander Oates's old rooms. She was so busy she didn't see him at first.

"Well, Mrs. Kewley, and how's the new granddaughter?"

She turned her head and raised a happy face in the direction of the Inspector.

"I'm sorry, sir. Didn't know it was you...."

She rose to her feet with difficulty, wiped her hands on her rough apron, and patted her hair to restore it to something like shape.

"She's fine, sir. Fine. Thanks to you, I got there good an' early. A lovely little girl.... Callin' her after me, sir, though I'll see to it she gets Margaret, and not Maggie, like I do.... Can I do anything for you?"

"Yes, Mrs. Kewley. I've called to see if I can borrow the picture I liked in Mr. Oates's old room. Where did you say it was of?"

"The Isle of Man, sir. I remember well Mr. Oates tellin' me, because of Kewley comin' from there. Did you want to take it away?"

"Yes; I'd like to keep it a few days. I'll see you get it back. Will Mr. What's-his-name object?"

"That he won't. If Mr. Brodribb does complain, it's all the same to me. I gave it 'im, didn't I? All he did was get a cheap frame on it. I'll fetch it...."

"Let me go up. If Mr. Brodribb says anything, tell him I'll make it right with him later. Here's my card if he asks who I am."

"I'll see to it, sir. Here's my key...."

Littlejohn caught the 'plane to the Isle of Man just after one o'clock from Northolt. The picture was wrapped up under his arm. He hadn't the faintest notion where to start looking for the scene, but he intended to find out as quickly as possible. He wanted to be back that night if it could be managed. Hunt's deliberate lie about the place being in Wales, when all the time he must have known it was Manx, had roused the Inspector's curiosity. Suppose Lysander Oates had made his hideout there. He seemed fond of it and it was the last spot anybody would think of going to, to find him. By a pure stroke of luck, Oates had forgotten the water-colour behind the wardrobe and Mrs. Kewley had remembered where the scene was. And then Hunt had played the fool with him....

Sitting next to Littlejohn in the Dakota was a ruddy-cheeked, stocky little man reading a copy of the *Isle of Man Times*.

"Excuse me, sir. I've a picture here with me. I wonder if you could tell me where the scene was painted. I believe it's somewhere on the Island."

The man looked at him over the top of his rimless spectacles and smiled a slow, kindly smile.

"Are you an artist, then? Plenty of lovely places on the Island.... Let me see it?"

He took it in his hands and eyed it over. Then he turned it upside down as if that might help him. He shook his head.

"No.... I can't say I know it. So many places like that on the little island. Gorse and hills.... No...."

Slow and musical of speech and full of courtesy.

"But I'll tell you who will know. See the parson in front there? That's the Reverend Caesar Kinrade, Vicar of Grenaby, a man who knows the Island like the palm of his hand. He'll tell you, sure enough. Walk along and tell I sent ye. I'm not coming with you; I don't approve of walking in mid-air."

The Rev. Caesar Kinrade was dozing and it seemed a shame to wake him. He was very old and his features were lost in a froth of lovely white whiskers. He opened one blue eye and fixed it on Littlejohn and then opened the other.

"Well, and what might you be wanting, disturbin' an old man's nap a thousand feet up? Sit down...."

There was a vacant seat beside the good man and Littlejohn took it. He opened his picture again.

"Snuff the Wind," said the Rev. Caesar, without hesitation.

"I beg your pardon, sir.... "

"The place is called Snuff the Wind.... See the road there, the old mine chimney, and the Wesleyan Chapel that somebody made into a cottage. Are you sellin' pictures, or what is this all about?"

"I'm a police officer, sir.... "

The thick white eyebrows rose, revealing more than ever the bright blue eyes.

"...I'm searching for a man who disappeared from London, sir. This is a mere clue, which might reveal his whereabouts. Can you tell me where I can find the place?"

"It lies to the west of Granite Mountain, not very far from my home. I'd take you there, if you wanted to go, but I'm a tired old man in middlin' health and I've been to a conference and I want to get home to my bed. But Teddy Looney will be meetin' me at the airport in his old taxi and can take you on after he's dropped me, if you're so minded."

"I'd be very grateful indeed, sir, if that could be arranged."

"I'll be seeing you when we land, then. Excuse me if I finish my sleep. I don't like this new way of travel, except that it prevents staying the night in Liverpool for to-morrow's boat, and I can sleep in my own bed tonight.... "

With that, the Rev. Caesar fell asleep again.

They touched down at Ronaldsway at 15.20. The Rev. Caesar Kinrade joined Littlejohn and led him to where the oldest contraption he'd ever seen was waiting to take the parson home. It looked as if Teddy Looney used it for a hen-roost when he hadn't it on the road. The sun was shining and great white clouds threw enormous shadows across the gentle purple hills, decked in heather and flaming gorse.

Teddy was a huge countryman with a round red face, blue eyes which looked right through you, and hands like hams. He touched his cap, which was decorated with cow-hairs, as though he'd been butting the cattle jovially as he milked them.

"Welcome back, Reverend.... You keepin' pretty middlin'?"

"Yes, thanks, Looney. And right glad to be home.... "

The vicar turned to Littlejohn.

"Believe it or not, this fellah's never been off the Island in his life...."

Teddy grinned broadly.

"An' don't want to, either. Got all I want here. Don't hold with foreign travellin' ...."

"Neither do I, Looney. Don't know why I keep going. And now, I want you to take me home and then run this gentleman out to Snuff the Wind ...."

"Snuff the Wind? Doubt if the old bus'll do it. What's he wantin' there for? Not much to see there ...."

"Was there ever such a man for an argument! Now, Teddy, do as you're told, ask no questions, and earn your money."

"All right. If you say so, Reverend ...."

They clambered in the old saloon, settled themselves on the hard seats, Teddy hoisted the parson's ancient Gladstone bag aboard beside him, and with a rattle and a shake, they were off.

"I don't suppose I'll be seeing you again, Inspector. So good-bye and God bless you ...."

Teddy carried the bag, shepherded the Rev. Caesar in the large old vicarage, and then resumed his journey with Littlejohn. They soon left the lowland farms behind, passed by deserted crofts and tumbledown houses on the intack lands, skirted vast tracts of peat, heather and blaeberry, all along an excellent road between high banks of turf, with gorse in full bloom crowning them. Then, round a corner, climbing all the time. More ruined houses of heavy stone, and, at length, an old chimney, slag heaps, mine-workings and a chapel.

"Snuff the Wind," said Teddy Looney.

"Do you live near here, Teddy?"

"Grenaby, where Parson Kinrade lives. Are you reckoning on picnicking here, or gathering blaeberries, or what, master?"

"I want to just have a look round and then perhaps you'll take me back ...."

"You'll have to be quick then, master. It's milkin' time and nature won't wait for us ... ."

"Could you leave me and come back pretty soon, then?"

"In about an hour and a half, if that'll do."

"Yes; I forgot to ask what time the last 'plane leaves ... ."

"Eightish, to Liverpool. You'll not get on it without you've reserved a seat. The full season's on ... . "

"Can you ring up the airport, Teddy, from somewhere? Tell them it's for Inspector Littlejohn, of Scotland Yard, on official business. Here's my card to remember it."

Teddy was quite unimpressed. He took and pocketed the card without so much as a look at it. Foreigners and their ways didn't disturb him at all. He touched his cap and departed to his milking.

Littlejohn stretched his legs, strolled around, and looked about him. On one side, the great mass of Granite Mountain with graceful hills rolling away on either side. Behind him the land sloped away to more fertile fields and beyond them was the sea, shining like silver in the sun of the late afternoon. He filled his lungs with the clean air, sharp with the freshness of the heights and scented with peat and gorse. A spout of clear water leapt from a hole in a wall and fell with a splash in a roadside brook. Littlejohn cupped his hands, drank, freshened himself by swilling his face, and dried himself on his handkerchief. On the heights it was still; down below an invisible train whistled and a little red bus came in sight and as suddenly vanished round a bend in the distant main road.

The chapel was built just off the highway. It had evidently at one time, perhaps in the revival after Wesley's tour of the Isle, served the now ruined cottages of the crofters and a miner's house or two, in days when it paid to work the copper and lead lodes. Behind, the neglected mine, the slag heaps, the chimney, looked like the memorial to a forlorn venture.

The chapel had been made into a country cottage by someone. It was in good repair, although some of the windows had been broken and were boarded up. The door was on the latch and opened to Littlejohn's pressure.

Just one large room, recently whitewashed, with another door to a kind of little vestry, with a paraffin stove and a sink without taps or water supply. Water evidently came from the spout in the wall. The larger room was thinly furnished. A camp bed, a wooden chair, a seedy chest of drawers, and a canvas chair for lolling in. A pile of blankets neatly folded on the bed. Somebody had erected a stone hearth and chimney on one side. An oil lamp hung from a beam over a wooden table.

Littlejohn strolled around. The cabinet held cups, saucers, cutlery, and a few tins of food. There was a pot of mouldy jam, a crust of bread, hard as iron, a bread knife and a corkscrew, a half-empty bottle of rum, some tea in a jar.... Other odds and ends, and, on the bottom shelf a rucksack...a knapsack, as Mrs. Kewley called it.

Under the bed lay a suitcase. Littlejohn opened it. A few articles of clothing; socks, a change of underwear, a box of paints, some drawing paper and pencils. Then a book... *The Compleat Angler*, with the name Lysander Oates on the fly-leaf. Yes; this was where Oates had gone to ground. And then what? The appearance of everything pointed to Lysander having been scared and suddenly bolting without so much as taking a clean pair of socks or his precious painting tackle. The place had been tidied, so it might have been a sudden alarm...a visitor, some poking stranger, the police...Or perhaps Lysander had made this his bolt-hole until he could arrange things. By now, he might have crossed to Ireland.

There was a folded paper on the otherwise bare table. The *Daily Trumpet* for April 29th. That must have been about the date of Lysander's departure, if he *had* departed. Obviously he hadn't been here for some time.

Littlejohn turned to the fireless hearth. A lot of grey wood-ash, damp from rain coming down the chimney. On the hearth, a half-burned screw of paper. Gingerly Littlejohn opened it. He caught his breath. The note had been burned diagonally, but sufficient of it remained for the purpose.

ander,

Thanks for your strange message. I really don't
you have taken yourself off to that god-
join you there immediately. Term does
am very concerned to finish it with
urgently need help, I will come
I will join you there at the end
catch the post and I hope
Something must have gone
cry for help.
ever,
Hunt.

The Inspector carefully folded the note as he had found it, took the copy of *The Compleat Angler* and gently placed it between the leaves, and in the large pocket of his raincoat. He turned over the rest of the dead fire, but found nothing more. Then he made for the kitchen and examined the cooking stove. No papers had been burned there, but the stones on which it stood attracted him. One of them had not been cemented-in like the rest. He returned for the bread-knife and prized the stone from its socket. There was a substantial little cavity beneath, evidently constructed by some former tenant for hiding money or other valuables. The old dodge of making the hearthstone one's strongbox. But this was quite empty, except for one tiny scrap of paper which Littlejohn spotted as he was about to replace the stone. A piece about an inch square, yellow, and bearing some words of print, part of a longer inscription.

ME COUNT

ICO BRA

He thought for a minute. Home Counties Bank, Pimlico Branch! That was it!

Suddenly footsteps sounded on the road, halting and shuffling, a pause, and then gently again. Littlejohn went to the vestry door and looked into the living-room. Through the open doorway a face was watching him, a tipsy-looking face, with many days' growth of bristles, many days' accumulation of dirt, rheumy-eyed from too much liquor. A tramp on the scrounge for what he could find.

"Hi, you...."

"Me?"

"Yes. Do you know this place?"

"No. I'm from the north of the Island. Don't belong here. Came over for the haymakin'. Trying to raise me fare home to Dublin. Spare a copper, kind sorr...."

"You've never been here before?"

"I said not, didn't I? I haven't..."

"If you wanted to hide a body, what would you do with it in a place like this?"

"I'd chuck it down the mine.... Here, what are you gettin' at?"

"You seem to know all about the mine. When were you here last?"

"End of April...Just passin' on the haymaking; going from the south to the north that toime...."

"Was anybody here, then?"

"Yes. A fellah drawing water from the spoyt there. He gave me a bob. I knew I wasn't welcome, so I didn't ask for so much as a bite or a drink, though the good God blesses those as shares what they've got with the poor and needy ones.... "

"That'll do. Is that all?"

"What more should there be? And now can you spare a copper...? Did you say a *dead* body?"

It had just dawned on him! He looked at Littlejohn as if he had a corpse to dispose of and was asking for advice in doing it. With one wild whoop, he took to his heels and ran until his leaping figure vanished behind turf hedges in the distance.

The mine! Yes; had Hunt been over, taken the money from the hiding-place under the stove, and thrown his friend's body down the shaft? Impossible to say, and the Inspector was in no position to go down the workings himself. Better wait till Teddy came back with his old rattletrap and send him off for help. But he hadn't to wait so long.

The sound of vigorous singing was borne on the air, coming nearer and increasing in volume as it came.

Victorious, my heart, yes, victorious!
    Away with our fears, away with our tears,
    In freedom more glorious love's bondman
    appears.
More glo-oh-oh-oh, oh-oh-oh-oh, oh-oh-ohorious,
    In freedom more glorious love's bondman
    appears!

It was P.C. Maglashen, doing his rounds on a remote beat, pushing his bike and practising his piece for the forthcoming Manx musical festival. The singing faded, he halted, looked sheepish, and then glared officiously as he saw Littlejohn standing smiling at the door of the chapel.

"The very man!"

He looked anything but love's bondman. He was a very hot, portly, exasperated bobby, scenting trespass, theft, arson and the rest, and frustrated by being stopped in the middle of a romping bass run.

"What you doing there?"

When Littlejohn introduced himself and explained what he was after, the constable's chubby, clean-shaven face lengthened. He was not greatly impressed by Scotland Yard, but he was concerned that things had been *going on* over his territory. He solemnly propped his bike against the wall and entered the chapel, followed by Littlejohn.

"It's been unoccupied for several weeks now, sir. It belongs to a man in Foxdale, who lets it for the summer, when he can find anybody who'll take it. Last year it was done up and let to a man from the mainland who said he was studying Celtic remains. Then, this spring there came another tenant."

"Did you see him, constable?"

"Yes. About end of April, he arrived. I saw him knocking around and spoke to him. But he didn't seem to want botherin'…. It was none o' my business to be sociable if he didn't want me, so I just passed the time o' day and went on. The weather was very bad and I don't see what he was wantin' here at that time of the year. He seemed decent enough…."

"What did he look like?"

"Medium build, rather stocky, glasses and a bit of a beard…."

"Lysander Oates, right enough. Did he spend all his time here?"

"Just went into Foxdale to shop a bit. They said he was an artist. Expect he was waitin' for better weather to be gettin' on with a bit of paintin'."

P.C. Maglashen eyed the place all over, uncertain what to do next.

"And then he went?"

"Yes. Hadn't been here more than a few days. I guess the weather got on his nerves. One day when I passed, there was no smoke comin' from the chimney, so I popped my head in at the door. The hearth was cold and the place deserted. They don't bother locking-up in these parts and he must have just walked out. Though why he left all his things was a puzzle."

"How deep is the mine-shaft here?"

"You weren't thinking he'd tumbled down that, were you? He'd surely have more sense than messin' about there. Besides, what sense would there be in ...?"

"How deep is it, constable?"

"Not very.... Looks pretty deep and gloomy from the top, but that's on account of the blackness of the hole. Not more than twenty yards, if that. They dumped a lot of rusty barbed-wire and old respirators down it after the war."

"Let's go and have a look."

They crossed the moor for a short distance, struck across the slag, and there was the mine, a shaft descending through a heap of rubbish and protected by a rickety fence.

"Some of the boys come walking out here and play about. No use fencin' it properly. They only break it down."

Attempts had been made at one time to board the top of the shaft, but the timbers had rotted and fallen in. Now it was gaping wide. Plenty of footmarks all round where the boys had ventured close and peered down to see how far the shaft went.

Littlejohn tossed a lump of shale down. A few seconds, and a thud.

"There's water down there, too, though they do say not much."

"I'm afraid someone will have to go down. I want to make sure before I go that Oates isn't at the bottom ...."

"It's as bad as that, is it?"

"Yes. That man had a small fortune with him. He fled from trouble on the mainland, came here with his cash and, I think, was followed by somebody who knew of the money. Now we've to find out whether he left peaceably or whether he was murdered and the fortune pinched."

"Murder! I never remember a murder here since I've been in the force."

"You *are* lucky. About one a day's my experience. Now what do you recommend?"

"I'd better bike back to the village and get some tackle and men ...."

But he was saved the trouble. Teddy Looney could be heard, miles away, flogging his old car up the hills, and soon he appeared, ruddy from his milking and eager to get back to his tea.

"Hullo, Charlie," he said to P.C. Maglashen, who winced at the familiarity in front of the famous stranger from "over". He told Teddy exactly what to do. Ropes, torches, gum-boots, and a couple of reliable men.

"H'is someborry tumbled down the mine?"

"Maybe; maybe not. Now, Teddy, sharp's the word."

And Teddy and his contraption made a noisy getaway. They were back in record time. All the paraphernalia, and a couple of stocky laconic farm-hands ready for anything. P.C.

Maglashen insisted on doing the job himself. He stripped off his tunic, put on his gumboots, slid the rope under his armpits, and they lowered him. The light of his torch indicated his downward progress. He hadn't been far wrong in his estimate of the descent. They heard him shout from below and started slowly to haul up again. The air was tense as they pulled the rope. Somewhere behind a curlew called and you could hear, far away, a bittern booming an eerie accompaniment.

Instead of P.C. Maglashen, there came to the light of day the twisted body of Lysander Oates. The back of his skull had been smashed in.

# CHAPTER TEN
# NO MORE TEARS FOR FINLOE

When Cromwell called on Montacute at Rodley, he found the Inspector half frantic from a surfeit of bankers and executors. Mr. de Lacy had completely turned the tables on him. He either called or rang up for news every half-hour.

"Anything fresh about the Oates case?"

It appeared that the manager of the Executor and Trustee department of Silvesters' Bank in London had turned out from his files an old letter from Finloe Oates saying he wished to make the bank his executor and would soon be signing a new Will. The Trustee Manager, therefore, called upon Mr. de Lacy in person. He was like a jovial undertaker until he heard the Will of Finloe Oates had gone; given up and vanished on the strength of a forged letter!

"Not that there would be much in it for you, Butterfield," remarked Mr. de Lacy, on whose mind recent events had preyed so much that he now tended to treat it all with levity and titters. "What next?" he would mutter to himself and laugh loudly. His wife was trying to persuade him to see the doctor.

"Not that there'll be much for you. All the estate has been pinched except the house and I wouldn't be surprised if somebody didn't move into that on a forged conveyance ...."

Mr. Butterfield took a firm grip of his umbrella, just in case Mr. de Lacy went off his head completely, put on his bowler hat, and hurried off to the station in a state of great perturbation. There, he took the wrong train in his confusion and later found himself at Dover instead of Charing Cross.

The same thing was happening at the Home Counties Bank, Pimlico. After Mr. Macgreggor's report, the whole case was considered and it was decided that, for the present, no action should be taken against the manager. But as a corollary, it was found that the Executor of Lysander Oates was the Home Counties Bank! And Lysander had vanished. Maybe, he was dead; in which case the Executor would start to function. The Rodley Police and Scotland Yard therefore began to receive telephone calls from Threadneedle Street.

"Any news of Lysander Oates?"

"I'm fed up to the back teeth with it all," Montacute told Cromwell. "And now, here's a fellow called Hazlett buzzing round, from a London firm of solicitors. He says he drew both Wills and he believes he can help as soon as he has authority to do so. He was here this morning. Little clever-Dick of a chap, trying to push me round. I sent him off and said I'd write."

"Inspector Littlejohn's gone to the Isle of Man to-day in search of Lysander. Perhaps there'll be news tomorrow.... "

"Isle of Man? Whatever for? Seems a waste of time to me."

"Don't you get fresh about the chief! He's forgotten more about police work than you'll ever know."

"Don't get shirty! I'm a bit nervy, that's all...."

Thereupon the 'phone rang again.

"Is that you, Montacute? De Lacy, here. Any news yet about...?"

Cromwell went out to Netherby on the branch line. He found the one man in charge of the station busy with a lot of calves tied up in sacks to their necks. They kept mooing and it was getting on his nerves.

"If there's one thing cuts me to the quick, it's calves cryin'," he told Cromwell. "Reminds me of the days when the kids was young. Grown-up and married now, thank God. Five of 'em, and every one between the age of birth and two, a howler—all night and every night…. Got a ticket?"

"Yes; here it is. I want to talk to you about tickets. The local police tell me you saw the late Mr. Oates leaving here early one morning. You thought he was off on a trip. Was that so?"

"Yes, it was. They seem to think I'm a born liar because I made a mistake. It looked like 'im, and he limped like 'im."

"But you didn't see his face?"

"No, I didn't. He were hurryin' for the train which was drawin' in at the time. That's Oates, sure enough, I sez to myself and I wondered what he were doin' so early in the mornin'. Didn't take no ticket. I sez to myself, he must 'ave booked through an agency. In any case, they'll ketch 'im at the other end if he's not booked. And with that I forgets it, see? First train at five in the mornin', it was, and me not so lively at that un'oly hour…."

He was a little man with sad eyes and a walrus moustache. He had a long neck which he operated like a concertina, extending it when emphasising a point.

"Will that be all? 'Cos I see a chap comin' fer these calves, and I'll 'ave to help him load 'em…."

The calves were all mooing in concert now, which demented the poor porter until he didn't know which way to turn.

"It's no use…. I'll have to get a move to a h'industrial arena where they's no livestock to carry on…."

Cromwell gave him a shilling, which he spat upon and placed in the pocket of his corduroys. The sergeant made a note of it in his diary. It would go on his expenses sheet as "Sundries", and the cashier would play merry hell before he paid it. So what!

He met P.C. Mee parading the main street of the village. He usually aired himself about this time, bullying the little boys as the school turned out for lunch.

"Hey, you! Don't cross the road till I say you can. You'll get run-over.... "

"Hi.... If you ring another door-bell, I'll 'aul you in..."

"Good morning, constable. I'm from Scotland Yard on the Oates case.... "

"Yes, I know," said Johnny Know-all.

"I'm interested in a note on the records.... You said you saw Finloe Oates leaving by the first train one morning.... Is that so?"

Mee breathed hard. Why couldn't they let it drop? He'd admitted it might be wrong, but they kept on at him.

"It wasn't properly daylight. Matter o' fact, I was mistaken. I admit it, though it's rarely the case. I'm generally right in my reports. Anybody'll tell you that. But this chap didn't come face on to me. I see him side-view. He limped and wore a slouch hat, just like Mr. Oates...."

"About his build, too?"

"Yes.... Hey, you! Get off that wall. You'll break your neck. Don't let me 'ave to tell yer again.... "

"What date would that be?"

"May 4th.... I told headquarters that already."

"I can't make it out at all.... "

"It's as plain as the nose on yer face, if you ask me," said Johnny Know-all confidently. "Lysander killed Finloe, or else Finloe died on 'is hands. He stayed long enough to gather in all Finloe's money an' then bolted. It was Lysander I saw. Like as two peas, they would be at that time in the mornin'... half-light, so to speak."

"That may be...."

"And now, if you'll excuse me, I've got to be off. Inquest on Finloe this afternoon at two-thirty sharp and I'm one of the principal witnesses...."

They bade each other a rather stiff good-bye and Mee, after holding up a horse and cart and a tractor with relish to let two children cross the road, went in the police house for his dinner.

Cromwell decided he'd better stay in the village for lunch and attend the inquest which was to be held in the village hall, greatly to the consternation of the members of the Women's Institute, who had booked it for a bring-and-buy sale. Mr. Sebastian Dommett, the county coroner, had made it plain, however, that the ends of justice were not to be defeated by rummages of any kind and the women weren't to start until he'd finished.

They provided a lunch of sorts for Cromwell at the Naked Man. It consisted of nondescript soup from a tin; hot corned beef and carrots; and stewed plums and custard. Unused to providing regular meals of this kind, it seemed they had rifled the larder of all its old tins and served them up in a succession of messes. Cromwell didn't know what to do with the corned beef which was atrocious, so, when the waitress's back was turned and the room empty, he lifted a large dusty aspidistra from its pot on the window ledge, soil and all, and dumped the whole soggy mass in the bottom. Then he replaced the plant. When the girl returned, he sardonically praised the dish and she left wild-eyed at his speed and prowess, to get the next course.

"Would you like some more?" she whispered over her shoulder as she left, but there was no reply.

Florrie Judson brought his tankard of ale.

"The inquest's to-day. I'm not mixed up in it," she said, bending over him to impart the secret. Sensuality oozed from her, and she smelled of cheap face-powder and perspiring armpits. This was what Finloe Oates had preferred to Marion, the girl all the boys were crazy about years ago!

"...Mr. Oates's lawyer's been here asking questions, though. It seems he knows the money should come to me, but as the Will's been lost, there's likely to be trouble. He asked if anybody knew, and I told him the police had asked me...."

"A man called Hazlett?"

"Yes. He's not long been gone. He's here for the inquest."

"Did he ask many questions?"

"No. I told him about me and Finloe. He'd have to prove we was friendly, wouldn't he, so that he could prove Finloe might have left me the money...?"

She'd been thinking it over and greed and conceit had driven out affection. No more tears for Finloe; just a rapacious struggle to get her dues.

At precisely half-past two, Mr. Sebastian Dommett arrived with his retinue. Two tubby little clerks accompanied him wherever he went. It was said they constituted a bodyguard against the threats of a past malefactor to swing for Sebastian, who had deprived him of a considerable fund of treasure trove.

Mr. Dommett cast a Mephistophelian look around the court-room. He was cadaverous and his waxed moustache bristled with aggressive zeal. The small place was full. Many of the audience consisted of members of the Women's Institute, acting as scouts. They signalled from time to time to members looking through the windows from outside. In the small garden which surrounded the Hall—a war memorial really—were piled the bring-and-buy goods which were to be sold as soon as Mr. Dommett had finished with the space. The scouts within tick-tacked to those outside and Mr. Dommett caught the eye of one of them in the very act of indicating that proceedings were under way. He glared and held forth against unseemly behaviour in his court.

"I have powers to commit you for contempt if it continues."

P.C. Mee gave evidence. He wasn't a great success. Mr. Dommett's daughter had married a village constable against his wishes and a man in blue was to him like a red rag to a bull. He reproached Mee for not keeping a proper eye on the bungalow when it was apparently uninhabited.

"You might have prevented this awful crime if you'd been a little more alert."

Mr. Dommett thereupon flicked a long, bony index at Mee to indicate that would be all.

Dr. Hough, the police surgeon, then gave evidence. Mr. Dommett at once notified him that he himself was not a physiologist, and he would be obliged for an opinion in the simplest terms.

Dr. Hough therefore summed-up very clearly.

"The body was fully dressed and had been weighted in every pocket. Two months' submersion in a stagnant old tanpit had reduced it to a sorry condition. All the same, the organs were moderately well-preserved. The deceased had been suffering from cardiac degeneration for some years and was likely to die at any time from overstrain or sudden shock. Such a shock must have happened and killed him. Apart from the manner of disposal of the body, death was due to natural causes; heart failure."

"Can you estimate the time of death?"

"I would say the body had been in the water six weeks or two months. That is merely surmise based on its condition, and on precedents in medical records. The police, I gather, found in the pocket a rate-notice posted from the rating offices in the middle of March. I concur in the inference given by that."

"Very well…. Natural causes. Call Ezra Jones."

Jones was the postman who had met Mr. Killgrass in the garden on the fatal afternoon which had started all this.

Jones was wearing his best official uniform, which was a size too large for him. The sleeves fell over his knuckles and the trousers hung in corrugated folds over his boots. He had his hat on.

"Take off your hat when you take the oath, and *keep it off!*"

Mr. Jones, his jaws rotating round the perpetual quid of tobacco, prised off the offending article and stood with a livid ring crowning his brow where it had sat. He swore to tell the truth with great difficulty for his chew of tobacco impeded the flow of speech.

"I cannot allow you to chew tobacco in giving evidence. Please remove it…. "

Mr. Jones looked round for somewhere to spit. He reminded you of a dog seeking a special tree.

"No, no, no. Take it outside and remove it. Then return."

Mr. Jones rushed to the open door, spat the quid on the grass, greatly to the discomfiture of the bring-and-buy contingent, and returned a new man.

He had little to say that was relevant, but it took him a long time to sort it out. Anxious female faces appeared at the windows and eyed him malevolently.

"Your name is Ezra Jones. You are postman in Netherby...."

Mr. Jones looked amazed. As if he hadn't known that for more than thirty years!

"No wonder taxation's that heavy," he told his cronies at the Naked Man later that afternoon. He had imagined fame awaiting later, as a result of his evidence. Instead, all he had told was that the house seemed occupied at the date guessed by the doctor.

At this point, Inspector Montacute had whispered to one of Mr. Dommett's attendant little men, who, in turn, had whispered it to his boss. That was police business; all they wanted was the cause of death, permission to bury, and an adjournment.

Mr. Dommett was annoyed, but he didn't show it. He gave a verdict accordingly, with the ineffective help of a small jury, whom he had impounded and prevented from doing a good day's work. After which, just to show the Women's Institute where they got off, he did a lot of writing on papers before him. Then he packed—up and went home. As he and his army were leaving the hall by one door, the bring-and-buy caravan with its bulky merchandise was entering by the other....

One thing the inquest had brought: Mrs. Titley, from the bungalow over the way from Finloe Oates's. She'd been away from home, staying with her daughter at Bexhill since before Finloe's death had been announced. The news of the inquest had hurried her back, greatly to the relief of her son-in-law. She missed nothing. Always peeping round the window curtains, she was able to state that on the date in question, she had seen Fish-lock take the key from its usual hiding-place, enter the house and...Well, she had begun to wonder if she had lost her skill at spying! He hadn't, to her knowledge, come out again in daylight. She wondered if he'd given her the slip. Confirmation of her continued prowess by the news that Fishlock had died inside and been hidden away, far from casting her down, seemed to invigorate her.

"I see that Flo Judson prowlin' around, too. The 'uzzy! No better than she should be. Strange goings-on there were at that 'ouse after poor Mrs. Finloe passed over. Nearly as soon as she was laid to rest, there was Finloe caperin' around like a young lad. Paintin' the outside and mowin' and weedin' all hours of the day.... Then, sudden, it stopped, and he shut 'imself up like an 'ermit. I couldn't make 'ead or tail of 'is goings-on. A time or two, I saw 'im prowlin' round just after dusk, as I was goin' to bed. The place seemed deserted at night. He must 'ave gone to bed when it got dark."

"Are you sure it *was* Finloe Oates, Mrs. Titley?"

"Who else could it be?"

She was a scraggy, peevish-faced woman, with the inquisitive features of a tapir. Her mouth opened and closed like a trap, and her thin, pointed nose grew red with the enthusiasm of turning over a lot of gossip, especially as it had a semi-official blessing.

"It might have been someone like him prowling around after dark."

"It might, as you say. I never went out to see him close to."

"Did you know Finloe's brother, Lysander?"

"Yes. He came over to Mrs. Finloe's interment. Didn't stay long then, but I saw him here later. He come one afternoon. I saw him go in, but I never saw him go out. Now that's another funny thing! My windows overlook the front. You'd think they'd another way out behind."

She said it with great indignation, as though resenting any attempt to avoid her close supervision.

"My guess is that Finloe went queer, threw himself in the water, and died of shock. They said he died natural, didn't they? Well...?"

"Yes; that may be a theory...."

They didn't tell her, though, of all the jiggery-pokery with Finloe's estate. She knew enough already. She hurried home, eager to make up for lost time in surveillance of Shenandoah.

Montacute pondered for a time on the various points raised.

"That seems to settle it. Lysander took Finloe's place till he'd sold the shares and collected Finloe's money. The one thing I can't understand is, him digging up the dog. I was a bit puzzled at the time I was told about it and I did a bit of digging there myself just to make sure Finloe hadn't been put there instead of the animal. I got Lysander's prints from the spade, too, so he *did* unearth the body. What he did with it, I can't for the life of me think. Perhaps it's in the tanpit as well."

Cromwell's mind flew back to one of Littlejohn's old cases.

"We once investigated a murder where a dead dog came in. It had been poisoned by the same poison.... Here; let's get back and go through the list of local vets. I've got an idea."

There were only three veterinary surgeons in Rodley and the third and most remote remembered a dog being brought for examination, post mortem.

"I recollect it well. In fact, I think I've still got the report on my files. I'll look."

He was a little bandy-legged man, dressed in riding breeches and hacking jacket. His hair was sandy and his eyes, too, with sandy eyebrows and eyelashes. He looked like a man with a great thirst and his complexion betrayed it. Behind the surgery stood a large building containing kennels and you could hear all the dogs yapping, barking and howling in misery.

"Here it is...."

"May I borrow it? I'll see you get it back. How did it come to be done?"

"I remember one night around late March a fellow..."

"What did he look like?"

"He kept on the doorstep in the dark while he talked, but I could see his spectacles and I think he wore a bit of a beard."

"Right. Go on...."

"He had the dog in a sack. Not a pretty sight, I'll tell you. It had been buried once. He seemed a bit upset. Wanted a post-mortem. I said he'd have to leave it, and he did. He came the next night...."

"What about the results...?"

"I'm not much of an autopsy performer myself, but I'm lucky in having a pathologist friend from the local infirmary. He said, being as it was me, he'd come and do it. He took out the organs and examined them in-his own lab. His report said poisoning by a fair quantity of arsenic. To amuse himself, he went further than that. He told me the dog had eaten some pork pie as its last meal and that had probably contained the dose."

"You passed that on to your client?"

"Yes, and he nearly went off his head. He ground his teeth. 'The swine,' he said, 'I'll kill him for this.' I didn't make much of it or take it seriously. I thought perhaps the dog had been a nuisance to the neighbours and they'd doped a piece of pie and thrown it over the fence. O.K.?"

"Yes, thanks. I'm very much obliged...."

It was late when Cromwell got back to the police station. There was a message there from Littlejohn saying he was getting the midnight back to London from Liverpool and would be glad if Cromwell would ring him at the Liverpool police office when he got in. The sergeant put through a call at once. Littlejohn told his colleague his story, and Cromwell told his. Montacute was surprised by a spate of exciting news. Lysander Oates had been found dead in the mine at Snuff the Wind, and evidence pointed to Theodore Hunt as the murderer.

"And the Inspector says he wants you to consider exhuming the body of Mrs. Finloe Oates. Her dog was poisoned by arsenic and it looks as if it died through eating the remnants of a pie which her husband must have doctored to kill her. Lysander found the dog, dug it up, had it post-mortemed, and jumped to the same conclusion that I did. He must have taxed Finloe with it and Finloe died of shock or fright. The swine must have been paving the way for marrying Florrie Judson...."

# Chapter Eleven
## Arsenic and Handwriting

Digging up a body is a horrible job, especially when there is little purpose except curiosity in it. The confirmation that Mrs. Oates had died from a dose of poison would really lead nowhere. It would simply settle the fact that her husband had poisoned her. But Finloe Oates was dead and past paying the price. Even Lysander, who was presumed to have found out the crime, and, in his fashion, avenged it, was not there to answer questions. He, too, was dead. All the same it had to be done. The necessary order was obtained to sanction the exhuming, which was performed by night. Nobody knew what was toward in Netherby churchyard, except P.C. Mee, three men from Rodley, one from the Home Office and the two Scotland Yard detectives. An old lady who lived near the churchyard rose at three in the morning for a dose of bicarbonate of soda, peeped through the curtains, saw lights cautiously bobbing among the tombstones, plunged back in bed, drew the clothes over her head and forgot her flatulence in her terror.

The organs of poor, neglected Mrs. Oates—once so fair and the cause of strife among friends—revealed arsenic and plenty of it. The experts said there had been enough in the food to kill five more women. And that was that. It added another shocking chapter to the drama of the Oates family, and little else.

Meanwhile, the handwriting experts at Scotland Yard had been busy, too. The writing on the note Littlejohn had found in the Isle of Man had to be established as that of Theodore Hunt beyond doubt. First, an authentic copy of the schoolmaster's handwriting was required. That was easier than they expected. Littlejohn telephoned to the Superintendent of Police at Bishop's Walton and asked for his help. The Superintendent laughed ironically. He had plenty of specimens. His son attended Dalbay Hall School and his copybooks were plentifully sprinkled with caustic samples of just the thing Scotland Yard were asking for. A special messenger arrived very promptly, bearing two grubby, ink-bespattered exercise-books with Superintendent Slatter's compliments. Both bore the stamp of Dalbay Hall, with a statement, in atrocious printing, that they were the property of Thomas J. Slatter, of Form IIIb, and then, in larger and more appalling lettering, "ALGEBRA" and "SCRIPTURE".

The handwriting expert, who had boys of his own and was also skilled enough to do their homework for them when they couldn't do it themselves, had to be reminded by his colleagues that they weren't concerned with the Journeys of St. Paul and Quadratic Equations, but with Theodore Hunt's comments on them. There were many, for Mr. T. J. Slatter's average mark out of a possible twenty, was about three or four.

"The chap at Bishop's Walton ought to blush at sendin' out stuff like this for others to see," said the calligraphist. "Ashamed of himself, too. My boys always get top marks. I see to it they do...."

They concentrated on two statements.

"See me after class. You don't seem to know what you are doing at all. Disgraceful! Do it all again."

"St. Paul, as far as experts know, never set foot in Cornwall! Do you mean Corinth? Shocking work! See me later."

Whatever young Slatter had suffered through quadratics and the wanderings of the apostle, he had elicited comments which settled once and for all that the note found at Snuff the Wind had been written by Hunt. This meant another trip north for Littlejohn, and a hasty one at that.

It was late afternoon when Littlejohn arrived at Bishop's Walton and he thought it best to call at the police station, thank the Superintendent and enlist his help.

"He's gone to Mr. Hunt's, sir," said the sergeant-in-charge. "There's been a fearful shindy there, sir, and they sent for him."

The sergeant had made no overstatement; the house in Abbott's Walk was like bedlam when the Inspector arrived. Slatter and two constables were in the stately drawing-room, and between them, battered, dishevelled and hysterical with rage, was Hunt. His clothes were dirty and disarrayed and his face was blackened like that of a chimney-sweep.

Littlejohn took Slatter aside and asked what it was all about. The Superintendent was very sheepish himself. A large, beefy countryman, he looked ready to explode.

"I sent off the copybooks on the quiet, so that my son wouldn't know; but he found out, it seems. He must have seen me taking and addressing them. I did it at home. He says he read the address on my blotter. What does he do, but goes and tells it round the school. Hunt must have got to know and jumped to conclusions. He packed a bag and was going to run away.... I don't often take a stick to my kids, but this time ..."

Slatter smacked his lips at the thought of the sufferings of Tom, junior.

"But why all this commotion?"

"His sister caught him packing and thought he was leaving her for good. She has outbreaks now and then, but this has beat the lot. She enticed him into the coal cellar some way and locked him down there till he promised not to go. Hunt tried to get out through the coal-hole in the alley. Good job one of my men was passing and heard Miss Hunt screaming and saw Hunt emerging from underground. He sent for me just as I was in the middle of giving my lad whatfor for letting me down...."

"Where is Miss Hunt?"

"The doctor's been, given her a sedative, and put her to bed. She'll be all right. A lot of this is just playacting to get her own way, if you ask me."

"I'd like a word with Hunt alone, if I may, but perhaps you'd better stay around, sir."

"With pleasure. Have him all to yourself. I've had enough of him. This isn't the first time we've been here on similar errands. He can't control her when she has a bad bout.... "

Hunt had quietened down. They'd given him brandy and he had recovered somewhat. After a wash and a change of clothes, he looked presentable again. Littlejohn had to tread warily, for the letter he had found in the Isle of Man had not altogether put a noose round the schoolmaster's neck. There were some features about it which required fuller explanation. The expert had said, for example, that under the microscope, it looked to have been burned systematically to suit somebody's purpose. At certain spots, the flame consuming it seemed to have been snuffed out by someone wearing gloves. But one thing of vital importance had been revealed. Whoever had written the letter had also forged the cheques and documents to Silvesters' Bank! And Hunt had written the letter!

"What made you wish to run away, sir?"

Hunt was sitting on the couch, as pale as death. His skin looked like parchment moulded on a skull. His pride and poise had gone and he knew there was a policeman standing on the other side of the door.

"I didn't want to run away. It was my sister's impaired imagination. She suffers from bouts of illness and fancies things when the attacks come on. She locked me in the cellar as I was going for coal...."

Hunt was so sorry for himself and confused that he started to weep. Tears ran down his cheeks and he shook with hard, distressing sobs. Obviously he was at the end of his tether.

"I'm sorry, Mr. Hunt, but this won't do. I have a number of things I want you to explain, please. You need not answer my questions, and if you do, I must warn you that anything you say may be taken down in writing and used in evidence...."

"Go on. Go on.... Give me full measure and overflowing. I've deserved it. My pride has brought me down again."

It was growing dusk outside. The streets were quiet and a lamplighter—quaint survival—paused to light a gas-lamp at the corner. Slowly, Hunt crossed the room and switched on the lights in a beautiful lustre chandelier.

"Well?"

"Please look at this, sir."

Littlejohn took the partly burned letter from his pocket and spread it on a small table.

"Where did you get that? I sent it to ..."

He stopped suddenly, his eyes vacant, the truth dawning on him.

"Have you been to the Isle of Man?"

"Yes. I found there the dead body of your friend Lysander Oates. He'd been murdered."

Hunt looked dumbfounded and then a sudden burst of energy, which he didn't know how to dissipate, seized him. He ran to the window, looked through it, as though contemplating another dash for freedom, cooled his forehead on the pane for a second, and then turned and ran back to Littlejohn with little prancing steps.

"I didn't do it. I didn't.... I never went to the Isle of Man.... I told him so...."

He seized the lapels of Littlejohn's jacket and shook the Inspector in a frenzy of strength.

"Control yourself. This letter implies that Oates asked you to join him there and you said you would...."

"I didn't.... I did not.... It's been burned to make it look as if I'd gone.... Somebody's been trying to hang me.... But I won't stand for it.... "

He took hold of Littlejohn and shook him again.

"If you don't calm down, I'll take you and lock you up for the night. Now, sir! Explain what you mean."

There must have been a streak of madness in Theodore Hunt as well as in his sister. From rage he turned to suavity, as if about to convince Littlejohn once and for all.

"Allow me to disabuse your mind.... "

Just as he might have done a class at school! You could almost see him gather his teaching gown round him in a pose of scholarship. He opened a drawer in the bureau and took a sheet of paper.

"Follow me closely.... "

Hunt placed the burned document on top of the plain sheet and, after a brief pause, started to write. His pen flew across the paper, piecing new words to those of the letter, restoring those destroyed by fire.

"There!"

A shout of triumph! The constable put his head round the door.

"All right, sir?"

"Yes, thanks...."

Littlejohn didn't even raise his head. He was so engrossed and fascinated by what Hunt had done.

Dear Lysander,

Thanks for your strange message. I really don't understand why you have taken yourself off to that godforsaken spot. I cannot join you there immediately. Term does not end yet and I am very concerned to finish it with dignity. Nevertheless, if you urgently need help, I will come as soon as possible. I will join you there at the end of May. I write this in haste to catch the post and I hope you will not mind the delay. Something must have gone sadly awry to call forth such a cry for help.

Best wishes,
Yours as ever,
Theo. Hunt.

"Well?"

Hunt was triumphant. He even smiled, forgetting his troubles.

"Very ingenious, sir, but not convincing enough. What made you write it?"

Hunt sobered down. He was beginning to realise that his position was dangerous. He grew excited again.

"I know you won't believe me. It all sounds absolutely fantastic. But I swear it's the truth. On the memory of my mother, I swear it. Oates telephoned me from the Isle of Man. He said he was in terrible trouble, and would I go there at once?"

"But couldn't you answer him by 'phone at the same time?"

"That's just it! I know you won't believe me. But you *must*. What am I to do, if you don't? You'll think I killed Lysander myself and I didn't. I swear..."

"You wrote instead of answering by 'phone. Did you want time to think it over?"

"No. Oates spoke to me. The line was terrible and I could only just make out what he was saying. Even then, I guessed some of it. He asked me to go to him without delay. Life and death, he said. I started to argue. 'I can't hear you,' he said. I got in the end shouting so loud that people in the street looked in at the window. Still he couldn't hear. It must have been the under-sea cable went wrong. In the end, he said, 'I can't hear a word of what you say. Write to me to-night and say when and how you're coming.' He ought to have known I couldn't just pack up and go right in term. I wrote at once. I felt very annoyed...."

"And you wrote in the terms of the letter you have just reconstructed?"

"Absolutely. Someone has burned it to incriminate me.

"You say the telephone call came from Oates in the Isle of Man?"

"Certainly. He was there. Where else should he ring from?"

Littlejohn went to the door and called in the constable.

"You have a local telephone exchange in Bishop's Walton?"

"Yes, sir."

"Please go there now and trace this call. Ask where it came from and what was the state of the line at the time."

The Inspector jotted down the time and date of the incoming call mentioned by Hunt.

"And now, Mr. Hunt. There was a picture of the Isle of Man hanging on the wall there last time I called. Why has it been removed?"

"Really, Inspector. I know you have certain powers, but surely not those of demanding details of how and why I choose to arrange the furniture of my home. One tires of pictures, you know. One likes a change, now and then."

"I suggest the change was due to your fear of the exact spot in the island shown on that picture being discovered. You told me it was in Wales."

"Did I? I must have been dreaming. I took it down for a change.... "

"That won't do, sir. I must warn you that unless you tell me the truth about your relations and your dealings with Lysander Oates, you run a serious risk of being charged with his murder."

Hunt's eyes glazed and he struggled again to keep his self-control.

"This is ridiculous! He was my friend. Why should I kill him?"

"For the fortune in his possession. The fortune you helped him to get by forgery!"

"This is fantastic! Murder! Forgery! What next?"

"I do not need to tell you, sir, that Lysander Oates appropriated all his dead brother's means by forging documents during the time he kept his death secret. He sold all his investments and drew his balance from the bank by documents which you helped him to forge."

"Utter nonsense! Utter rot! Have you gone mad?"

"Very well, sir. You will be taken to the police station and there charged with the murder of Lysander Oates and with the forgery I've mentioned. We have proof of your guilt there, too. We have tested your handwriting...."

Hunt suddenly made a wild spring at Littlejohn, like a savage animal at bay. The Inspector stretched out a long arm and held him off, whilst Hunt clawed and flailed the air trying to grip him by the throat. Littlejohn seized him by both arms, lifted him bodily and sat him down hard on the couch.

"Now behave yourself, or I'll handcuff you. For the last time, do you wish to tell me the truth, or do I call the constable and have you arrested?"

Hunt sat there, panting and twisting his lips. He couldn't keep still; shuffling, waving his arms, flexing his legs.

"What do you want to know?"

"About the forgery, first."

Hunt was on his feet again, walking up and down, halting, turning on his heel, gesticulating.

"I did what a real friend would do. I helped Oates right a wrong, that's all."

"How?"

Up and down, up and down. Hunt paced the carpet with little prancing steps, recovering his control as he related his ethical venture into crime.

"Lysander quarrelled one night with Finloe about the way he'd treated his wife.... I didn't go into the full details. I hate sordid domestic squabbles. I was too amazed, too, at what Lysander asked of me. In the course of the quarrel, Finloe dropped dead. Lysander came to see me all the way from London. He was in a terrible state. Would I help him?"

Hunt, half a madman, was reciting it with gestures and pompous little postures, just like a cheap melodramatic actor.

"Be as brief as possible, if you please."

Hunt didn't seem to hear. He was like one in a trance.

"It was all like a fantastic story. Lysander had discovered from some neighbour of Finloe's that his brother had been indulging in an adulterous affair with a local barmaid whilst his wife was alive. He feared that Finloe had left all his considerable wealth to the hussy and was determined she shouldn't have it. He wanted to be certain. If he made known his brother's death, the law would take its course and the estate might go to the barmaid. He wanted to get the Will and make sure."

"When did he call here?"

"The night his brother died. He came by road in a hired car. He had left his brother's dead body in the house."

"Well?"

"He had looked through his brother's papers and found that the Will was at the bank. He wanted to write for it in Finloe's handwriting, but was no use whatever at forgery."

"That was where you came in?"

"Frankly, yes. I had been a friend of the Oates family ever since we were children. I had a natural aptitude for forgery, though, believe me, I never used it illicitly.… "

"Until Lysander asked you."

"Until Lysander asked me."

Hunt seemed to be enjoying himself.

"He asked me to copy Finloe's hand and tell the bank to send the Will to Finloe's home by post. I remonstrated with Lysander. We argued. He told me of the harlot in the village inn, how she would inherit what now was morally Lysander's birthright.… Ten thousand pounds!"

"What did he offer you as your share?"

"What do you mean, sir? I was not to be bought against my conscience! Eventually, I agreed. I wrote to the bank, the Will was sent to my friend at his brother's house, and he found that, as he suspected, the barmaid had inherited the lot.... "

"Finloe Oates must have been mad!"

"So Lysander said when he returned here the next night. And then he told me the awful scheme he had initiated. He had thrown his brother's body in a pond behind the house and was going to impersonate him, live in the house as his brother until he had realised his assets, and then go abroad and retire in peace. He didn't seem the least upset. His brother had died a natural death, he said, and was past caring where he was buried. In any case, he hated him and didn't mind disposing of the body. Once in possession of the money, he proposed to hide his trail, living a little while in a house he knew—the one he painted and gave me—and then off to the south of France via Ireland ... ."

Hunt was still pacing about excitedly. He paused now and then for effect, picking up one of the many little Dresden figures which ornamented the room, putting it down again, blowing dust from the mantelpiece and helping himself to drinks from the brandy bottle without asking Littlejohn to join him.

Superintendent Slatter thrust in his head.

"Finished yet?"

"No, sir. But you needn't wait. I'll see you later at the police station. There's a constable about, is there?"

"Yes. He's sitting by the kitchen fire.... "

Hunt was eager to be getting on with the tale in which he was the hero, the clever one. He was out to clear himself in his way and avoid a night or more in a cell.

" ... All that prevented Lysander from succeeding fully was that he couldn't do more than forge his brother's name. He'd have to write letters of instruction to the bank. To use a typewriter, he told me, would have aroused suspicion, because his brother never even possessed a machine. He wanted me to do the writing for him. He said it wouldn't be forgery. He'd take the responsibility of forging the name, if I'd write the letters. As he needed them, he'd send me draft copies of the letters, which I would re-write in Finloe's hand, from specimens provided, and return at once. We did that and continued to do so till Lysander had acquired all the money which was, by rights, his own."

"How much of it did you get?"

"There you go again! You are a cynic, Inspector. I did it all because I thought Lysander was right and I wanted to help him. He was a truly decent fellow, a lifelong friend."

"How much?"

Hunt sighed. He turned his back and started to wind a little French clock on the mantelpiece.

"Five hundred pounds," he said over his shoulder. "But ... but Lysander insisted. I didn't refuse. I'm penniless except for my salary, Inspector. I spend all I get on my sister and her comforts ... ."

He rested his elbow on the marble mantel, and gripped his brow melodramatically between his fingers.

"That is all, Inspector. I've made a clean breast of all I know and all I've done. The crime was committed ... the forgery, I mean, by the late Lysander. I only wrote the letters; he signed them."

"Did you see him again after his second visit, sir?"

"No. The rest was done by mail. With the last letter he sent, he told me he was through and was immediately putting into operation his plan to leave the country. I knew then he'd gone to the Isle of Man and I'd never see him again. I little thought he would die."

"Murder is the word, Mr. Hunt."

Hunt turned savagely on the Inspector.

"Well, what of it? I didn't do it."

"You say you haven't been away from home this year?"

"That is true. I haven't been to the Isle of Man, if that's what you're hinting at. You can't catch me there."

"You're forgetting the three days I spent with Mrs. Swailes, aren't you, Theo? The time you went away and didn't say where you were going, except that it was on business.... "

The voice came from behind the door and was followed by Miss Hunt, clad in a long white nightgown and house-coat. She had grown calm, deadly calm, and spoke in a wheedling, malevolent voice.

"Where've you come from, Constance? Get back to bed at once. I order you. The doctor said ..."

"Don't get cross, Theo. You know it upsets me. I came down to find you. Nurse is talking with the constable in the kitchen and I was all by myself. I stopped behind the open door to listen and you seem to have forgotten that you were away for three days at the end of April. I can never forget that. You left me, Theo, you left me ..."

She began to cry and grow wild again.

"Nurse! Nurse! What do you mean by leaving my sister? You know it's not safe to leave her! She might do herself harm in her present depressed state. Get along and put her to bed. And *stay with her....*"

The constable, his ears red, came rushing out with the nurse. She was pretty and he'd just been starting to enjoy himself. The girl tossed her head.

"If I can't relax a little when the patient's asleep ..."

"You can't .... What do I pay you for ...?"

The nurse and her constabulary admirer started to usher and persuade Miss Constance up the stairs again.

"Is it true what your sister said?" asked Littlejohn as they returned to the drawing-room.

"Inspector! Inspector!"

It was Constance in hysterics, calling for him.

"He was away with that Susan Fairclough. He thinks I don't know. Ask him. Ask him about that Fairclough woman .... "

She started to scream and they had to get her in her room by force. Hunt did not attempt to help them. He was beside himself with rage at this latest outburst.

"Don't heed my sister. She's beside herself sometimes. She imagines things."

But the last shot had got home. Hunt was anxious to pass it off.

"Who is Susan Fairclough?"

"A friend of ours."

"Your sister didn't seem very friendly disposed. Who is she?"

"Wife of one of my colleagues at school. I am friendly with her husband. Constance is terribly jealous of all my friends."

"You were away on the days Miss Hunt stated ... the end of April ... the time Lysander Oates was killed?"

"What are you getting at?"

"I want an answer. I warn you, I can confirm this by inquiries at the school. You went away?"

Hunt turned his head hither and thither. He was trying to find a way out and none presented itself.

"Yes. I forgot. I was away .... "

"Where?"

"I'm not disposed to say."

"Very well. Get your hat and coat. You are under arrest...."

"But I've told you, I didn't kill Oates. Why should I?"

"Where were you?"

Hunt had reached breaking point. He started to shout and bawl.

"I went to the Isle of Man! Now are you satisfied? I went to the Isle of Man! I couldn't get Oates out of my mind. I wondered if he were in danger. He had so much money with him. A fortune.... I went."

"By 'plane?"

"No. I got the morning boat. Stayed overnight in Liverpool."

"Were you away three days?"

"Yes; damn you! How much more?"

"How did you spend the three days?"

"Coming and going. I was only on the island one day. I stayed a night in Liverpool coming, and one going."

"Where?"

"The Crescent Hotel."

"You went to Oates's cottage?"

"Yes. It was deserted. I never saw him. There was nobody about. I didn't see him. You've got to believe me!"

"Did anyone see you?"

"You can check at the hotels."

"Was anyone with you when you went to the cottage?"

Hunt thrust his face close to Littlejohn's. He had the eyes of a madman.

"Meaning what?"

Littlejohn had his answer without any more questions.

"Mrs. Fairclough was with you, wasn't she?"

"Don't you dare mention that sweet woman! The association of Susan with the police is distasteful to me in the extreme.…"

"All the same, Hunt, you'll hang unless she gives you an alibi."

"I'll what?"

"Hang."

"But I'll deny it all. They can't prove I killed him if I didn't.…"

*"Did you take Susan Fairclough?"*

"Yes. Yes. I did. But I won't have her brought in it. Her husband is cruel to her. A boor! A hog! Yes, a hog wallowing in a sty! She is the sweetest woman on earth, the comfort of my darkness, the…"

"That will do. Calm yourself, sir. I shall have to see her."

"If you go near that sweet woman, I'll kill myself. I will. I swear it. I've nothing to live for anyhow. Constance has got worse and worse. I'm tied to her hand and foot. Daren't leave her. She goes mad if I'm away an hour longer than usual. Susan and I love each other. I'm getting Constance in a home and we're going away together. I'll make up to her what that swine Fairclough…"

"Was she with you all the time you were in the Isle of Man?"

"Yes. It was our first trip together. It was beautiful. Spiritual.… Nothing sordid…nothing of the flesh. Just the love of kindred souls.…"

"She will be able to give you an alibi then.…"

"What! And bring that swine Fairclough in as the outraged husband! Not likely! I'll hang first."

"I'm afraid you have no choice, Mr. Hunt. You are coming with me to the police station where you will remain in custody on a forgery charge. The bank have called in the police on the case and you are self-condemned."

"You swine! You've trapped me. I'll deny it all."

"Come along, sir. The constable will go with you and you can put a few things in a bag.... "

"I won't go."

"It would ill become the dignity of an educated man like yourself to be forcibly taken there. Come along now. Be reasonable, Mr. Hunt."

"Very well. But you shall pay for this. I do not suffer fools gladly, let me tell you."

Then began the business of getting Hunt away and making arrangements for his sister. Constance was removed to a home that very night. She thought she was going on a holiday and took kindly to it. She remained there for the brief remainder of her life and, strange to say, never asked for her brother again.

As Littlejohn left the silent Hunt house much later and for the last time, the telephone bell rang. It was the police. They'd traced the mysterious call from Oates.

" ... It wasn't put in at the island at all, sir. It came from a call-box at Speke Airport, Liverpool, and was timed two-fifteen.... "

"That looks like a point for Hunt," said Littlejohn to himself. Someone had incriminated him by the doctored letter in his own writing. They had decoyed him to the island, and at the same time got him to write to Oates at Snuff the Wind.

Had it been Oates on his way to the Isle of Man? Or had it been his murderer, trying to implicate Hunt? Two-fifteen.... That was about the time the Northolt 'plane would touch down at Speke on its way to the island. Someone on that 'plane had sent the message.

# Chapter Twelve
# Mrs. Fairclough

The Faircloughs lived in a large semi-detached house near Dalbay Hall and took in some of the boys as boarders. On his way there, Littlejohn wondered what kind of a woman he was going to find. He had tried to dismiss from his mind visions of young and flighty masters' wives, or women past their prime desperately clutching at a last chance of romance with the fantastic Hunt. But he couldn't stop himself from playing the mental game of find-the-lady. It was past the hour of school and he had already rung up Mrs. Fairclough to make sure that no complications would arise from the presence of a jealous, complacent, or even unsuspecting husband.

A young maid opened the door. She wasn't at all prepossessing. A pitiable girl with a chlorotic complexion, chronic catarrh, close-cropped hair, like an inmate of some penal institution or other, and a large smear of blacklead across one cheek.

"Whad nabe shall I say?"

"Inspector Littlejohn...."

"Oh...."

It hadn't registered but that didn't matter, for Mrs. Fairclough had evidently been listening for his arrival and now appeared in the doorway, smoking a cigarette. Littlejohn's flights of fancy had not been far wrong!

Susan Fairclough was well past forty and there was grey in her dark hair. She still bore considerable traces of the good looks she must once have possessed. She was small and probably, in her heyday, had been slim and energetic. Now, her figure had thickened, the flesh around her chin and throat had started to sag, she depended on careful make-up for her complexion, and her former charm had turned to studied coyness. She wore a long blue house-coat and had obviously groomed herself for the interview.

Littlejohn was at a loss to understand the reasons for an intrigue between this woman and Hunt. He seemed too fastidious and she too vain to suit one another. Surely, no mad surge of passion, no reckless determination to squeeze the last few drops of excitement from life whilst the going was good had impelled these two middle-aged people, responsible and set in their ways, to commit the folly of running away together, risking their own security and the happiness of those dependent on them and then, strangest of all, running back to resume the life they had left behind in Bishop's Walton!

"Come in, please."

She said it without removing the cigarette. The voice was dry and affected and the hand with which she closed the door was white and podgy with red-painted nails. The maid disappeared into the kitchen and you could hear her banging about with a brush and dustpan. Mrs. Fairclough led the way into a small morning-room where a fire glowed dimly in the hearth and a Siamese cat lounged voluptuously in an armchair beside it. This place was known as the Den. The boy boarders were allowed in most parts of the house, but this room was sacred to Fairclough and his wife. It bore signs of strange, exotic taste. The easy chairs, the curtains and the divan were upholstered in folk-weave of red, blue and gold. The carpet was expensive Chinese. The only other ornaments were three pictures on the walls and three large cases of books.

"Sit down, Inspector…. You are looking at the pictures?"

She was right. Littlejohn was trying, in his way, to discover what they were all about. One was composed of pieces of coloured paper stuck in geometrical patterns one on top of the other. Over the fireplace hung an oil painting of what might have been anything from a garden in spring to a canal winding its way through fields the colour of verdigris. It looked as if the artist had squeezed his colours, willy nilly, from the tubes and rubbed them in the canvas with his thumbnail. The remaining water-colour showed two elongated neuter figures, with shapely legs, but whose bodies were made up of vertical and horizontal lines with no substance.

"My husband is a collector. There are hundreds of pounds worth in value in those three works…. The dealers say they will be worth twice that in a few years."

"Will they, now? I'm afraid I don't know much about modern pictures, Mrs. Fairclough."

"It's an acquired taste, I must admit. They grow on one. I would miss them now if they went. Cigarette?"

She lit another from the stub of the old one.

"You said you wanted to see me alone…. I can't think why, but I'll help if I can."

She knew very well what it was all about. There was fear in her large, fine eyes; the pupils were shifty and she couldn't keep her hands still.

"This is going to be rather embarrassing, Mrs. Fairclough, but if you'll be frank with me, I'll make the affair as little trouble to you as I can."

She stiffened and tapped the ash from her cigarette nervously, and waited.

"I think I ought to tell you right away that your friend Mr. Hunt has been arrested."

She tried to brazen it out. She giggled as though the idea of Hunt in gaol was comic.

"On suspicion of murder.... "

She switched to anger. She dug her nails in the palms of her hands and stimulated rage.

"What has that to do with me? Why mix me up in it and take the trouble to call here whilst my husband is out? You ought to have conducted this interview with him here. He would have known what to do about it."

"I'm sure he would, Mrs. Fairclough, but it would have been very unpleasant for you. Mr. Hunt claims an alibi. He states that he was with you in Liverpool and the Isle of Man at the time of the crime and that you can swear that he didn't leave you for long enough to murder anyone."

She turned pale under her cosmetics and Littlejohn thought she was going to faint. In her anxiety, she looked ten years older. Then, she pulled herself together.

"Of all the impertinence! As if I..."

Littlejohn was going to have no more beating about the bush.

"Mrs. Fairclough, I called here to keep this matter as quiet as possible and avoid a scandal. Your name has been mentioned in this case and I wish to ask you some questions. If you refuse to help us, the case will be aired in court, that's all. Take your choice."

She crossed to a cupboard, poured out a liberal glass of gin, drank it and looked a bit better.

Her voice changed. She was going to try the helpless woman tactics.

"...I admit we were friends. Nothing wrong in that. I thought a trip to Liverpool to see the shops and the sea would do me good. I'd had a hard winter and the boys were away. My husband was going to an exhibition in London, so I decided to take the opportunity. Why I should be mixed up in this terrible business, I can't say...."

She tried to weep a little, but the tears wouldn't come.

"May I ask you a question or two, Mrs. Fairclough? It might be easier that way."

She sat down, still clinging to her gin glass, tensed herself, opened her eyes wide and tried to look a model of truth.

"Yes, I've nothing to hide."

"You were away at the end of April, the 28th of April onwards?"

"Yes. I was in Liverpool."

"And the Isle of Man?"

"It was a nice day; I thought the sail would do me good."

"You went with Theodore Hunt...?"

She bit the nail of her index finger, but did not answer.

"Come, Mrs. Fairclough. I want the truth. If you won't give me proper answers, I may as well go and find them elsewhere. But I assure you, if I do, your name will have to be mentioned and the results will be your own responsibility."

"I did go with Hunt..." she burst out. It was as though she spoke it in a hurry before she decided not to tell it. "As I said, there was nothing wrong in that. He was going. We travelled together. He looked after me and made things much pleasanter by his kindness."

"You were together all the three days?"

"What do you mean by that?"

She was afraid again, but trying to bluff it away.

"You stayed in the same hotel?"

"Yes. We had separate rooms. There was no sordid little intrigue. As though I'd do such a thing with a man like Theodore Hunt! I mean..."

"I know exactly what you mean, Mrs. Fairclough. You aren't in love with him. He thinks you are. But that doesn't concern me. Please give me some particulars of where you went and what you did."

"That's simple. It was late when we got to Liverpool. We had dinner and retired. The next day was fine and sunny. Mr. Hunt said he had an errand in the Isle of Man. We crossed on the morning boat, crossed back on the midnight, stayed the next day in Liverpool, resting, and returned on the morning after. Is that all?"

"Not exactly. It's the island part I'm interested in. What did you do there?"

"Theodore wanted to see a friend who had a cottage in the wilds. Why, I don't know. But once there, I began to get bored and a trip to one place was as good as another. We went almost to Peel, took a taxi, and drove into the interior to the cottage."

"Do you remember where it was?"

"I can't for the life of me remember. It was a sort of chapel very nicely converted, I reckoned, into a cottage. There was a deserted mine not far away."

"That is right."

They seemed isolated in a strange world. The servant girl had suddenly grown silent, there were no sounds from outside, the room was fantastic, and even the cat was unlike the usual homely kind. It glared at Littlejohn who had taken its favourite chair, took a bound and landed on the mantelpiece, where it settled down sedately.

"Tell me, please, exactly what you and Mr. Hunt did then."

"The taxi stopped at the cottage and Theo went inside. I followed. It was quite deserted. Theo shouted, but there was no answer."

"Did you look around?"

"Just casually. The owner, a man called Oates, I think, was nowhere about. Theo said he'd rung him up a night or two before and asked him to come urgently. He was in trouble. I'm sure nobody would get me on such a wild-goose chase. Even if they were dying. It was just silly."

"And then?"

"Theo left a note on the table. 'Call again when you're out,' or something such, it said, in Theo's sarcastic way. He thinks it funny; I don't. We left the note and went to Peel for tea. I wanted to get the afternoon boat back, but Theo was determined to try again. There was a midnight boat, so I finally said yes, we'd get it. God! It was rough later and I wished I'd never agreed. It was the same again. Nobody there; Theo's note where we'd left it. Not a sign or a soul. So we came back. Theo said he'd have been furious if it hadn't given him such a lovely time with me. I didn't find it very thrilling. It was evident he'd something on his mind and wouldn't tell me. He was a bit distraught...."

"So, you can assure me that all the time you were at the cottage, Hunt was not out of your sight?"

"Certainly. We were together all the time we were on the island. We left the cottage, had dinner, went to the pictures, walked along the promenade and then joined the boat about eleven o'clock. I swear it."

"Very well, Mrs. Fairclough. You will be prepared to sign a statement to that effect?"

"Yes...."

She started to wring her hands until the fingers turned blue.

"...Er...Will my husband need to know?"

"That depends, Mrs. Fairclough. It is necessary to clear Hunt of the suspicion of a murder in the Isle of Man on the date you were with him. It all rests on developments how much becomes public."

"I beg of you, Inspector. There will be such a row. I didn't tell him Theo was with me...."

She scuffled with a cigarette packet, took one out, lit it unconsciously and drew nervously at it.

"But if, as you say, the trip was quite harmless and the fact that you and Hunt were together was purely fortuitous..."

"My husband is terribly jealous. He hates Theo, too. They are such different types. He might even...even...try to divorce me."

"But there are no grounds. What are the relations between you and Hunt?"

This was necessary, although the question seemed a bit impertinent. If they were in love, they might have concocted a story.

"We were merely friends. Theo produces the plays at the school and, as there are no girls there, the masters' wives sometimes take the ladies' parts. We met often there and, as we had tastes in common, we got friendly. Nothing more...."

So that was it! A little affair, maybe an innocuous one of hand-squeezing or kissing in corners, under the stimulus of grease-paint and footlights. And Mrs. Fairclough was an amateur actress. Littlejohn might have guessed it! Her behaviour all the time reminded him of a Pinero melodrama. *His House in Order!*

"You do believe me?"

"It's no business of mine, if the account you've given me of what happened in the island is true. It will clear Hunt and that is what I want. Did you notice anything unusual at the cottage?"

"No. It was cold and deserted and a bit untidy. I wanted to get away.... "

"I must be going now. I will call again with a colleague and take a statement, which you will kindly sign."

"I beg you again, please don't let my husband know. It would ruin everything. He is a violent and jealous man. He would kill Theo.... "

As if to confirm it, the door suddenly burst open and a large, flabby man stood panting on the threshold. He was livid with rage and his eyes protruded, showing the whites. He was fair, pink, and clean-shaven and his hair was clipped close to his head. He wore a tweed suit and a foulard bow-tie, in keeping with his artistic pretensions. He thrust himself towards Littlejohn and faced him angrily. He looked huge, with his arms raised above his head and his legs at full stretch. Littlejohn felt no fear. The intruder was made of little muscle and a lot of fat.

"What are you doing here? Answer me. I demand an answer. Tell me what you're doing here.... "

He cast up his words rapidly, as if trying to work himself into a fit of genuine violence.

"Modley told me he saw the police entering the house as he was passing.... "

"Who's Modley?"

Littlejohn asked it by way of putting in his motto somehow. Mrs. Fairclough wasn't saying anything. She sat there, nursing the cat as though it gave her strength and security, and glaring at her husband. Littlejohn wanted to be off; he had no stomach for a nasty domestic scene.

"Never you mind who Modley is.... "

"Don't be silly, Charles. He's the school porter. Control yourself."

She was sneering. It was evident there was little love lost between this queer pair; the art connoisseur and his play-acting wife.

"You keep out of this. I've had enough from you.... You...you...Jezebel!"

It seemed to relieve Fairclough. He said it again.

"Jezebel!"

"Go on. Say it again if it pleases you. And then tell me what all this nonsense is about."

Her voice was like ice and had coarsened. If Littlejohn hadn't been there, the two of them would probably have settled down to a vulgar brawl.

"I know what it's all about. I know Hunt's in gaol and you're involved, too, somehow. Otherwise, why talk to the police behind my back. After all, I'm only your husband, am I? The complacent cuckold...the laughing-stock of the school. Well, I've finished. I'm through...."

It was like a poorly rehearsed play; Fairclough overdoing it and Mrs. Fairclough, in her efforts to control herself before a stranger, making little stilted gestures like a bad actress.

"I'm through!"

He repeated it, but it was evident he was enjoying the situation too much to leave the stage, yet.

"I've been watching you and Hunt for a long time. Don't think I'm a fool. I saw you at the play, throwing yourself at him and him beside himself that any woman should even notice him. Well, you can have him. I'll give you your freedom and you can take him and his loony sister on for a change and see how you like that. I'm through!"

"Don't be vulgar, Charles. You know you can't make ends meet without my income. Where would the money come from to buy your nice pictures, and your fancy food and wine, and your little trips to London? Tell me that? From your salary as part-time art master at Dalbay? I don't think so...."

"I'll never touch a penny of yours again. I'll make my own living. I'm not too old for that...."

Littlejohn made for the door. He'd had enough!

"I must be going. I'll call again for a statement...."

"Wait! I want you to hear this. You've heard part of the tale. How much, I don't know. I expect she's been excusing herself for her sordid intrigue with Hunt...."

"How dare you, Charles!"

"Don't speak to me, you...you Jezebel!..."

"Can't you think of another name...? Call me a loose woman, a betrayer, a vampire...."

"Oh, shut up! Don't think I haven't had my eye on you for a long time. I know all about your little trip to Liverpool with Hunt and your staying together in an hotel.... I had you followed."

"You what?"

"I had you followed. All the way. Liverpool, the Isle of Man and back, Liverpool again, and home. Why did you come back? Why didn't you bolt with your lover and leave me alone? I wouldn't have cared. I think you'd a damn' cheek coming back."

"You had me followed? I might have expected it! Very well; I won't stay here another day. I'm going...."

"And take your precious Hunt with you...that is, when he's finished his term in gaol."

"Will you please let me speak, and then I'll go and leave you to settle your own affairs."

Littlejohn had to raise his voice to make himself heard above the domestic pandemonium.

"You say you had your wife followed, Mr. Fairclough. By whom?"

"What's it got to do with you?"

"Quite a lot. Whoever did the following can confirm your wife's statement."

"Well, of all the nerve ... ."

The fact that it displeased his wife made Fairclough all the more obliging.

"A fellow called Stroud. A private agent I had recommended for discreet inquiries."

"I know him. Discreet's the word."

Littlejohn had a picture in his mind's eye of Mr. Stroud. He'd once been a policeman who'd been gaoled and sacked for turning a blind eye to certain matters happening on his beat. Beef in a bowler hat, Cromwell had once called him.

"And you've had Mr. Stroud's report?"

"Yes. It arrived at school to-day. I had it addressed there. My wife always opens my letters at home ... . "

At this Mrs. Fairclough's tight reserve left her. She rose and began to pour a torrent of invective, oaths, blasphemy and epithets from the gutter upon the head of her husband, and, in the midst of it, Littlejohn made a speedy exit.

He didn't return for Mrs. Fairclough's statement, for he heard she had left town that day. Instead, Mr. Hubert Stroud, discreet inquiries, was persuaded by Cromwell to sign a copy of the report he'd already sent to the outraged husband, and also add a few more details of his own. This gave Theodore Hunt a good alibi, but that was a doubtful blessing to him.

# CHAPTER THIRTEEN
# BLUE SPECTACLES

Hubert stroud had an office in the Strand. By cricking your neck and looking at the very top of the building almost facing The Savoy, you could just see "STROUD'S INQUIRY AGENCY" in gilt letters on a dirty window-pane. Inside, there was a cheap table, two chairs, a cane hat-stand and a resplendent filing-cabinet. That was all Mr. Stroud needed, for the bulk of his work was done elsewhere. Cromwell had to telephone five times before he caught Hubert; whereat he ordered him to stay where he was until he could cover the distance between Scotland Yard and the discreet inquirer's office.

"What's all the fuss about?" said Stroud. "Not often we 'ave the pleasure of a call from the Yard."

He looked to be sitting in mid-air, for his huge body completely hid the small chair which supported him. His face was a choleric red, his head bald, with two white tufts like cotton-wool over the ears, his small moustache was waxed in points and he wore a shabby navy-blue suit with dandruff liberally sprinkled on the collar. His tie was looped through a gilt ring with a large sham diamond glittering in the middle.

"Hullo, Hubert. I'm just after a bit of information from you, that's all. All contributions gratefully received."

"You are, are you? Well, let me tell you mine's a confidential job. My reputation depends on my discretion. So, it all rests on what you're after."

"A little matter of a divorce case in Bishop's Walton; or if it isn't quite that, it's precious near it."

Cromwell sat on the other chair and the noise it made caused him to leap to his feet again in case it collapsed under him. Mr. Stroud looked angry. He didn't like the police since his involuntary departure from the force. His cirrhotic nose with its network of livid veins grew redder out of temper.

"Look here, this is my bread and butter. It's not fair to ask me to blab about what I find out. Live and let live ... ."

"I quite agree. Fair's fair; all the same we know all you found out about a fellow called Hunt and Mrs. Fairclough in connection with what looks like being the case of Fairclough v. Fairclough in the courts. The angry husband told my chief all about it."

"Then why bother me? I should be on a case at this minute. I might be missing an important lead, wasting my time here."

And to show the urgency of his labours, Mr. Stroud rose, put on a bowler hat and took a large rolled umbrella from the hat stand.

"Quite simple. Just a word and I won't detain you. Your report gives an alibi to Hunt. At the time, you were watching him in the Isle of Man .... That right...?"

"Yes ... ."

"At the time you were watching him, he was supposed to be murdering one of his friends."

"Well, I can assure you he didn't kill anybody while I 'ad 'im under my eye. I never left him from the day 'e left Walton to the day he returned. Liverpool, as well. I stayed in the same hotel as that pair. Open and shut case. Collected all the evidence from the hotel staff and gave 'er husband the 'ole lot served up on a plate. Between you and me, never was on an easier mark. Just like a couple o' babes, they were. Chap was delighted. Fairclough, I mean. Been after a divorce for a while. On the Q.T., he's got a little bit o' fluff of 'is own on the Chelsea Embankment…a girl who paints modern pictures…and 'e thinks 'e'd better be gettin' married to her to cut down expenses. He didn't tell me that, o' course. But I've ways of me own, see?"

Mr. Stroud tapped the side of his nose, which resembled a piece of ornamental purple pumice. Then he opened the filing cabinet, took out a bottle and invited Cromwell to a drink. When the sergeant refused, he helped himself liberally. It was evident that he'd expected something more damning in the nature of police inquiries. This one relieved him and made him feel in better shape.

Cromwell smiled to himself. Littlejohn would laugh when he heard about Fairclough and his painter-girl. The Inspector had told him about the pictures at their house in Bishop's Walton. Most ingenious! Fairclough investing his wife's cash for a rise in price in paintings probably made by his light o' love in Chelsea.

"So, you'll give us a signed copy of the report you made to Fairclough about his wife and Hunt. That ought to clear Hunt."

"Yes, it ought. But you'll have to give me a fee for what you get. The labourer's worthy of 'is 'ire, you know."

"You're telling me! What sort of a place was the cottage you followed the pair to? A bit isolated, I hear."

"Yes. They took a taxi there. Right into the wilds, it went. I nearly slipped-up on it. There wasn't another taxi to be had for love or money. Lucky for me a farmer drove up in an old tumbledown car. I stopped 'im and persuaded 'im to take me on as a fare."

"Did you see anybody else about?"

"Plenty on the main road, but only an odd car or two after we left it…oh, and a chap picnicking not far from the cottage."

"Oh. What about him?"

"Well; what about him? A chap can picnic, can't he? I didn't know him from Adam. He seemed a queer bloke, though. He was sittin' in a car with 'Hire and Drive' printed on the mudguard. The sun was blazin' hot, but there he was, with the top of the car shut and him inside, munchin' his sandwiches. It must 'ave been like an oven sittin' in that thing."

"Think hard, Hubert. Tell me more about him."

"Why? What's he got to do with it?"

"Just tell me some more."

"Let me see …."

Stroud looked a figure of fun sitting there in mid-air, his hat on, his umbrella clutched, going through the gestures and grimaces of racking his brains.

"I could only see his 'ead and shoulders. He wore a cloth cap…a check pattern, shading his face. Yes…and 'e had a pair of binoculars in one hand. It was a rare place for viewing the country round…lovely view…I didn't blame him. In the other 'and he'd got a sandwich. Oh, yes…and he had dark glasses on. The sun was shining bright. Nothin' funny in that, either."

"No, maybe not. All the same, you might have given us a valuable lead there. I'm much obliged, Hubert. Maybe, someday I'll be able to return the favour. Anything else you can think of?"

"Not at the moment. Sure you won't have a drink? Just one for the road?"

"No thanks...."

Cromwell left the discreet detective drinking his own very good health. Littlejohn had gone to the airport to make some inquiries and now Cromwell was due back at Netherby on an inquisition of his own.

Florrie Judson, the barmaid at the Naked Man, was at her place among the assorted bottles. She was frustrated and perplexed. Finloe Oates had left her his money, according to what she'd heard. The money had mysteriously disappeared and the police were on the job. She couldn't find out from anywhere whether the legacy had been spent or not. Was it real, or just a mirage? Florrie dreamed dreams about what she would do with the money. First, she'd resign from the Naked Man and throw a pint of beer over her boss, who was always making passes at her when his wife's back was turned....

"Good afternoon.... Any news?"

"Good afternoon, Miss Judson. Sorry, nothing fresh. But I'd like a pint of beer, please."

Cromwell took a sip, entered the cost in his notebook for inclusion in "Sundry Exes." and smiled at Florrie.

"If we could only discover who saw Mr. Finloe Oates about the time he died. His brother was here, of course, but there must have been somebody else. Did nobody call and ask for him?"

"Not a soul. I lie awake thinkin' and thinkin'. If only I could think of who might have wished to see him or do him harm. Then we'd know who'd taken the money, wouldn't we? I could do with that money.... It's undignified here serving beer and puttin' up with people's insinuations and all that money waitin' somewhere for me...."

She sighed and looked reproachfully at Cromwell. He might have taken it and hidden it himself! Cheap scent, face powder and a sweaty feminine aroma hung on the air round Florrie. Mr. Chubleigh, the landlord, entered in his horsey attire, nodded suspiciously at Cromwell, as though the sergeant might have designs on Miss Judson's virtue, and gobbled her up with his own eyes.

"'Ot," said Mr. Chubleigh, à propos either the state of the weather or Miss Judson herself.

But Florrie was immersed in her own affairs.

"I remember Mr. Lysander in the village. He called in here, but 'e didn't approach me. We was busy, I recollect, and the barman served 'im. I found that out since you was here before. Not that Joe ... that's the barman ... could tell me much. Mr. Lysander must 'ave been a cautious one. Joe saw him later talkin' to Mr. Lapwing, who lives just over the road. I asked Mr. Lapwing, but 'e looked at me queer, and dried-up. Some people get a bit above themselves. He's only the sexton and undertaker here, but you'd think he was Lord Almighty since he made that garden. Swankin' and showin' people over it. Proper pest he is ...."

Cromwell finished his beer and promised to report news to the heiress very presumptive, should there be any developments. She escorted him to the door and speeded him like an honoured guest.

The sergeant crossed the road to find Mr. Lapwing. It might turn out worth while. He did not need to seek the sexton far.

Mr. John Henry Lapwing had been a modest and humble servant of the church, digging graves and making coffins, until one day the devil tempted him in the shape of a plot of stony ground under the churchyard wall. To Mr. Lapwing had suddenly come the idea of constructing a rock-garden, summer-house and lily-pond in his spare time. The diversion had become an obsession. As the vast structure of this New Jerusalem of crazy-paving, granite chippings, plaster figures, exotic plants, pools and little streams, water-wheels and summerhouses, had grown under his hand, his pride had waxed accordingly. He spent all his time there. He regarded coffins, corpses and graves with contempt, except as a means of raising more money to invest in his fantastic enterprise. When not at work among the dead, he stood at the gate of his grotesque paradise, inviting visitors from their bikes, charabancs and private cars to step inside and view his landscape o'er. Tips or fees he dismissed with scorn, seeking only the appreciation of his clients and feeding on their admiring cries.

"Come in the garden," he said to Cromwell as soon as the sergeant asked his name.

They commenced the grand tour. They ascended a flight of crazy stone steps, the interstices of which were filled with rare mosses. Mr. Lapwing told Cromwell their English and Latin names but Cromwell forgot them both. The palm-walk, the monkey-puzzle, the mock orangery, the love-lies-bleeding, the lobelia borders. Mr. Lapwing paused to tell the visitor of the medicinal properties of lobelia. Then came the first rest-house, a miniature of the Place of Peace of some Eastern Emperor, constructed exactly to scale, said Mr. Lapwing. The pair of them thereupon sat down on a carved seat facing a lily pond in which goldfish lay like lifeless models, and Mr. Lapwing told Cromwell all about how he came to erect his masterpiece, how long it had taken him and how many parts of the earth he had combed—from an armchair of course—for ideas for its glorification.

"All with me own 'ands, too...."

Cromwell expressed his amazement and asked Mr. Lapwing about Lysander Oates.

"Oh, yes. I showed 'im round, sir...."

Mr. Lapwing looked incongruous amid all this wealth of curious edifices and flora. He spent all his money on it and his dress suffered. He wore a shabby suit, made up of trousers of grey tweed, a waistcoat of blue serge, and a coat of green broadcloth which had once been black. On his head, a black billycock. In his garden, in his workshop, amid the shavings of coffins, in the mortuary laying out corpses, down the graves flinging up earth, he always wore his billycock. It was suggested that he slept in it. The only time he removed it in public was in church when there was anybody there; otherwise he kept it on—and at funerals during the committal. The wire round the brim of the hat showed in many places.

"Yes, I showed 'im round. Didn't know 'is name at the time, but tumbled to it later. Remembered seein' 'im at the funeral of the lamented Mrs. Finloe.... Bad business that. Was present myself at the disinterment of the poor woman...."

He rose, pulled crumbs from his pocket and started to feed the fish, which he addressed in familiar terms through the water. Cromwell remembered that one was called Walter.

"They all know me.... That Walter's an artful one..." he said as he returned. "Shall we be gettin' on? Lots more to see...."

"Wonderful! A great credit to you, Mr. Lapwing. Just before we move—I don't want to talk while we're going round; I like to hear of things from you—just before we go, will you answer me another question?"

"Certainly, sir. If you're thinkin' of making sich a place round your own 'ome, I'll be very pleased to put you wise as to 'ow to begin...."

"It's not that, Mr. Lapwing. Did you, by any chance, show anybody else around who was interested in Oates or his brother? Somebody seeking information about one or the other?"

"Mr. Lysander, of course, was more interested in his brother's affairs than in wot I was showing 'im. I don't like those sort. I show 'em over here free; it's up to them to enjoy it, not talk a lot about outside things...."

Cromwell felt a bit rebuked, but persisted.

"You don't say! Impolite, to say the least of it. You mean he found mere gossip more interesting than all this wonderful place you've made with your own hands and brains?"

"He did. That Judson woman from the bar of the Naked Man was the same. I told her nothing, though Mr. Lysander Oates brought 'er into the picture, I can tell ye. Asked if I knew his brother. I said yes, for many years. Had 'e been happy with the late Mrs. Oates? I said, yes, though there was some talk of his bein' a bit sweet on Florrie Judson and meetin' her on the quiet. I wouldn't 'ave told him that, only he asked if there was any other woman in his brother's life. He said he wanted right to be done, whatever he meant by that. Well... I must confess that when I'm in me garden, I kind of feel friendly to everybody and I told Mr. Lysander. He said he appreciated it and wouldn't say a word. You see, he didn't ask me angry like. He was laughin'. 'With 'is money, I bet our Finloe's a pretty lady or two after 'im,' he says. 'Eh?' That laughin' sort of put me off my guard. I laughs, too, and mentions Florrie. Then he stops laughin'. Looks mad enough to murder somebody, and off 'e goes without so much as a thankew...."

"This Oates business seems to have taken possession of the whole village. It's become a sort of horror sideshow, hasn't it?"

"It has. This garden 'ud do 'em far more good. Good for the 'eart and mind, is a garden. There was another funny little chap come here, too. Got me fair wild. No use for the flowers and sich. All on about the Oateses. I kept tryin' to turn his mind to loftier things, like plants and the wonders o' nature. But no; all he wanted was the Oates tale. He didn't get much change from me, I can tell you."

"What was he after? I'm surprised he persisted among this ... this ... feast of beauty and industry ... ."

Cromwell was growing lyrical in his efforts to appease Mr. Lapwing.

" 'E asked how Mr. Finloe was after his wife's decease. Then, after I'd passed that off in a sort o' defunct manner, 'e starts again. 'Ad I seen Mr. Lysander about of late? I says, yes, he'd been 'ere in the garden, looking round, and had been appreciaytive. A sort of 'int, like, you see. But it didn't sink in. He walked round, quizzing me, not looking to left or right, just quizzing. Then, he asks, was Finloe thinkin' of leavin' his bungalow ... sellin' up and goin' elsewhere? I told him, not that I was aware. Why, I told 'im, Mr. Oates was very interested in my garden and what I'd done and 'ad only a week before, asked me for advice on puttin' up a summer-house, a sort of mandarin's place. 'Come up, John Henry,' said Mr. Finloe. 'I'm thinkin' of smartening up my place and you're the very one to 'elp me.' 'Any time you like, sir,' I tells him. But after that he got himself killed, or dropped dead seemly, and nothin' happened."

"You got the idea that the stranger had heard that Finloe was selling out?"

"Yes. But it wasn't true. Now I know what Finloe wanted my 'elp for. There's gossip in the village that he was plannin' to wed that Judson woman—the 'ussy—and he was goin' to make his place smart for 'er."

They started their perambulations again. Another monkey-puzzle, hydrangeas, palms, little cokernut trees,

Japanese dwarf oaks, fuchsias and japonicas. Then, another tiny crazy stone staircase, beside which a little stream descended a series of steps, bordered by exotic grasses and weeping willows. It was quite a little wonder!

"What was this rude fellow like...I mean the one who asked about Finloe removing and selling up?" asked Cromwell as they entered a pagoda made of tree branches and guarded by two almost life-size Chinese figures in plaster of Paris.

"Eh? Oh yes.... Little slip of a fellow. Sports coat, flannels and check cloth cap. Said his eyes were weak and wore smoked glasses. I recollect 'im well, because I kept lookin' him all over. It was them smoked glasses. I told 'im he'd better take them off. It's shady here and he never see the colours and sights o' things with 'em on. But no; his lordship wasn't here for seeing the garden. He'd come to gossip and quizz. So, I soon got rid of 'im. Had the cheek to offer me a pound note as he left! A pound note! 'No,' I sez. 'My reward is the pleasure this place gives to them as sees it. You haven't seen much in them glasses, if I may be so bold. Why come 'ere at all?' Just like that, I sez it. He took off at that."

They visited other fishponds, this time full of murky-looking carp.

"Got 'em from an old mill reservoir, one as they was fillin' in. Saved their lives, I did. Them old carp's hundreds o' years old, if they're a day. Whenever I feel a bit beside myself, I come to look at 'em, lyin' there all still and wise in the water. Very 'umbling, is carp. Wot is man, with 'is three score and ten beside them carp with their 'undreds of years...?" He threw crumbs in at the fish, but showed no familiarity out of respect for their great age.

The surprise of the tour was when the rockery and crazy paving suddenly levelled into a lawn like a green velvet carpet, with another pool in the centre and a bird bath and a plaster faun in the middle of it. There were other statues, too, peeping through the surrounding willows. It made you think that Mr. Lapwing had been robbing graves of their embellishments. That would be an unkindness, however, for in the course of his labours as mortician, he came across bargains in monumental masons' yards and bought them cheap to peer from behind his bushes like angels guarding or marvelling at his handiwork.

Mr. Lapwing made Cromwell a freeman of his maze. He bade him return as often as he minded and seek peace in his grottoes, thickets, pagodas and gazebos and practise humility whilst contemplating the ancient carp. He inquired concerning Cromwell's facilities for erecting summer-houses, pools and exotic gardens around his own home and, on hearing that few such opportunities presented themselves in the neighbourhood of Shepherd Market, he urged the sergeant to remove to more suitable parts when he would come and superintend operations personally.

It was only when they were parting that Mr. Lapwing, as an afterthought, divulged some more startling news.

"I saw that feller in the smoked glasses again.... Nosin' round Finloe Oates's place, he was. I'd been to look over the garden there, as requested by Finloe. I found nobody about at all. I was on my knees in the little thicket pickin' up a bit of rare moss, when suddenly up pops the little chap, looks through the window and then, findin' nobody in, starts to examine the fastenin's of the sashes. But just then, somebody passes... the man with the laundry, I think... and smoked glasses ups and offs...."

"When was that...?"

"I can't exactly say.... No use sayin' I can.... But it wasn't more than a couple of days after Finloe Oates vanished. I know that because of what I told you about Finloe askin' me up to see the garden. I gave it a day or two before I went, just to make it seem I wasn't runnin' after him. The place was empty."

Cromwell pressed a few more questions on Mr. Lapwing but without success, and wishing him well, left him with promises to return soon.

Littlejohn was back at the Yard when Cromwell arrived. He had been to Northolt examining the passenger lists of 'planes leaving for the Isle of Man on the fatal dates around the death of Lysander Oates. He had not had any success, as far as a superficial scrutiny went. The bookings all seemed harmless enough. It was hardly likely that any of them would be involved in the murder.

"It was obviously somebody closely in touch with what had been happening previously," he told Cromwell. "Someone who found out—presumably by accident—that Lysander had amassed a small fortune from his brother's estate, someone who had access to information about the liquidation of the estate, the death of Finloe, Lysander's hide-out...."

"Gamaliel?"

"Yes....? He moved in Lysander's orbit. You recollect, too, that he saw Nellie Forty about Lysander's whereabouts.... Our man must also have discovered Hunt's connection with the frauds...."

"Come to think of it, sir, Gamaliel doesn't seem to tally with the man in smoked glasses, who Stroud saw and who snooped round Lapwing, also who probably quietly broke in the house after Lapwing went and left the coast clear for his return. Perhaps he was inside when Fishlock let himself in with the key. Lapwing said the intruder was looking for a likely window to get in by.... No, it couldn't have been

Gamaliel. Once we lay our hands on the little fellow with the cap, sports suit and dark glasses, the rest'll fall into shape, sir...."

"No doubt. It's not a coincidence, is it, that the same man should be asking about Finloe, spying on the bungalow and trying to get in, probably killing Fishlock and later, watching the mine and chapel at Snuff the Wind? Of course, it may have been a team of them again, with Gamaliel as a sort of scout, spying out the land. We'd better call at Pimlico Hospital and see if we can get any more sense out of him. He's obviously scared to death of someone and I'll bet my last dollar it wasn't Lysander he carried a gun for. It might be check-cap who scared him and, if what Gamaliel says is true, tried to kill him by throwing tiles off the roof at him."

"So, it all boils down to this, then, sir: Lysander found out that Finloe had poisoned his wife so that he could marry Florrie. They quarrelled and Finloe had a heart attack and died. Lysander, suspecting that Finloe might have left all he'd got to Florrie, got hold of the Will from the bank to make sure and found he was right. He couldn't destroy the Will, say Finloe had died intestate, and cash-in as next of kin, because the bank knew there was a Will. So, with the help of Hunt, he frauded and forged and realised Finloe's assets, pretending his brother was still alive and doing it himself. The meter-man called unexpectedly and looked like ruining the whole affair, so Lysander..."

"Wait a minute! Fishlock died *after* Lysander, if the meter-book and the old newspaper I found at Snuff the Wind *and* Hunt's story are to be credited.... No; our friend check-cap comes in there. He must have been the one who struck down Fishlock. He must have been in the act of seeking information about Lysander's doings or whereabouts when Fishlock, poor chap, walked right in on him. So..."

"That could be it...."

"It fits. Finloe's dead; so is Lysander. Hunt is in gaol and has a double alibi. I couldn't imagine his killing Lysander in any case. He's too soft and fastidious. Poisoning his quarry's wine or smothering him in his sleep—the woman's way—yes; beating his brains in and then carrying him to a pit shaft and dumping the body down it; no. I thought I might have got a lead from the passenger list on the Manx 'planes, but it's blank at Northolt. Five passengers one day; four another; and six another. In all, seven of them were native Manx; four were women on holidays, including two nurses; two children, an American, and a Chinaman. Not a very fruitful lot for a killing. I'd better be off to try Speke, Liverpool, to-morrow. Finding check-cap will be like hunting for a needle in a haystack. He might have crossed by boat. In which case, it's a forlorn hope; no passenger list and a ship-ful of holiday makers. All the same, while there's life there's hope. Let's go and see what's really biting Gamaliel...."

The matron of Pimlico Hospital saw Littlejohn and Cromwell herself and she was very grave and embarrassed into the bargain.

"I'm sorry to say Mr. Gamaliel died this afternoon. I've tried several times to get you and I left a message for you to come as soon as you could."

"We didn't get it. We've been out all day and just called for a few minutes at the Yard. What's happened, Matron?"

"I really can't understand it at all. You see, it was the grapes you sent him, Mr. Cromwell. He ate a few of them and then became appallingly ill. We did all we could, but it was too late. He died of strychnine poisoning in half an hour."

Cromwell stood transfixed.

"But I never sent him any grapes. Why should I?"

"Just after lunch, a box was handed to the girl at the reception desk. A small boy brought it and said he'd just to leave it. He'd been sent by a man from Scotland Yard. There was a card of yours on it, Mr. Cromwell.... Here it is...."

The matron had collected the box, the string and paper in which it had been wrapped, the grapes, or what remained of them, and Cromwell's card, with "Good Luck" printed on it in capitals.

"Where have they got that from?" he asked, holding the card by its edges. "I haven't handed one out for... Oh, yes. I gave one to Gamaliel. He must have left it there and the murderer broke in and got it."

Littlejohn turned over the wrappings and the box. On the neat brown piece of paper was written in good block capitals: "Mr. Gamaliel, Pimlico Hospital."

"No fingerprints, I guess, but we'll take these and try. Now, Matron, tell me how it happened, please."

"The girl at the reception, it seems, sent up the box without more ado. The sister, knowing that Mr. Cromwell had visited Mr. Gamaliel, and seeing the card, naturally thought the fruit above suspicion. She gave Mr. Gamaliel half of the bunch. There was no harm in his eating them and he seemed happy and reassured by the thought that you'd remembered him. A quarter of an hour later, he became violently ill. We couldn't understand it. At first, we thought he'd had a fit. Then it became obvious he was suffering from poisoning. We did all we could, but it was too late.... He died without a word. The doctor will see you later if you like. He thinks the poison was injected hypodermically in some of the grapes. He's found some suspicious specimens in the bunch and they have them in the laboratory now. Would you care to go there?"

"In just a minute, Matron. What about the man in the next bed... or whoever it is?"

Cromwell awoke from his brooding.

"There was a chirpy little Cockney there, I remember. I didn't see him, but heard his voice. There were screens round his bed, but he sounded quite all right. Would he know anything?"

"Let us go and see."

The matron led the two detectives to the ward Gamaliel had shared with six others. The sister joined them and together they made for where Gamaliel's bed had been. Already, there was another patient asleep in it. They were so busy at Pimlico. The bed was the last in a row and in the next one the same Cockney was lying, reading with the help of a bedlight. He seemed surprised to have visitors at that hour.

"Pity about Gamaliel, as he was called," he said after they had greeted him. "Awful nervous.... Tossing and crying in his sleep. Now, he's got 'is long rest, God 'elp 'im. It was awful while it lasted. I'd got a ringside seat, as you might say. I'll never get 'is face out of my mind. When he found out he'd been done for...!"

"Did he say anything?"

"Not a word. Gave up the ghost straight away. As though what he'd expected had caught up with him."

Cromwell approached the bed.

"How are you, chum? You seemed pretty bad when last I was here. Screens round your bed..."

"I wasn't so bad as all that, really. Just been through an operation that...well...caused a bit of embarrassment. Get me? Sister was very good. We'll make you private, she said, didn't you, Sister? And with that round comes the screens and I've a snug little cosy corner of me own till the part that makes you blush is over. I remember you comin', sir. You was the only visitor that poor cove had from comin' in till the time he pushed off."

"I heard you talking, too. You have plenty of visitors?"

"Can't say I'm short of 'em. Wife and grown-up family of six. Never a dull minute, eh, Sister?"

The sister smiled at him.

"I'd a parson with me when you called, sir!"

"Your own vicar?"

"No. Sort o' haven't any vicar of me own now. No private and personal chaplain, so to speak. We sort of got out of it after the old rector of St. Mark's died. The one as married me and my missus and christened the kids. No, I never saw this one before. He crept round the screens, all quiet and meek, like, and asked how I was. Seemed attracted by your conversation, sir, as if he knew your voice."

"Perhaps he did. What did he look like?"

"Timid chap. Spoke as if he'd got a sore throat, high-pitched, like. Knelt down, and said a silent prayer to his-self for me. Lasted pretty long, too. All the time you were talking, nearly. Then he got up, said God bless, peeped round the screens and tiptoed out."

"Did you see this fellow, Sister?"

"No. He'd no business coming in like that, especially behind screens without a nurse. Just a moment. I'll inquire. I'll look at the rota on ward duty and ask the girls."

Nobody had seen the little parson. It was admitted that he wouldn't have had much difficulty getting past the doors. Parsons were always coming and going, but they hadn't the run of the wards, of course; and to insinuate themselves behind screens round the beds was quite unheard of.

"Had he a clerical collar?" asked Littlejohn.

"Yes; but come to think of it, a queer-looking one. I recollect it looked like an ordinary one turned back to front."

"Anything else peculiar?"

Littlejohn and Cromwell knew the answer before it came.

"Yes. He said he felt he just had to call and see us all, especially blokes like me, isolated and not able to see what was goin' on around. He'd been the same. Just come out of hospital himself after an eye operation. He wore dark glasses."

# Chapter Fourteen
# The Anxious Passenger

Mr. Pipe, the Cockney patient at Pimlico Hospital, hadn't been very helpful in giving a description of the clergyman in blue glasses. All he knew was that his collar looked queer, he was on the small side with a thin body and face, and his hair was plentifully plastered with sticky stuff like vaseline. He confessed that the smoked glasses had fascinated him and he hadn't taken particular heed of other features; especially when, for the most part, the clergyman had been kneeling by the bed with his face in his hands.

"Whoever he was," said Cromwell as the two detectives made their way to Gamaliel's shop in Risk Street, "he'd got scared. He even took the risk of following me right to Gamaliel's bedside to listen in and see if Gamaliel was betraying him. There must have been something between them and the chap in smoked glasses couldn't let Gamaliel live to tell us what it was...."

There had been a key among the dead bookseller's personal effects in the hospital and they descended to the basement and let themselves in. The first thing to greet them was the frantic cat which, in his haste, Gamaliel had forgotten to put out when he fled. It had been imprisoned several days and bolted before the newcomers and sought refuge in a side alley.

The place smelled damp and musty, there was even a trace of leaking sewers on the air. And, of course, cats! Outside, the walls looked camouflaged, for the painter, finding the owner gone, had left his job half-done, and departed to another where his bill was more certain to be met.

Nothing had been disturbed; the dirty dishes from Gamaliel's last meal, still on the table; a half bottle of milk gone sour; a catalogue or two propped against a teapot; and a part of a pork pie now in a high state of decomposition.

The place had been locked; the windows were fastened and intact; only Cromwell's card which the sergeant remembered the bookseller had stuck in a letter rack on the wall and which was still there when last he called, had gone.

"Somebody's been here, very quietly, since Gamaliel went in hospital. Perhaps my card gave him an idea.... "

"He must have had a key, Cromwell. There's no sign of breaking in...."

"What about the painter you mentioned? Would he be likely to have one?"

The question was suddenly answered by the appearance of the melancholy housepainter himself. First his trousers appeared descending the cellar steps; then his white coat; and lastly, his sad face with its drooping moustache. His cheeks were spotted with green, like the symptoms of a mysterious disease.

"Hey!" he shouted and hurried towards them, as though they might be preparing to bolt at the sight of him. "Hey! I hear Gamaliel's dead. 'Oo's goin' to pay me the three pounds 'e owes me?"

"How should I know?" snapped Cromwell. They were in the middle of a very baffling case and here was this spotted intruder hunting for his blooming three quid! "You'll have to find his executors. I'm not giving it you. But we want you. Were you here the day before Gamaliel went to hospital?"

The painter sniffed and helped himself to a half empty packet of cigarettes left by Gamaliel. He caught Cromwell's bellicose eye and decided to content himself with a single one of its contents, which he lit and almost set his whiskers on fire in the effort.

"Yes, I was. I did three quids' worth of work…"

"Never mind your three quid. As far as I could see, you watched all that went on in this place…"

"Look 'ere…"

"Don't trouble to deny it. You know you did. Now throw your mind back to Gamaliel's last day here…."

You could see the painter throwing it back. Littlejohn smiled to himself and said nothing. It was a treat watching Cromwell handling London characters, his speciality.

"Did anything particular happen?"

"I did three pounds' worth of paintin' on tick…"

"Cheese it! Something more important than that…"

"You mean customers?"

"Anybody."

"The usual lot arrived. I never understood how Gamaliel made any money. Most of 'em seemed to come for a free read. Now an' then, somebody'd buy a book, but not offen. Let me see…. Yes…a chap in a cap an' glasses arrived. 'E pretended to be lookin' at books till the shop was empty, then he goes up to Gamaliel and they start talkin'. Gamaliel got excited, as 'e always did when money or such was mentioned. They looked like a pair o' plotters, specially the chap in the cap…."

"Smoked glasses?"

"Yes…. How do you know?"

"Go on…."

" 'E seemed to be askin' Gamaliel a lot of questions and Gamaliel gettin' crosser and crosser and flappin' 'is 'ands, like he usedter.... It was about eleven and I was wantin' my tea. I come down the steps and they ups and looks daggers at me. 'Wot you want?' sez Gamaliel. 'Me tea water,' I sez. With that the chap in the specs decides to be off. 'E bends 'is head, so I can't see 'im proper.... I'll bet 'e was a Communist. Always thought that Gamaliel was up to no good. Only Communists could paint some of the pictures 'e hung on these walls. Look at 'em...."

With a paint-stained hand he metaphorically swept away a row of framed lines, blobs, splashes and fantastic washes masquerading as works of art. One of them had a cigarette-end gummed to it as part of the contents of an ash-tray.

"Did you overhear anything they said?"

"Yuss. I got good 'earin'. The chap in the cap whispers 'One word about this and you're for it. You know what I mean. An' out you go from 'ere, bag and baggage...' remember that because I'd just done three pounds of painting without seein' me money, and I thought 'another county court summons brewin'.' "

"How did Gamaliel take it?"

"Not so good. He took queer an' pale, 'ad a good drink from 'is bottle and told me to go to 'ell and take me tea with me."

"Well, if I get to know the names of the exors. I'll let you know..."

"You won't get to know, just because 'e owed *me* money. Just my luck.... "

On the way back to the Yard they called at Lysander Oates's old rooms.

"Hello, sir," said Mrs. Kewley. Littlejohn was evidently one of her favourites.

"Hello, Mrs. Kewley. I'm here bothering you again. How's the granddaughter by the way?"

"Fine, sir. An' they say she's just like me, the little love. What was you wantin', sir?"

"Did anyone call here inquiring about Mr. Oates before I called, but after he left?"

"One or two people. I forgot to mention it when last you was 'ere. I was that bothered about the baby comin'. That Mr. Gamaliel called to ask where 'e was, but I couldn't tell 'im anythin'. Oh, yes, an' another little fellow came, too. It seems Mr. Oates had done 'im a bit of work an' he wanted to pay 'im. When he heard he'd left, 'e got interested in Mr. Oates's rooms. He wouldn't take No, even when I said they was let, or as good as. We always 'ave a waitin' list for these rooms. He asked if I'd let 'im see the rooms, just in case…. Offered me ten shillin's…. So I took 'im up."

"What kind of a man, Mrs. Kewley?"

Littlejohn knew the answer.

Mrs. Kewley who had been peeling potatoes, dried her hands as though the answer demanded all her attention. She brushed a wisp of hair back from her face.

"'E said his eyes was very bad. Wore sun glasses. But 'e didn't miss much, I can tell you. He spotted that picture you borrowed…. You'll let me 'ave it back, I'm sure, when you've done with it…."

"Certainly. You may depend on me…."

"He asked where that was. I told 'im, Isle o' Man, a favourite spot of Mr. Oates's. 'What part?' 'e sez. I couldn't tell 'im. An' with that, he takes out a pencil and sketches it on the back of an envelope…. "

There was little more to ask. Littlejohn gave Mrs. Kewley a ten shilling note.

"Buy the baby something, Mrs. Kewley…."

And he left her calling down blessings on his head.

Littlejohn and Cromwell parted at Victoria, the Inspector to take a taxi for Euston and Liverpool; his colleague to pick up some fingerprint men and visit Gamaliel's shop again.

At Lime Street Station, Liverpool, Littlejohn joined a party leaving for the Lingus 'plane for Dublin and got a free ride to Speke Airport. The officials there were very helpful and efficient. They produced the schedules of bookings on the day before Oates's death. It was like hunting for a needle in a haystack. There were scores of names. He decided on another tack.

"Who would be likely to see each passenger on these trips? We'd better try two days before, and the actual date."

The official wasn't perturbed.

"The officers at the ticket bureau will be best. I'll get them along when they've finished weighing-in for the Dublin 'plane, though I can't swear the same men were on duty then.... "

Two polite, good-looking young men in blue uniforms eventually arrived and apologised for being so long.

"We're busy, you see, sir," said the taller and better-looking one.

Littlejohn gave as good a description as he could of the mysterious man in blue glasses. The smaller officer spoke without hesitation.

"Yes.... I recollect him. Let's look at the schedules, sir."

He ran a finger down the names.

"Here he is...."

Mr. J. F. Curtin.

"He didn't arrive by the airport 'bus, I remember. He suddenly appeared, asked for the phone in a squeaky voice, and went off to telephone. He kept himself away from the rest of the crowd for the 'plane, right until they'd all gone to join it. The hostess had to hustle him. He looked a bit anxious. In fact, that's how I remembered him. We get a few queer cards here, with havin' the 'planes from Eire coming and going. Smugglers, even fugitives from justice sometimes. He looked like a fugitive, right enough. With his glasses and his cap pulled down. All the same, we'd nothing on him...."

"His ticket was for Ronaldsway Airport?"

"Yes...."

"May I see the schedule again, please?"

It had been the last 'plane of the day before Oates died.

"Did this fellow have a ticket?"

"Yes; he booked at London Office...."

"Ah...."

"The last seat we had, too. There was a football team crossing, so it made things a bit awkward."

"Could I have a word with London from here?"

"Certainly. Just excuse me, I'll put a call through."

They turned up their records at London and luckily the booking clerk who had made the reservation in question was in the office.

"Do you remember a passenger...J. F. Curtin...on the last 'plane on the date I gave you? A little fellow in dark glasses...."

"We get so many," answered a robust voice, "but, as luck will have it, I do remember him. We'd quite an argument. I told him before I phoned for his seat that he'd be lucky to get a place on the 'plane. I recommended he went from Northolt, where passengers weren't so heavy. He didn't want that. He was a bad passenger in the air. So, I told him that if he missed his chance at Speke he could always get the boat next morning. I was trying to be helpful, but he took it wrong. 'Never!' he said. 'I'm a worse sailor than a flyer. I'd die of mal-de-mer....' However, we got the last seat. Someone had given it up through illness...."

"Thanks very much...."

The schedule showed a block booking for the football team and their followers, returning to the island, the officials said, in triumph, five goals to one. Then, the rest of the passengers:

Nostro and Orton, a music-hall turn.
Mr. J. Qualtrough, obviously a Manxman.
Mr. & Mrs. W. Quiggin, no doubt about where they
    came from.
Mr. J. F. Curtin...
and...

Littlejohn chuckled at the next name.

Rev. Caesar Kinrade. What a stroke of luck! The old parson, who hated travel of any kind, had turned up again!

"That means I have to cross on the next 'plane myself," said the Inspector.

"You'll be lucky if you get a seat, sir."

"I'll travel as freight, if needs be...."

And he showed them his warrant card again and said it was vital. They tucked him in with the crew.

# CHAPTER FIFTEEN
# THE VICAR OF GRENABY

M r. Looney and his fantastic vehicle were nowhere about and Littlejohn therefore made a more comfortable and respectable journey to the parsonage at Grenaby. They had not got far from the airport before the taxi took the road to the interior of the island and began to rise steadily through rich farmland and neat, prosperous-looking homesteads. The neighbourhood grew more and more lonely, and they passed ruined cottages and deserted crofts until finally, the road descended through fine, leafy trees to a sturdy, compact stone bridge spanning a clear trout stream. On one side, a ruined mill and on the other, a forlorn-looking mansion, once the home of the mill-owner. Another rise, and then the taxi took to the private lane, locally known as "the street", which led to Grenaby Vicarage.

The parsonage was quite a distance from the church, which Littlejohn during his trip never saw at all. The house itself was large, strong and foursquare, built of local stone with a fine doorway and fanlight and square sash windows, now reflecting the light of the late afternoon sun. The trees and plants in the garden were lush and neglected, the parsonage looked ready for a coat of paint, and the tumble-down outbuildings, surmounted by a crazy weathercock, hinted that the vicar's neat trap and spanking pony had given place to Mr. Looney's ramshackle chariot more or less permanently.

Littlejohn tugged at the bell-pull and after a lot of shambling about indoors, a very old lady greeted him on the threshold.

"Speak up. I'm a bit deaf."

Littlejohn asked, fortissimo, for the vicar and the strength of his request brought the good man himself into the hall. The whole place, although neglected outside, was spotless indoors. Fine, heavy mahogany pieces furnished the hall.

"Hullo," muttered the Rev. Caesar Kinrade. "I thought I would be seeing you again. Come inside."

He stood aside to give Littlejohn entrance into a large majestic room, which he apparently used as a dining-room and study combined. There was a beautiful Regency dining-table there, and five small Trafalgar chairs and a carver round it. Beside the good log fire, two comfortable wing chairs. The walls were covered from floor to ceiling with books of every shape and size, old, new, dirty and clean. Manuscripts for a sermon on a little table under the window.

The table was set and the vicar bade his housekeeper lay another place.

"Manx lobsters for supper," he said, waving aside Littlejohn's polite excuses. "For what we are about to receive, etc.... Sit down and make a start. I thank you beforehand for your company, Inspector."

"This is really too good of you, sir...."

"It's a treat for me. I'm a lonely man. Five children and my dear wife once sat round this table. Now, I'm all alone. My wife has been gone nearly twenty years and all my children are married, happy and thriving, *deo gratias*. I see you like my picture."

Littlejohn was facing the fire over which hung an oil painting of what must surely have been an island scene. Great rolling hills in browns and purples and greens; the gorse, the heather and the bracken. In the foreground, rich cultivated fields, gradually shading off to the uplands where nature held sole sway, scattering her own colours with a lavish hand. Just where the cultivated joined the wild, two figures and a horse, all stocky and strong, were burning gorse and the light mist of smoke trailed away over the hills into nothing... .

Littlejohn feasted his eyes on the picture, giving himself an antidote and new faith against the monstrosities he had seen in the home of the Faircloughs and in Gamaliel's book-shop.

"Especially refreshing after some modern daubs I've just encountered in what we might call the course of duty. Who painted it and where is it?"

"It was done by our own splendid island artist, William Hoggatt, commissioned by my parishioners for my eightieth birthday. I'm eighty-four, now. Just a bit deaf, but otherwise... I can read, walk as far as suits me, and I can still compose and write out in a fairish hand a sermon for my diminutive congregation. As for the scene itself..."

He rose and drew back the curtain of the window.

"Behold!"

And there it was! Now in its summer clothing, whereas the artist had caught it in its autumn glory.

"And now, to come down to earth. Here are the lobsters... ."

The Rev. Caesar Kinrade refused to discuss business until the pair of them had disposed of the very excellent meal which the housekeeper had given them. The lobsters were fresh, the salad home-grown, and they finished off with a blackcurrant tart and fresh cream, and then local cheese. Littlejohn remembered that meal for many a day afterwards.

Parson Kinrade favoured tea instead of coffee, and Littlejohn, enjoying the housekeeper's brew with spring water, agreed with him. They lit their pipes and sat in the chairs by the fire.

"Are you staying the night or getting the last 'plane back, Inspector?"

"I must get back to-night, sir. I've booked on the eight o'clock. I can't leave the case at this stage, though I'd very much like to ...."

"Come back and tell me about it when it's all settled. And now, let me tell you what you've come after ...."

"You know then, sir?"

The Rev. Caesar Kinrade removed his glasses, stroked his froth of whiskers and looked Littlejohn full in the face with his piercing, kindly blue eyes.

"Yes. I knew you'd come back after you found the dead body of ... let me see ... Oates, was it? ... at the mine. Murder will out, Inspector, and I stand right across the trail which leads you to the murderer. But first, I want to know what it was all about. My conscience must be clear before I tell you what might easily hang a man."

So, Littlejohn told Parson Kinrade the whole story, from the death of Wainwright Palmer, the defaulting bank cashier, on to the reason for his own presence in the Isle of Man. And he told the events which had led up to the strewing of the bodies of Finloe Oates, Jack Fishlock, Lysander Oates and Mortimer Gamaliel on the way ....

"I have talked with the murderer," said the vicar in a whisper to himself.

The incongruity of the situation struck Littlejohn. The quiet parsonage filled with gracious furniture from other days, the painting hanging like a blessing over the mantelpiece, the glorious view outside, the saintly bewhiskered vicar of Grenaby, sitting like a patriarch, calmly and relentlessly telling his story, and around them, the misty, lovely beginning of a Manx evening, the "little everin'" as the old folk called it.... Difficult to believe that not far away violence and death and a murderer were skulking....

"I knew you would be back, because of the picture you showed me of Snuff the Wind. I little thought then what you would find at the end of your little trip. But Looney called here with the news as soon as he could get away. He's a rare boy for a gossip."

"He was a great help at the time, sir."

"I'm sure he was. Well, I thought little about the incident of the picture, although I thought quite a lot of your meeting me on the 'plane and what you found afterwards. No; I forgot it, until suddenly I remembered that someone had asked me about Snuff the Wind before. It was long before your arrival and...well, Inspector, I must confess that private events had driven sense out of my old head. The first time I saw a picture of the chapel and the mine was on the aeroplane you mentioned. The footballers were on it, and a merry lot they were, because they had won. Suddenly, I became aware that a man sitting across the gangway from my seat was looking closely at me. He was, I think, sizing me up...."

"What did he look like, sir?"

"All in good time... all in good time...."

These old folk are rare storytellers, but they must tell their tale in their own way.

"I'm sorry, sir...."

"There is a current belief, I know from experience, that old whiskery gentlemen, particularly if they happen to be clergymen, are in their dotage and are weak in their wits. The man of whom I speak—so much the worse for him, I'm afraid—evidently came to that conclusion. He tapped me on the shoulder and showed me a rough pencil sketch of Snuff the Wind. 'Could you tell me if such a place exists in the Isle of Man?' he said. I recognised it at once, and I told him so. He must have been very eager to know, because he asked his question whilst the navigator was warming-up his engines. We weren't even in the air."

Parson Kinrade rose and sadly looked at the evening falling over his garden and the hills beyond.

"Very beautiful, isn't it? You wouldn't think sin existed in such a lovely world, would you?"

Littlejohn agreed with him and said so.

"I have been vicar here for almost fifty years. I could have gone elsewhere, a larger parish here or a living on the mainland, but I love this place and its people. I elected to stay. As I was saying, and yet, even amid such beauty, evil exists. In my humble ministry, I have encountered, I suppose, every item in the devil's catalogue.... Here, in this very parish. Men's hearts are the same wherever you find them dwelling. To make my point, sir, I'm an old man and, as I say, I know evil when I see it. My calling has given me a nose for it. I scent it like a good gun-dog. I certainly scented it that afternoon in the 'plane. 'Those who plan some evil, from their sin restrain'... remember the childhood lines? I knew the man planned some great evil, yet, miserable that I was, I could do nothing to stop it. There he sat, showing me a sketch, asking me its location. I couldn't, or I hadn't the courage to say, 'Hold.' I told him and he forthwith went and killed a fellow man there."

"You couldn't pretend to know, sir...."

"But I did.... Take a fill of this tobacco. It's ship's tobacco...my grandson in the Navy keeps me going. That day I had hastily crossed to Liverpool to hold the hand of a dying friend, a boyhood friend, in a Liverpool hospital. He had died and I was so upset that the incidents on the 'plane seemed to me like a faint dream until you found the dead man at Snuff the Wind. Then, I knew you would return without my asking you."

"And about the man himself, sir. Did you take much heed of him?"

"Yes. As I say, he thought me in my dotage and, in his folly, singled me out for his question. There were others there who looked much more intelligent. Had he asked Johnny Qualtrough who was sitting in front of him, he would have received the same answer, and it would have been forgotten.... But the mills of the gods grind slowly, don't they? God isn't mocked, you know. Through asking me, the man sealed his own doom. He wore dark spectacles and a cloth cap. The passage, though short, was what is technically known as a bit bumpy. The man was sick in one of the little bags provided for such emergencies. He must have had a very ticklish stomach; nobody else was much upset. Qualtrough looked a bit green, but the footballers kept up their merry banter all the time."

"We know he preferred train travel. He refused a seat from Northolt, preferring the short air trip from Speke and he dreaded the idea of the boat. So..."

"Yes. His glasses slipped down as he...in his contortions.... For a moment I saw his evil eyes, his mean features, and then he slid them back, looking at everyone but me, to see if he'd been spotted, ignoring me because I was an old dotard. He had green eyes and a mean, straight nose, his hair under his cap, which he surreptitiously raised to mop his sweating forehead, was dishevelled, wiry stuff which one can't control for long. It reminded one of a ... a ..."

Littlejohn held his breath.

"A shaving-brush .... Why, whatever ..."

Littlejohn had jumped to his feet in surprise.

"I ought to have known ... ! Whatever was I thinking of not to have remembered him ...?"

"The devil looks after his own ... just as long as it suits him to do so; then he destroys 'em."

"So, Hazlett, after all!"

"No, Inspector. That's not the name. It was Mathieson ...."

It was Parson Kinrade's turn now to look puzzled and disappointed.

"Mathieson, Inspector. He took a great risk when he thought I was stupid with old age. In looking at his pencil sketch, I held it gently to the light. There was an address on the other side of the envelope. I could just make out the name Mathieson and London, in typewriting on the reverse side."

"Yes, sir. Mathieson & Co., Gedge Court, London. He is sole partner of a firm of solicitors of that name."

"I see. This means, of course, that you have solved your case, Inspector."

"Far from it, sir ...."

Mr. Kinrade looked very disappointed.

"You see, we have to prove he committed these crimes. It may look very suspicious and circumstantial for Mr. Hazlett to be over here just at the time Oates was killed. There are other incriminating items, too, as I've already told you. But there is more to do, yet. I'll have to have a word or two with Mr. Hazlett ...."

"Rather an understatement, a word or two!"

"Perhaps. If he is brought to book, it will be mainly through underestimating his antagonists, sir."

"You mean..."

"You and me, sir. You say he thought you were in your dotage and slipped-up. He must have thought I was a fool, too, last time I saw him. He boasted that he knew all about me and recited what he'd learned about my history and mode of living. He must have been sizing up the opposition."

"He must be a wily brute, though. This plot was very cunningly laid, wasn't it?"

"Yes; and there is still much more to do. If necessary, would you cross to England to identify Hazlett? He's a lawyer and likely to prove a slippery customer."

"With pleasure."

"And now just to check up one more point. Are there many garages who do hire-and-drive car business on the island?"

"Two or three, I imagine. They're all in Douglas."

"Do you know their names, sir?"

"I don't. But if you're getting the eight 'plane, you'll need to leave in half an hour and you'd better get friend Looney's contraption to take you to the airport, if you can bear it for a brief distance. As you ring up Looney, ask him about the hire-and-drive people...."

Mr. Looney was in and, yes, he would be delighted to bring his vehicle for Littlejohn. He reeled off four hire-and-drive garages and apologised to Littlejohn for not being legally in a position to hire out his own tumbril to Littlejohn for driving in similar fashion.

Littlejohn started to ring up the addresses given; it was high season and they were all late on duty. The second shot landed home.

Yes; a fellow called Curtin hired a car on the date in question. The man looked it up and checked it in his books.

They remembered him quite well because he proved an awkward customer.

"Why?"

"Well, he haggled about the price for a start. And then it turned out he hadn't a Manx driving licence. We can't hire out without one. He got mad and a bit abusive. I told him all he needed to do was to go to the Highway Board office a few hundred yards down the street, show his mainland licence, and they'd issue him one right away."

"Had he a mainland licence?"

"He said he had, but he'd left it at home."

"I'll bet he had!"

"Beg pardon?"

"How did he get the car, then?"

"It ended by him hiring one of our men to drive him. They went as far as Foxdale and then Mr. Curtin said he was staying there a bit. He set out for a walk with a map, got back two hours later and then they came back."

"Was that all?"

"No. He turned up again next day for the same outing. But this time, he did a dirty trick on us. He sent Kinnish, the driver, in one of the Foxdale stores for some postcards and while Kinnish was there, drove off with the car on his own. He threw a note out at Kinnish as he went off—'See you in an hour,' and went tearing towards the plantation."

"Is that near Snuff the Wind?"

"Aye; what of it?"

"He came back later?"

"Kinnish had to wait over two hours in Foxdale. Curtin paid him well, but it might have been awkward for us. The car wasn't insured for Curtin driving and he'd no Manx licence…."

"What kind of man was he?"

"Middlin' built, thin, squeaky voice, argumenta-tive.... Wore dark glasses all the time on account of the sun, he said. Check cap and light suit..."

"Thank you very much.... "

Littlejohn returned just as the sounds of Mr. Looney's old car became audible in the far distance.

"Did you get what you wanted, Inspector?"

"Yes, sir. I did. One more link in the chain. It was 'Curtin' all right who laid in wait for Hunt after he'd tricked him into crossing to Snuff the Wind."

"He used a hired car?"

"Yes. He presumably walked from Foxdale the day he killed Oates. Would that be far?"

"An hour's walk almost."

"I guessed so. The second time he went, he bolted with the car. They had to send a man with him because he daren't show his mainland driving licence to prove he could drive."

Mr. Looney was making a noisy arrival at the vicarage gate.

Littlejohn thanked the grand old man for all his help and hospitality.

"It's been a privilege, Inspector, and I hope we'll soon meet again and you make a successful end to this sorry affair. This has been quite an exciting chapter in my rather quiet life. Not that I don't keep abreast of things. I read a lot and the world comes to me in my armchair. At present I'm reading some of the best stories I've ever come across. They're by Damon Runyon. Most amus-ing.... Most.... As you fly away, imagine me in the quiet of my study enjoying myself with Milk Ear Willie and Harry the Horse!"

"I know them well, sir."

Looney noisily took Littlejohn through the misty lanes to Ronaldsway. The dew was heavy on the grass and the sun had just fallen behind the hills as they took off for England, and long after they landed, the Inspector thought with a chuckle of the saintly vicar of Grenaby following Damon Runyon down Dream Street and into Good Time Charley's Joint in search of adventure.

# CHAPTER SIXTEEN
# THE ARRIVAL OF
# MR. CARDONNEL

On the morning of the day when Littlejohn crossed to the Isle of Man, a large furniture van drew up at the gates of Shenandoah. It was followed by a great flashy car from which emerged a little fat man followed by a buxom blonde young lady who seemed to know all the answers.

"There it is. Like it?"

"Nope."

"You won't know it when I've finished with it, little gel."

"I hope not," said the little gel with emphasis and, taking out a large portable make-up outfit, she began to improve her looks.

Mr. Cardonnel had bought Shenandoah. He had other larger—much larger—places up and down the world, but here he planned to build a remote love-nest for his latest parasite. He was an ignorant, choleric man, with a leathery skin, puffy figure, hanging paunch and poached shifty eyes overhung by large pouches. He wore a light grey flannel suit, a white linen cap, and brown shoes with cloth tops. He made money in London as an importer, Rouen as an exporter, Manchester as a merchant-converter, and Buenos

Aires as an operator, all of which occupations had elastic implications. His impudence made everybody fear him, except the Collector of Taxes who had sworn to get him yet.

"We'll pull it all down an' put it up again. All you need is somethin' to start on, these days. You won't know it when I've done with it...."

"You said that before."

Mr. Cardonnel shrugged his shoulders. He'd bought the house cheap and was getting a bit fed up with Sadie and her whims. Not a bit of gratitude in her; and after all he'd done for her! If she didn't behave he'd have to sell it. At a profit, of course. Meanwhile...

He took a key from his pocket and flung it at the chief remover.

"Shift the lot," he said. "I bought it all, lock, shock and barrel."

Mr. Cardonnel's origins and nationality were a bit of a puzzle, but he prided himself on his idiomatic English.

"Shift the lot to the saleroom where I told you. I hope there's a few antiquities there to raise the price of moving them."

Three men were carrying all the remaining belongings of the late Mr. and Mrs. Finloe Oates and stowing them in a van when P.C. Mee passed on his bike.

"'Ere," he said dogmatically. "What are you at? That's not yours..."

"It's *is*. 'E's bought it," said one of the strong men who was bearing a large wringing machine on his back. He wanted to jerk his thumb over his shoulder but circumstances forbade it.

The light suit, white cap, cloth tops and big cigar rather put Mee at a disadvantage.

"What's goin' on 'ere, sir?" he said to Mr. Cardonnel.

"Eh?" snapped the cosmopolitan round his cigar. "Mind your own businesses ... ."

"There's been a murder 'ere and till it's cleared up this place hasn't to be disturbed."

"I bought it ... ."

That seemed conclusive as far as Mr. Cardonnel was concerned. What he paid for was his.

But the blonde had heard as well. She paused in her make-up operations.

*"What did you say?* A murder ...?"

"Yes. A nasty one, too."

This was just the excuse Sadie was waiting for. She was fed-up with Mr. Cardonnel who thought he'd bought *her*, as well. Besides, a certain young film producer had been telling her how well she'd look on celluloid.

"You never told me."

"Of course not. Why worry your pretty head about it, my pet? What's a murder now and then. Doesn't make the house any worse, does it? Doesn't spoil the nice country round, does it? You won't know this place when I've done with it. Change the name, rebuild the house, new garden, garage for four cars. Won't be the same. No trace of murder ... ."

"So *you* say. It'll be haunted, for all that ... ."

Miss Sadie, for all her materialism, was superstitious. She carried a rabbit's foot everywhere in her handbag and wore a lucky talisman next to her fair skin.

"Pouf!"

"Pouf yourself. I'm going back ..."

"You're what?"

Mr. Cardonnel had bought all the furniture, fiddled a substantial building licence, paid for the place, and insured it ready for a fire.

All the same, the flash car later returned to Rodley. The old furniture had been put back in the house, the van had gone, and here was Mr. Cardonnel summoned to appear at Rodley Police Station and give an account of himself.

"There's nobody to sell the place yet. Surely whoever sold Finloe Oates's securities, hasn't sold his house and furniture, too. It's the bloomin' limit," said Montacute after Mee's report.

Mr. Cardonnel and Sadie weren't on speaking terms when they arrived in town. In separate places, they counted their ready money. Early next morning, he planned to leave her, still sleeping, in Rodley's best hotel, The Swan with Two Necks. He would put £100 on her dressing table and leave her with the clothes he'd bought her. Sadie, finding she had twenty pounds, three shillings and fourpence in her bag made up her mind to bolt to London in the car whilst the Old 'Un, as she lovingly called him to her private circle, was tied up in the police station. A murder house! What crazy thing would he be wanting next?

So, Mr. Cardonnel saved quite a bit in £ s. d., but lost his flash car.

"I want my lawyer," said Mr. Cardonnel stubbornly. "I ain't sayin' anything till my lawyer gets here.…"

"But nobody's accusing you of anything, sir. All I want to know is, how did you buy the place? The owner's been dead quite a while and, as far as I can see, there's nobody to sign the transfer."

"I want my lawyer," intoned Mr. Cardonnel, who was still wearing his white cap and smoking a large cigar.

"Very well, then. Where is he…?"

"I 'ave several. I don't keep all my chickens in one hatch. In this case, Meager's the man. Send for Meager."

Mr. Meager lived, it seems, in Brighton, and it took them a couple of hours to get him to Rodley. He came post haste for he was making a good thing out of Mr. Cardonnel. Mr. Meager was a real forensic smart-Alec. On the way there, he imagined Mr. Cardonnel arrested for something terrible and already he had decided who to employ as counsel and how much to charge for the initial fees.

"Tell 'em all about the bungalow I bought.... I'm goin' to sell it, but first of all, they're tryin' to say it's not mine after I paid for it. Tell 'em I paid for it."

Mr. Meager told them. He looked like the manager of a smart week-end hotel. Black jacket, grey trousers, patent leather shoes and white linen, just as if he attended weddings every day. He was swarthy with a look of the Middle East about his face and hair, and before he uttered a sentence, he hissed like a cobra.

"Certainly you bought it, Mr. Cardonnel. I arranged the conveyance."

"Who with?" said Montacute.

"With the vendor's solicitor...."

"Who might that have been?"

"Slope and Ryleigh of Holborn, London. The title was quite good. They acted for the vendor."

"How was it all done? Please tell me how the transfer..."

"Conveyance, you mean..."

"Conveyance, then. How was it signed?"

"H'ss. As a rule, all the parties meet at a common meeting-place, pay the money over, and sign the documents together. In this case, however, the deeds were sent to me for examination of title, then Slope & Co. sent me the conveyance signed by their client. They are a firm of good repute, so I accepted it that way."

"So you never saw the seller, then?"

Mr. Meager looked a bit uneasy. His bloodshot eyes turned to the poached ones of Mr. Cardonnel and he read trouble in them. He hissed in a low, coaxing key this time.

"I assure you Mr. Cardonnel, all was quite in order."

"It 'ad better be. Nobody pulls a fast one on me. I paid my money and I'm havin' what I paid for. Remember that, Mr. Meager."

"Of course."

Mr. Meager stroked his oily hair.

"Well, Mr. Meager, I think you'd better get full details of that transaction from the seller's solicitors, here and now," said Montacute.

"Here and now," said Mr. Cardonnel ominously. "And I don't want to be here all day, so look sharp."

Mr. Meager thereupon telephoned to Holborn and held a very technical conversation about conveyances, vendors, consideration money, ultra vires, fi. fa., mutatis mutandis, and searches in land registries, eventually returning to impart the news that Slope & Co. knew as little of the vendor as he did himself. Their contact had been personal, however, and in order.

"But that's all very irregular, isn't it?"

"Well, gentlemen, it's this way...."

Mr. Meager sat down, crossed his legs, joined the tips of his exquisitely manicured fingers, and prepared for a long explanation for which he proposed to charge Mr. Cardonnel a handsome fee in course of time.

"Cut the cackle an' get to the hens," said Mr. Cardonnel idiomatically.

Mr. Meager raised his eyes to heaven and looked at Montacute and his attendant shorthand-typist constable as though to indicate that all his clients weren't on the Cardonnel level.

"It seems that Messrs. Slope received a letter from the vendor, Finloe Oates..."

"When?"

"Early in May. It was to the effect that he had a house to sell. He enclosed a copy of an advertisement which I had previously inserted in several local papers on behalf of my client..."

"Me!" said Mr. Cardonnel, biting the end of another cigar.

Mr. Meager leapt to his feet and lit the cigar for his client with a silver lighter.

"Go on...."

"He said he had the house for sale. Would they contact me, offer it, and say that as the vendor wished a quick sale, he would sell for five thousand pounds...!"

"Outrageous!" bellowed Mr. Cardonnel. "Meager would 'ave 'ad me pay it, too. I beat 'em down a thousand.... Paid four..."

Mr. Meager waited patiently until his client had finished, like a spaniel waiting the word or the whistle to begin operations again.

"The key was sent, we looked the place over roughly...."

"Did you go in the loft?"

Mr. Cardonnel looked amazed.

"Whatever for? I only wanted the place to pull down and remake. Wanted to find a place to start on. Get somethin' to start on these days, is my advice. No use buyin' plots of land and expecting any 'elp with 'em. Get a place to begin on.... That's the stuff! By the way, if either of you gents want a nice little place, I'll sell that bungalow to you cheap. We can come to some arrangement if you like..."

"May we hear the rest of your account, Mr. Meager?"

Montacute was fed up with Mr. Cardonnel. He tainted the air.

"The deal went through, Slopes sent the documents of title, prepared the conveyance and posted the lot to me. The conveyance arrived signed by Oates and witnessed by Slope & Co. That was good enough for me. I sent a draft and that was that."

"But what I'm interested in is Slope & Co.'s client. How did he contact them?"

"As I said, it was all done personally."

"But how could it be?"

"Slope & Co. obtained the signature of Mr. Finloe Oates in their office. He called and signed in their presence. He had previously handed them the deeds and identified himself by showing his identity card. All was straight and above board."

"It had better be," said Mr. Cardonnel.

They didn't stay much longer. Mr. Cardonnel left them after renewing his offer to sell them the bungalow cheaply. He was back not long afterwards concerning Sadie, whom he said had stolen his car, but, after a whispered conversation with Mr. Meager, he decided to withdraw the charge.

Cromwell, armed with a tale from Montacute, made his way up the steep, seedy stairs of a Holborn block and found at the end of the trail, the dingy chambers of Slope & Co. They were the last fruits of an old firm whose aristocratic clients had all died or lost their substance in death duties. They were glad to do odd jobs of conveyancing and copying for other firms. The staff consisted of a dried-up managing clerk, because there were no Slopes or Ryleighs left, and the firm functioned as a subsidiary of a large partnership in the city.

"Yes, Mr. Oates called here. He signed the deed all right. I can assure you on that point."

The clerk had his sandwiches spread out on a half-finished conveyance and seemed glad of somebody to talk to.

The windows of the place were hermetically sealed and there was a strong, hot smell of sealing-wax, liniment, moth balls and cheese sandwiches on the air.

"What sort of a man was Finloe Oates?"

"Shy, very shy."

Mr. Tuffin, the factotum, nibbled his sandwich like a mouse and took a swig of tea from a large beaker.

"Yes.... Very shy.... Seemed afraid of the law. Healthy sentiment, what? I could tell you a thing or two. He, he, he."

He thereupon swallowed a crumb down the wrong tube and became convulsed with choking and coughing.

"...Oh, ohohoho...."

He drank some tea and subsided.

"Never drink with your mouth full.... And never talk while eatin'. That's what my dear mother always taught me, sir. She's still alive. Chirpy as a bird at eighty-eight.... What were we saying, sir?"

Mr. Tuffin looked as old as he said his mother was. His copious hair was snow white and fluttered round his head like silk. He wore an old-fashioned suit with narrow stove-pipe trousers and a high collar which looked ready at any moment to decapitate him. He tottered about on his long shaky limbs and his body and hands were thin and bony. There must have been some spirit inside him which burned like a lamp, though, for he never stopped smiling. He looked a good man, whom somebody had placed in his high garret of an office and forgotten.

"We were saying something about Finloe Oates, Mr. Tuffin...."

"A shy man, I was saying, wasn't I? He wore dark glasses. He said he suffered from cataracts, poor fellow. My Uncle

Reuben had them for years and then somebody recommended him to try a decoction of Eye-bright...."

"Mr. Oates was nearly blind then? He could see to sign the papers?"

"Oh, yes.... He signed them and I sent them off to Brighton. The draft was here by return and I had it ready for him when he next called."

"He identified himself?"

"Well.... He called with the deeds himself. And I asked him for formal identity, too. He showed his National Registration card. The signature more or less tallied."

"More or less?"

"He'd forgotten his pen. He borrowed a quill one.... Said he liked them.... Naturally it differed a bit from a fountain pen, but the signature on his Identity Card and the one he gave were pretty much alike. I use quills for engrossing deeds. A bit old fashioned but then, I'm old fashioned, and I like a nice quill...."

"Nothing else you can remember, sir?"

"No. Why? Is anything wrong?"

"I think the man who called on you wasn't Oates at all. He was a rogue who stole and liquidated all Oates's property. Stock, bonds, bank account, and now his house.... He got the lot...including Oates's identity card, seemingly."

"But.... This is terrible...."

"Don't worry, Mr. Tuffin. I think I'm right in saying that no title passed on a forged signature..."

"You are, sir. But this might mean I shall lose my place."

"Not if we can help it. I'll call again and tell you what happens...."

"Fortunately, I only do this for a hobby now. I don't know what I'd do, sir, without my job to occupy my mind. I don't *need* to work, really..."

"You're lucky, Mr. Tuffin ..."

"Money is a mixed blessing, you know. Take my case, sir. For years, fifty or more, my Uncle Reuben lived with my mother and me. He used to go out to work every day, but my mother and I just thought he did something in the City. At times, he hadn't a penny to bless himself with and my mother and I would help him with our own savings till he earned more ... ."

"Must have been a bookie?"

"How did you know? You're right, sir. He daren't tell my mother because she's a very strict Particular Baptist and he was afraid she'd turn him out. He was fond of us both and had nowhere else to go, you see. When he died, he left us all his money. My mother didn't like it, but as I said, what would happen if we didn't take it? Besides, I said, Uncle Reuben would feel it very keenly, if we didn't accept his legacy ... ."

Cromwell waited ... and it came!

"He left us eighty thousand pounds."

Mr. Tuffin said it without excitement or alarm. Just as though Uncle Reuben might have left them a lot of debts or an odd five pounds!

"We don't know what to do with it ... ."

Cromwell bade the clerk good morning and left him still pondering abstractedly on the fortune which baffled him. Cheese sandwiches, indeed!

"Whoever did this crime seems to have aimed at completely skinning Finloe and Lysander Oates," Cromwell told Littlejohn the following morning. He had met the midnight from Liverpool at Euston in the small hours and they were on their way together in a taxi to the Yard. "It's a wonder he didn't sell the old clothes as well ... ."

He then told Littlejohn about the forged conveyance of Shenandoah and how it had been done.

"We're up against a clever antagonist but he made one slip and, through that, we'll get him."

He then gave Cromwell an account of his travels and how he had stumbled across the amazing truth, the fact that Hazlett had been in the Isle of Man at the time Lysander Oates was murdered. He was the man in the dark glasses.

"So it all ties up...."

"Theoretically, yes. But we've to find a motive. A real motive. Not just that Hazlett wanted the money. Why did he want it; and why did he want it so badly as to strew the way to it with a lot of crimes?"

"He's a lawyer. Perhaps he's been fiddling his trust monies. That's what seems to turn all good lawyers bad, sir."

"We've also to find out the train of events leading up to this crime epidemic. For instance, how did Hazlett know about Finloe's death and Lysander's tricks; about Hunt and his share in it; and how came he to be connected with Gamaliel?"

"I might have a quiet look around his office and the staff there. Perhaps we might get a crumb or two of information...?"

"Do that after breakfast. I don't need to tell you how. Meantime, I'll try to get some more background about Gamaliel and Lysander."

"Hadn't we better put a man on keeping an eye on Hazlett? That fellow seems to have eyes in the back of his head. If he finds out we're on his trail..."

"Right. But don't let him smell a rat, that's all. If he knows we're after him, as you say, he'll bolt..."

"He'll wriggle out of it, if he can. For sheer getting out of trouble, give me a shady lawyer any day."

At Scotland Yard, although it was only eight o'clock, some startling news was awaiting them. The Bishop's

Walton police had telephoned to say that Theodore Hunt was dead. Fairclough had been arrested on suspicion of murdering him, for the man's head had been battered in by a stick or other heavy object. A Mr. Stroud, Mr. Hubert Stroud, had found the body and was calling in the Yard with a full account of it all. Meanwhile, the police were investigating the affair and would report later, inasmuch as it was connected with the Oates murders. In fact, Theodore Hunt had been out on bail when he got himself killed.

Mr. Hubert Stroud was already at the Yard, complaining bitterly about being kept waiting to tell his tale. Littlejohn invited him to breakfast with Cromwell by way of recompense. Mr. Stroud graciously accepted.

"Kippers fer me," he said rubbing his hands.

"Well?" said Littlejohn when the brief repast was over. "What's it all about?"

Mr. Stroud inserted a small cigarette in his large mouth and puffed hard.

"I went up last night to see Mr. Fairclough. He owed me quite a bill. He told me about little Hunt. I was sorry... 'armless sort o' chap. Fairclough was a bit under the weather. His wife 'ad left 'im..."

"I could have told you all that. What about the murder?"

Mr. Stroud put his hat on, the better to ease his flow of thought.

"It turns out Fairclough was ready to forgive his missus if she'd give up 'unt. That's what he intended all along; just to scare her by knowing a lot about her amoors, put 'er in a bad position and then seem big 'earted by forgivin' and forgettin' on condition she behaved in the future. Well, it didn't come off like that. She cleared out and left 'im."

"We know that...."

Mr. Stroud sharpened a match and picked his teeth with it.

"Hunt was let out on bail almost at once. Not havin' been actually charged with murder and only on suspicion of forgery, a lawyer pal of his gets securities for 'im, and Hunt's out in no time. It turns out that Hunt came straight away down to London to find a first-rate lawyer for himself; another pal of his, it seems. That's what the solicitor in Walton told the police while I was there. Then Hunt comes back to Walton."

"Well.... It's taking you a long time, Hubert...."

"Don't be in a 'urry, Mr. Cromwell. Let me get it straight. Now, havin' seen Fairclough, I think after what Fairclough says about Hunt, I'd better call there at Hunt's place and tell him to watch himself...."

"You mean you called to see if you could touch him for a fee to keep your mouth shut....?"

" 'Ere. I'm supposed to be helpin' you. Not that the police ever did anythin' for me. On the contrary, I can assure you. I said I called on Hunt to warn him."

"All right. Go on...."

"I found 'im dead in the garden. He'd been battered on the head. He wasn't cold.... Now, Fairclough had been breathin' threats all over town about Hunt. In fact, as I told the police, the last thing he said to me before I left his house was: 'I'll kill Hunt for this.' What more could you want?"

Stroud was still picking his teeth with his hat on. He looked malevolent at his own thoughts.

"What are you brooding about?"

"Fairclough's a poor fish, but you never know what a man'll do till he's driven to it. He must 'ave loved his wife."

"It pleased you to put a noose round his neck, I guess, almost at once," said Littlejohn. "Many a man's said he'd kill his wife's lover. It's a way of keeping up his spirits and show-ing his manhood. Fairclough couldn't kill a rice pudding!"

"Sez you!"

"Wouldn't he pay your bill, or something, that you should suddenly testify about his threats?"

"Look 'ere. I won't stand for your insinuations. I told the whole truth when the police asked me. This is what I get. I'll be going. I'm not co-operating if I'm not wanted."

"Was Hunt in the house on his own?"

"Yes...."

Mr. Stroud was sulking. His bottom lip thickened to twice its size and his moustache dropped from offence.

"Was he wearing outdoor clothes?"

"Yes. A sports suit, check cap, and dark glasses."

Mr. Stroud played his trump card triumphantly. He leered at Littlejohn and Cromwell, removed his hat and then put it on again to show he was going.

"Think that one out! Good day, gents."

# Chapter Seventeen
# The Café in King's Road

Mr. Teale was anxious to talk. He'd been conveyancing clerk at Mathieson & Co., for nearly forty years. He'd never had a wrong word with any of his principals until recently and Mr. Hazlett had now started talking of dispensing with his services. And simply because he'd told Mr. Hazlett he couldn't do *all* the work of the firm and, added to that, not be sure of his pay when it was due.

"I remember Mr. Leader, Mr. Curtiss and the Mathiesons, father and son, and they all spoke very highly of my work," he told Cromwell.

The sergeant had kept a long vigil to get hold of Mr. Teale. First, he'd gone to the Home Counties Bank in Pimlico, where nice Mr. Macgreggor had told him the name of Mathieson & Co.'s head clerk. He had also asked Mr. Macgreggor a couple of questions in passing.

"Do you know if the late Lysander Oates and Mr. Hazlett, of Mathieson & Co., were great friends?"

"Yes, I've seen them paying in here together. As a matter of fact, Mr. Hazlett was in here once, early in the year, when Mr. Oates was paying in one of his big cheques. Mr. Oates looked as if he wished old Hazlett would drop down dead ..."

"You mean he was bored with his talk?"

"No. Just annoyed. Old Hazlett's a great busybody and was looking over Lysander's shoulder at his credit slip. Any more news about the murder, Mr. Cromwell? Our people have been very decent about my share in the forgeries.... So far! If it turns out the money's napooh...well...it might be a different tale."

"We're doing our best, sir. I hope it won't be long now...."

"So do I...."

Luckily, Mr. Teale went out for lunch instead of eating sandwiches at the office. He'd nobody to make sandwiches for him. He'd not been married very long; a girl thirty years younger than himself. She was always in bed asleep when he left home in the mornings. Mr. Teale called regularly at a café in King's Road, Chelsea, but they didn't treat him very well. He had an orange-shaped head, with fair hair, redolent of brilliantine, plastered across it. His face reminded you of a bloodhound; great baggy eyes, loose chaps and hanging dewlaps. He looked ready to burst into tears in his solemn moments. You got quite a surprise when he began to articulate; you expected him to bark. His wife said he was her living; you would hardly have expected her to marry him for looks or love. So, it is understandable that the waitresses at the café made him wait whilst they served the bright boys and smart men who came there.

Cromwell had been wondering how to scrape an acquaintance with Mr. Teale. He took the vacant seat at the little clerk's table and said it was a fine day. Mr. Teale preferred to brood over his paper.

"Welsh rarebit and tea," said Mr. Teale to the waitress, who ignored him and took the order of a corner-boy who had just arrived.

It happened twice again and then Cromwell spoke.

"Waitress!" he called in a voice of thunder, and everybody stopped eating.

"Yes...?" said the waitress losing some of her impudence.

"Did you hear my friend here order a rarebit and tea?"

"No...."

"Well he wants one, and has said so about five times. Please get it at once and bring me the same."

The orders—not that they were worth the trouble by the shrivelled looks of them—arrived in no time and Mr. Teale was a definite admirer of Cromwell's.

"You know, sir, I wish I had your courage...."

"It's just my way of keeping the old flag flying, Mr.... Mr...."

"Teale's the name."

"Mr. Teale. It seems to have become the habit for the world to push middle-aged nobodies like you and me around and for these bad-mannered youngsters to treat us with contempt. Well, sir, I've nailed my colours to the mast and I'll go down fighting. Nobody's going to push me around...."

Cromwell was amazed at his own verbosity. So was Mr. Teale. He said so.

"I wish I could tell folk off like that. I'd have told my boss what I think of him...."

And he told Cromwell how, after a lifelong's faithful service with Mathieson & Co., and after earning the appreciation of all the deceased partners one by one, he had fallen foul of the survivor, Mr. Hazlett, simply because some months ago, he had complained about his salary not being available on its due date.

"And the boss spending money like water. He said I'd have to wait a week or two until some securities he'd sold came in. The truth was, he'd overspent our income and we had to wait till more bills were due."

"He's got a nerve, Mr. Teale! What kind of a fellow is he? A young wastrel, I guess...."

"Not at all, Mr .... Mr ...."

"Pook's the name. Cuthbert Pook...."

"Not at all, Mr. Pook. You see, Mr. Hazlett had been used to a good income apart from his legal one. In his day he was quite a big shot writing for the newspapers. Earned a large income. Now, though, they don't want him any more. He's heavy and what you might call learned. They don't like that stuff nowadays. Too much thinking required about it. They want what they can read while they're listening to the wireless or having an argument with the wife, Mr. Pook. He just got outdated and they didn't accept his writing any more. I know, sir, because I've been there when he's got his manuscripts back from newspapers and he's sworn something horrible."

"But he still goes on spending? What on?"

"Keeping up a big house, treating his family... He's not married but he shows off to a lot of nieces and nephews. Then he got speculating and didn't do so well. It was then we had to wait for our money...."

"You got it eventually?"

"Yes; he seemed to get it from somewhere. Then he started staying away from the office quite a lot. It was when I complained that there was too much for me to do, that he said if I didn't like it, I could go. As if I'd get another job at my age. But he needn't think I didn't know what was going on. There was a woman about or I'm a Dutchman."

"What do you mean, Mr. Teale?"

"One day I got fed up with doing so much on my own. I sort of rebelled and boiled over. I put down my pen and said to Lucy—that's the typist—'Lucy,' I says, '*I'm* takin' a day off myself. This weather's just in my line, and as we weren't paid last month, the old man can't say I'm doing it in his time.' So I up and off. I decided to go and see my sister in Rickmansworth. I went to Euston, and lo and behold! there I see the boss taking a train to somewhere or other. But it was the way he looked that struck me of a heap. Him that always was so proper in his dress, togged up in sports suit, cap, and wearin' a pair of sun spectacles. He beat it quick when he spotted me. Ignored me, he did, and never spoke of it after. Neither did I, for at the time I wasn't exactly on speaking terms with him, on account of my pay. But if he thought he was disguised, he'd better try again with me. I always was observant. I'd know the boss's ears anywhere. Bears' ears, I call 'em. No lobes..."

"Did you know anybody called Oates, client of yours?"

Mr. Teale grew secretive. He'd been in the law all his life and the confidence of clients was second nature to him.

"Yes...."

"I knew two of them. Finloe and Lysander...."

"That's right."

"Both dead now."

"Yes. We were their solicitors. Did all their work. But they gave their executorships to banks, I believe. We lost touch with them, although Mr. Finloe's house deeds were with us till quite recently. I remember him writing for them shortly after his wife's death. Mr. Hazlett delivered them himself, because he was a lifelong friend of the family. Took them out to the country where Mr. Finloe lived..."

"Would that be before or after Mr. Hazlett started to stay away a lot from the office?"

"What's that to do with you? No offence, I'm sure. But we have to be careful in the law, you know. Come to think of it, it all started about then. Taking days off, almost a week he was away once."

"Do you know two friends of the Oates brothers... Gamaliel and a man called Hunt, Theodore Hunt?"

"Yes. Gamaliel kept a bookshop not far from us. A nasty bit of work, he was. Died in hospital the other day. Come to think of it, a lot of our old clients seem to be dying.... Quite an epidemic..."

"I knew Gamaliel. Used to go in his bookshop..."

"Yes, so did I. We were agents for the property on behalf of some trustees. I collected the rents and held a duplicate key. The boss talked of chucking Gamaliel out, because of the rent, but Gamaliel came in and they had a terrible row. I heard part of it; my room's right under Mr. Hazlett's. From what I could gather, Gamaliel had followed the boss on one of his days off and was being a bit facetious or perhaps blackmailing a little. The boss shouted he'd have him in gaol if he said another word. And I heard Gamaliel laugh till he coughed."

"What about Hunt?"

"Yes; we were his lawyers, too. I believe the Oateses, Mr. Hunt, Mrs. Finloe Oates, and many others were friends together in their youth. They seemed to stick to one another. Mr. Hunt called the other day. He wanted some legal advice, I believe. Very hush-hush. He and Mr. Hazlett were closeted and whispering for quite a while. I didn't overhear that, but I know the boss was very upset when Hunt had gone.... "

Cromwell was mentally rubbing his hands. He'd never expected striking oil like this! Just as when you back an outsider on the off-chance and it romps home at a hundred to one! He paid for Mr. Teale's lunch and said he hoped they'd meet again before long. In this he was not insincere, for here was a star witness for the Crown in a murder trial!

On his way back to the Yard, Cromwell suddenly was struck by Teale's funny bewildered look when it dawned on him that a lot of their clients were dying! In fact, it was nearly a massacre of their clients! Now that the probable murderer had been spotted, it all seemed so easy. They were all clients of Mathieson & Co.

Littlejohn didn't smile when Cromwell reported to him.

"It's got to stop at once. The man's gone mad. He's started killing right and left now to save his skin. I'd better go round and see Hazlett with a warrant, though I'll have the devil's own job persuading the Chief about it. We don't have to arrest lawyers every day. I want a friend of mine to be in at the kill, too. The Rev. Caesar Kinrade is the only one who's had a proper look at Hazlett in his murdering clothes. I'd better 'phone the vicar and see if he can make it.... "

The telephone rang.

"Yes.... Who? ... Send him up.... "

Littlejohn smiled at Cromwell this time.

"You're in for a treat now, my friend. Do you know who's at the desk below asking to see me?"

"No.... "

"Hazlett!"

"Well, of all the cheek!"

"He's on his way. You'd better stay and listen to this."

There was a knock on the door.

"Come in.... "

There stood Mr. Hazlett, a model of legal rectitude in his black suit, spats, bowler and with his hair standing up *en brosse*, like a shaving brush.

"Good morning, Inspector. You're engaged?"

"No, sir. This is my friend and colleague, Cromwell."

"Good afternoon, Mr. Hazlett.... "

"I called to inquire about the Oates matters. I take it I can speak freely before Mr. Cromwell if he's your colleague."

"Certainly, sir."

Littlejohn looked Hazlett in the face. Strange, how after his talk with the Rev. Caesar Kinrade, he saw what the old parson had been getting at. Hazlett was an evil man. It was there in the green eyes, the thin nose, the mean lips, the cynical smile. The face of one old in pride and evil doing. Yet, without a warning, it might be taken for the face of any racing tout, black market operator, confidence trickster, or preacher of a cranky religious sect. This man was overflowing with conceit. A little notoriety as a writer, a little power as a critic to make or mar, and the evil was done. Then, suddenly, he had found himself shorn of his petty glory. He had become out-of-date and his editors and literary friends had returned his manuscripts. His pride had turned sour, he had hitched it to evil, and now the devil was rendering the account.

"As you know, I was the Oates family lawyer. I think I've a right to keep myself informed. I hear, too, that Theodore Hunt, another client of mine, has been violently done to death by a jealous husband."

"Who told you that, sir? The news certainly isn't in the papers yet."

"The police found my name in some papers in his desk. He has no other relatives but his own mad sister, now, I regret to say, quite off her head..."

"In what way can I help, sir?"

"I wished to tell you that poor Hunt had a kind of vendetta against the Oates brothers, particularly Finloe. You see, Finloe stole the girl he loved and Hunt often swore he would get even."

"But Finloe died a natural death, sir."

"Yes, but did Lysander?"

"No. But Hunt had no grudge against him."

"Not on the face of it. But, on inquiry from the Rodley police, I learned that Lysander had appropriated quite a lot of Finloe's funds after Finloe's death. I don't say it was right, I don't say it was wrong. But there you are. Hunt was impoverished; Lysander employed him in this forgery business and didn't pay him what Hunt thought were his dues...."

"How did you know that?"

"Hunt told me. Allowed out on bail after your arrest of him, he hurried straight to me and asked me to undertake his defence. He made a clean breast of it all to me...."

Hazlett looked almost compassionate. The devil a saint, trying to save his own skin! Littlejohn was interested. He wondered what fantastic excuse this man was concocting to cover himself.

"...He told me how he forged the letters for Lysander. He made a full confession of that. But he did not tell me he murdered Oates in the Isle of Man, which I'm sure he did to get the money.... "

"Did he tell you how he sold Finloe Oates's house, too, sir, on a forged conveyance?"

"Yes.... About the solicitors in the City..."

"And how he disguised himself...?"

"Yes. In the dark glasses and ridiculous suit in which they found him after Fairclough had murdered him. Yes, he told me of that. He admitted all his part in the forgeries, but did not, of course, mention the murders..."

"In the plural, sir?"

"Of course...Gamaliel. He killed Gamaliel, I'm sure of that. You see, Gamaliel caught Oates...Lysander, I mean...right at it. Somehow or other, he got a letter written by Hunt to Lysander about a document Hunt was to work on. He started a nice little blackmail business. Naturally, when he found out the police were watching Gamaliel, he had to do something..."

"Yes. Rather cunning to poison the grapes...."

"He did it that way? Most interesting."

Littlejohn almost laughed at Cromwell's astonished expression. The audacity of Hazlett was staggering. Here he was, the killer himself, calmly seated in Scotland Yard, showing off in helping them to solve the crime he'd committed!

"And now, sir, is there anything more you wish to know?"

"I want you to find the money Hunt stole from Lysander Oates, of course. That belongs to the estate. As family lawyer, it's up to me to watch their interests, even if they *are* dead."

"And what are those interests, if I may ask, sir?"

"The legacies. Nellie Forty and others, and then, all Finloe's estate to that dreadful Judson woman ..."

"But you are not executor, sir ..."

"I am their lawyer. But we'll not discuss that now. I really called to urge you to find the money and to appease my curiosity about the state of the case. I suppose your investigations into Hunt's affairs will lead you right to him as murderer."

"That depends, sir. You see, we've not got so far yet. We haven't looked into Hunt's affairs ... ."

"No doubt you'll see it the same way that I did when Hunt talked with me the other night. The poor man was off his head from worry. It just unhinged him. He committed murder under the spell of madness. His sister and his own frustration drove him to it ..."

"You think so, sir?"

"I'm sure of it. And now I must be going, gentlemen. Perhaps you won't mind keeping me informed. I'm extremely interested in this case and the way you're handling it so competently, Inspector. The principal parties are my clients, you know ... ."

It was Cromwell's turn to smile. He thought of Mr. Teale. The massacre of the clients of Mathieson & Co.

Mr. Hazlett fixed Cromwell with a stern eye.

"I regret I don't see anything funny in it, sir. On the contrary. Neither do I see anything funny in your questioning my confidential clerk, Teale. I happened to pass the teashop where you were enjoying a meal with him and, no doubt, plying him with questions about my deceased clients...."

Mr. Hazlett clicked his tongue against his teeth.

"I am surprised at you! Why not come to *me*? I would have told you. Instead, as Teale told me when I reproached him for it, you tried to get a picture of the Oateses and the Hunts from a mere clerk. As if he was any use! He almost fainted when I told him that his boon companion of the teashop was a policeman.... Come to *me* next time.... "

Cromwell felt a glow of satisfaction inside him. Teale hadn't told Hazlett everything. That was certain. Especially the part about the lack of wages and the threat of the sack!

Hazlett bared his long teeth in a smile and bowed himself out.

"Seeing how the wind's blowing?" said Cromwell.

"Making Hunt his scapegoat and at the same time, searching me—trying to plumb my thoughts. I trust he didn't succeed. There's a fascination about evil, you know. He's like a serpent and tried to make me like the mesmerised bird. To-morrow there'll be a showdown. We'll face him with incarnate good in the shape of the Reverend Caesar Kinrade—a saint if ever there was one. Then, we'll know. Meanwhile, we must wait on events, but see to it, and this is vital—see to it that the man who's tailing that serpent doesn't lose him. Make that quite plain. If you have to put half a dozen of them on the job, see that Hazlett's there to stand judgment to-morrow."

# CHAPTER EIGHTEEN
## SIMPLE EQUATION

The sun was shining in Gedge Court as Littlejohn and Cromwell made their way to the offices of Mathieson & Co. The old carp lay immobile in the brown pool in the centre of the square and the old sundial indicated that it was about nine-thirty, although you could just hear Big Ben striking half-past ten. They were on their way to see Mr. Hazlett.

They climbed the first flight of gloomy stairs to the general office, where they obeyed the notice to "Come In," and they found Mr. Teale anxiously peering round the screen to see who wanted them at that unearthly hour.

"Good morning," said Teale mournfully. He was more like a melancholy hound than ever, for his face had lengthened and looked ready for copious tears. He gazed reproachfully at Cromwell, who himself had been doing some hard thinking on behalf of Mr. Teale the night before. In the room beyond, a typewriter was going hard at it, the little bell tinkling in record-breaking speed.

"Good morning. Why didn't you tell me you were from the police, Mr. Pook...?"

Littlejohn grinned. Of all the names to choose! It was that of Cromwell's great-aunt from whom he said he had expectations!

"The name's Cromwell, Mr. Teale."

Poor Teale shrugged his shoulders as though it didn't matter much what Cromwell's name was after the great deception already perpetrated on him.

"Mr. Hazlett saw us together yesterday. He put me through it when I got back, I can tell you. I didn't tell him much, but it's got me the sack. I'm on a month's notice. After all the years I've served this firm, to boot me out like that, just because I happened to be a bit friendly with a policeman! Although, mind you, you shouldn't have done it to me, Mr. Pook."

"No other way, Mr. Teale. I'm sorry. But I expected this would happen after I heard your boss had seen us. So I've got you another job."

"You what?"

"The flats near me want a man in the office.... In fact to take charge. Somebody who knows, as you do, how to run property, collect rents, and with a bit of legal knowledge.... The very job for you. Three-fifty a year.... "

"What! Hey! Miss Minter...."

He ran round the screen to break the news and you could hear him telling the invisible high-speed typist that he'd got a new job and you could hear Miss Minter making noises of wonder and joy, punctuated by the ringing of the little bell on her machine.

Then Mr. Teale re-appeared. He had changed his jacket from a battered office coat to a seedy-looking black one. He was like a beetle busy moving house.

"When do I start?"

"Next Monday, if you're ready...."

*"He'll* never let me. Make me serve my month's notice or else pay up...."

Mr. Teale pointed upwards either to indicate his employer or the Deity as resisting his hopes.

"He won't," said Littlejohn ominously. And with that they asked Teale to let Mr. Hazlett know they had called. The clerk blew through a tube with a mouthpiece from which he first removed a sort of metal cork and you could hear someone at the other end shouting: "Whatissit?"

Teale told them to go up and immediately started to clear up his drawers in which reposed the rubbish he had accumulated over nearly forty years.

"Good morning," said Hazlett, rising from the table piled high with documents, books and papers. "This is an early call, gentlemen. Are there important developments in the Oates matter?"

He indicated two decrepit chairs on which the two detectives rather gingerly seated themselves. The windows were all closed, the sun was shining in and making the air hot and heavy, and the place smelled of old papers, dust and floor polish. Mr. Hazlett gathered together the documents he had been reading and placed them under a paperweight, a green glass jar filled with lead shot.

"After your call yesterday, sir, I thought quite a lot about the case and I thought we'd better discuss it together again. I have a theory about it; I know you have one, too. Perhaps we could help each other. You stated much of yours yesterday. It implicated Hunt. Maybe, it *was* Hunt. In any case, I'd like to get the matter in proper sequence ...."

Mr. Hazlett wasn't quite as comfortable this morning. In the first place, he wondered why *two* police officers had called this time. And again, he had an ominous feeling that the initiative had passed from him.

"Pray go on, then. I'm all ears, Inspector. What is your theory? I have followed your cases closely in the past and am very gratified to see you actually at work."

"In the first place, Mr. Hazlett, we might not have known anything about the Oates brothers and their untimely deaths even now, had it not been for a quite fortuitous bank fraud in Rodley. This necessitated the calling-in of hand-writing experts who discovered that cheques withdrawing the balance of Finloe Oates's account had been forged...."

"I am well aware of that, Inspector.... "

"I'm sure you are, sir."

Hazlett cast a peculiar look at Littlejohn.

"This eventually led to a search of the house, but instead of finding the bodies of either of the brothers, the police found instead that of a meter inspector, who had access to the place because Finloe Oates told him where to find the key if ever he and his wife were out and Fish-lock, the meter-man, called to read the meter. It looked to us to be one of two things. Either Fishlock was there when a third party, intent on no good, entered; or else the third party followed Fishlock in the house and killed him."

"It must have been Lysander Oates...."

"No; Lysander had left the place before then."

"Ah! Hunt."

"But how did Hunt get there? What business had he there?"

"He knew about the plot concocted by Lysander to realise and appropriate Finloe's estate. Hunt did the forging. He told me so."

"For reasons of my own, mainly because I think Hunt quite incapable of working out and seeing to its end all this complicated plot and crime, I want to leave him out. Perhaps my argument will amount to what we used to call when I did Euclid, *reductio ad absurdum*, in which case, Hunt may be proved guilty, theoretically. Meanwhile, let's call our criminal 'X'."

"Ah, solving the equation?"

"Yes, sir."

"Very well. Go on, Inspector."

"Let's begin right at the start, then. Finloe Oates becomes infatuated with the barmaid of the Naked Man at Netherby. He gets deeper and deeper in, and finally, poisons his wife to free himself."

"How do you know that? I never heard such a monstrous accusation...."

"Come, come, sir. You know Mrs. Oates's body was exhumed, surely. They found enough arsenic...weedkiller, by the way...to kill a dozen."

"I knew of the exhumation, but not that Finloe killed her. That is mere inference."

"Let us take it as such, then. Mrs. Finloe is buried and he is free to marry Florrie, the barmaid. Suddenly, he vanishes. Florrie sees him no more, but cheques and letters start pouring in his bank at Rodley, realising and removing the funds. What has happened? I think you know, sir."

"I know what Hunt told me. Finloe and Lysander, who called on him, had a row.... "

"Yes; Lysander had himself been in love with Mrs. Finloe and kept a kindly eye on her even after her marriage to his brother. Lysander heard of his brother's philanderings with Florrie and had a vague notion of what might have happened. When he heard the dog had died the day that Mrs. Oates died, he dug up the body and had it examined. The animal must have eaten the remnants of the pork pie and arsenic which killed its mistress. Lysander went and accused Finloe who, having a bad heart, dropped dead. Lysander found himself in a quandary...."

"I could tell you the rest. Hunt told me. He said Lysander felt that Finloe would have left all he had to Florrie. He couldn't stand for that. To make sure, he wrote to the bank in Finloe's hand and got the Will. It was as he thought. He therefore did not disclose his brother's death, but hid the body and stood in his brother's shoes until he had collected all his estate. Then he fled."

"But why did he flee so hastily?"

"I do not know. Do you?"

"I think he found someone else nosing on his trail; Mr. X."

"Hunt?"

"I grant Hunt knew about the forgery. Oates couldn't sustain all the forging; he sent for Hunt who made a hobby of it. But let us assume someone else found out what was happening, that Lysander was playing around with a small fortune in cash…. Someone who desperately needed funds, either to keep up his old state of living, or else to make good defalcations in other directions…."

"Hunt would fill the bill…."

" 'X', I said, sir. Now how did 'X' chance upon Lysander in the act of appropriating his brother's funds?"

"He must have called at the house and found him there. It all ties up for Hunt…. "

"Or for 'X', who might have called, shall we say with the deeds of Shenandoah, which Finloe asked for before he died. Or again, Lysander might have asked for the deeds…."

"But the deeds of Shenandoah were in the possession of my firm. Finloe asked for them by post and I sent them by post. I hear the house has been sold. Presumably another of Lysander's efforts. By the way…"

Hazlett thrust out his face in Littlejohn's direction.

"By the way…. You're not suggesting that 'X' might be me. Because, if you are, tell me your reasons and I'll refute them."

His eyes lit up with an evil light. He had hedged himself round with logical excuses and reasons and he thought himself beyond suspicion.

"No, sir. 'X' is, as yet, the unknown quantity. You yourself suggested him as the doubtful algebraic factor; the *unknown*, which juggling with the *known* might reveal. At any rate, 'X' discovered Lysander's game. He kept him under close watch; he might even have communicated with the bank from a privileged position and got to know that Finloe's funds had all been withdrawn. A friend of his might have told him that Lysander was operating vigorously in Netherby, seemed to be in the money, and was leading a strange life.... "

"And who might Lysander's friend have been?"

"A bookseller called Gamaliel. He played chess, *inter alia*, with Oates. He also did a trade in forged modern masters, which Oates painted and Gamaliel disposed of. 'X' called on Gamaliel to find out what was happening to Lysander. Gamaliel suspected 'X' of intervening for his own benefit and tried a little blackmail. 'X' reacted vigorously. He threatened Gamaliel, scared him to death, and as Gamaliel had a bad heart, gave him an attack of such terror that the fellow had to be taken to hospital...."

Hazlett was listening with rapt attention. He even clicked his tongue against his teeth in pity of poor Gamaliel.

"Poor fellow. What did Hunt threaten to do to him?"

" 'X' somehow had a key to the premises. He went on the roof and threw slates and bricks down on Gamaliel. Then, when they'd put the bookseller out of harm's way in hospital, 'X' disguised himself as a parson, hid behind the screens of the next bed and, discovering that Gamaliel hadn't yet recovered enough to tell what he knew, he sent him poisoned fruit, including with it the official card of my colleague, which he took from Gamaliel's shop with the help of his key. How did he get that key? Could 'X' have had something to do with the property, or.?"

"There was one hanging on a nail...tied to a bobbin with string, in the shop. Hunt must have taken it on one of his visits."

"Maybe..."

"My dear Inspector, you are a very stubborn man. The case against anyone here will be purely circumstantial. Everything points to Hunt. His poverty, his full knowledge of all that was going on, his collaboration with Lysander, and his resentment at the miserable sum he got as reward, his hatred of the Oates brothers on account of Marion whom he loved. He knew, too, where Lysander was likely to hide, because Oates had given him a picture of the place he always hoped he'd be able to buy in the Isle of Man and settle down in..."

"Others knew of that place, too. There was a rough copy of Hunt's finished painting in Lysander's old rooms. Certain people inquired about that and where it was...."

"Who did that?"

"We don't know. The landlady couldn't give a proper description. Certainly someone called and even copied it in pencil."

"Rubbish. The woman's romancing...."

"That's what she told us. Someone copied it...."

Cromwell listened fascinated. It was a duel...a duel to the death for Hazlett. He admired the cool way in which Hazlett picked holes in Littlejohn's arguments, parried his thrusts, attacked in his own skilled forensic way. But Cromwell knew from the start who would be the winner. He hadn't been a colleague of Littlejohn for nearly twenty years without knowing all the signs of the coming deadly stroke.

"...And, having discovered from someone or other where the cottage was situated, went there, found Lysander Oates hiding, and struck him down in cold blood...."

"Don't dramatise it, Inspector. It may not have been in cold blood. Lysander was no coward. He might have fought like the devil."

"He did nothing of the kind. His murderer came on him from behind and beat his head in just as he did poor Fishlock's. That done, he carried him to an old mine and flung him down it. There we found the body. And that is not all...."

Littlejohn paused to light a cigarette. He offered his case to Cromwell and Hazlett. The sergeant followed suit, but Hazlett waved it aside impatiently. He looked annoyed.

"Well? All these pauses for dramatic effect have no influence on me. I'm a lawyer and am used to this kind of thing."

"That is not all. The money was taken, but in the fireplace were the remains of a note, written by Hunt to Lysander. Part of it was burned; the other could be read to mean that Lysander had appealed to Hunt to join him in the island and render help of some kind. And Hunt had gone there. Our experts, however, state that it seemed to have been burned with a measure of artifice. There were signs of snuffing to ensure that portions were destroyed and others remained for us to read."

"Surmise. Lysander might have fingered it. I would regard it as another nail in Hunt's coffin, had he not already qualified for such a receptacle at the hands of the jealous Fairclough...."

Pleased with his macabre joke, Mr. Hazlett took a pinch of snuff from a silver box engraved like a cockleshell.

"But here comes another point, sir. I interviewed Hunt. In fact, I was rarely off his doorstep until we arrested him for forgery.... Hunt told me he received the request to join his friend, one might say confederate, in the island, but the line was so bad that Lysander, or whoever it was, told him to write and say when he could come. Hunt, however, was disappointing. He declined instead of obliging, and thus arrived a letter which instead of being on the face of it, a death warrant, had to be doctored to make it so."

"It made no difference, Inspector. I'm surprised you were taken in by Hunt's tale. Can't you see, he was just excusing himself, making up a story to cover. He had a good brain, you know."

"Yes, but he was too ladylike and fastidious to knock a man's skull to pulp on one hand, and follow another into a hospital and plan to poison him, even robbing his shop to get my colleague's card. All this is not true to type."

"There you are wrong. Hunt had plenty of guts. Did you know he was the most desperate of our little group when we were all together—Hunt and the Oateses and Marion, who later married Finloe...?"

"I know all that. Or rather, I'd understand it. If you taunted him, maybe he would do desperate things on the spur of the moment. But all this is planned in cold blood. Hunt was too much of a coward. He couldn't plan anything. He couldn't even plan the disposal of his sister in an asylum. They had to *take* her; then he agreed. He couldn't plan a real love affair, with a woman he fell in love with. He arranged a sordid little week-end and then ran home because he couldn't face it."

"All the same, I think he did it."

"We discovered that the telephone message, said to have come from Lysander, was put in from Speke Airport, Liverpool, not from the Isle of Man.... "

"There you are! Lysander telephoned on his way to the 'plane for Isle of Man. He told Hunt where he was going and Hunt was quick to follow."

That was a good one in Hazlett's favour! He was putting up a good show. His quick brain seized on the points and swiftly turned them to his own advantage. Cromwell smiled to himself. Littlejohn was only playing with his quarry, he thought. Soon...

"Let us take the point of view of 'X'...."

"You are indefatigable! And, by the way, I haven't all day, Inspector, though this is very interesting. It's turned eleven now; I must go in a few minutes. I've to be at court before twelve."

"Let's think of it as 'X' would have done it, sir. He has found out where Lysander is hiding. He makes for the place. To his subtle mind comes a chance to put an end to the chase which, to say the least of it, is becoming a nuisance to him. He simply wishes to collect Lysander's fortune and use it for his own purposes. He must find someone on whom he can pin the crimes and sacrifice for his own peace. He knows Hunt's part in the game. He either came across letters at Shenandoah, whilst he was there, revealing Hunt's share in the forgery, or else he knew Hunt's former fidelity to Lysander and took a chance. He telephoned Hunt from Liverpool and, by pretending to be speaking from the Isle of Man and by saying the line was bad, he induced Hunt to write this letter. Meanwhile he had killed and disposed of Oates. He waited for Hunt's letter—the death warrant. 'X' must have been furious when it arrived, for it was a refusal. On examination, however, it was found to be adaptable to burning and mangling and could thus be made into the type of letter 'X' wanted. He arranged it accordingly."

"A wonderful feat of official imagination, if I may say so. I still back my own view. Hunt did it."

It was like the passing bell. Hunt did it! Hunt did it! Littlejohn felt like playing all his cards and hoping for the best. But it would not do, yet.

"I said, he arranged it accordingly. When we arrived and found Oates dead, we also found the letter incriminating Hunt."

"Quite right, too. It was the genuine article. Why persist in defending Hunt?"

"I'm anxious to be just, sir."

"I admire your impartiality. Snuff?"

"No thank you, sir. 'X' had now, as he thought, completely caught Hunt in the toils. The police would examine the letter and find that it not only connected Hunt with the crime at Snuff the Wind..."

"I beg your pardon.... "

"The mine was known as Snuff the Wind. Rather queer, don't you think?"

"H'm. Go on.... Hurry!"

Hazlett was fascinated. You would have thought that now he scented trouble. The wild ride which would end in his doom was in progress and he was panting to get to the finish for better or worse.

"Hunt's connection with the forgeries would be manifest. He would be proved beyond doubt to be the partner in crime of Lysander. Thieves fall out and ... well ... Hunt scoops the pool. 'X' had thought it all out."

"I think you might drop this 'X' tomfoolery, you know. Hunt is dead; his extensive guilt is clear.... "

"But what did he do with the money?"

"I told you. Or didn't I? He said when he came here the other night, he'd lodged it in a safe deposit."

"Where? And where is the key? A key to such a treasure would probably have been in his pocket. From what we hear from Bishop's Walton, it wasn't. I asked them by 'phone for details of the contents of his pockets and desk. I thought there might have been letters. But there was nothing particular."

"That is a job for the police. Find the safe deposit. It's hardly likely he would treat so lightly money which had cost him so much to acquire."

"There are one or two more interesting features of the case, too, if you care to hear them, sir."

"Of course. You are a very capable officer, Littlejohn, if I may say so. When I heard you were on the case, I looked you up and inquired about you from friends at the courts; they said you were a very formidable proposition. Now I know what they meant."

"I appreciate your interest, sir. But why trouble to inquire about me so extensively? Surely, I wasn't so important. Now I could understand an antagonist trying to measure me up, but..."

Hazlett gave Littlejohn a straight, evil glance from his deep-set green eyes in their leaden sockets. Both men knew that battle was joined. It was one or the other of them for it!

"The other points I mentioned.... Our friend 'X', having got all the ready cash, looked round for the leavings...any odds and ends remaining. He found the house, Finloe Oates's bungalow, Shenandoah. Lysander hadn't dared try his hand at liquidating that. His brother had asked for the deeds before his death, but Lysander, knowing it usually involved a personal settlement, shied off. Not so 'X'. He'd dare anything. He sold the place for quite a fair sum. He wasn't actually present at the settlement, but he introduced himself to a quiet firm of solicitors in the City and they saw it through for him. 'X', however, attended in person for the part at the solicitors'...."

"So, his identity is known?"

"Hardly, sir. He wore a cheap suit and cap and dark glasses. He signed his name, or rather that of Oates with a quill pen in such a thick and confused scrawl that handwriting experts would find it no use in identifying him or his writing."

"You know 'X' as the man in the cheap suit, cap, and dark glasses, and that is all. What of his build... his ways, his walk...?"

"Unluckily, those who saw him weren't very good at observing. We're quite in the dark about it."

"Did he tally with Hunt?"

"I dare say he did. He wasn't tall. Medium built, they say. It could have been Hunt."

"But Hunt was found in such a get-up. He wore dark glasses, cap and a light suit."

"Hunt was in the habit of wearing light suits, I admit. I can't imagine him in a cap, but he may have put his scruples on one side. What was he doing, however, prowling about in dark glasses on the night he was killed?"

"Probably he had designs on Fairclough or somebody. Hunt seems to have fancied tinted glasses when he was operating."

"We also heard of 'X'—shall we still call the man in the dark glasses—we also heard of 'X' picking up information about Finloe Oates and Lysander and about Florrie Judson in Netherby. He was also seen as the parson in Pimlico hospital. Yes. He reversed his collar but kept on his glasses. On that occasion, too, he showed his hair. Rather unruly, but controlled by pomade of some kind. A very enterprising customer our 'X'...."

"You are most annoying, Inspector. You persist in calling Hunt 'X' when all the time, every scrap of evidence points to Hunt as the criminal.... "

"I don't call Hunt 'X' at all, sir, because he wasn't 'X'. They were two different persons. They were seen together, 'X' and Hunt, and I can assure you it was no optical illusion, but two bodies, unaware of each other's presence within a few yards of one another."

"What do you mean?"

For the first time, Hazlett looked angry. It was slowly dawning on him that Littlejohn was playing a game against him. He rose and leaned across the table and thrust his face close to Littlejohn's.

"What do you mean?"

"Unfortunately for Mr. 'X', a character of whom he was quite unaware joined the drama. There was 'X,' everything nicely planned, the money was his, and Hunt apparently securely nailed, when suddenly Mr. Hubert Stroud, ex-policeman, now private inquiry agent, enters. Luckily, 'X' was unaware of his operations. Stroud was the invisible man. Had 'X' known of Hubert Stroud's existence, he would have murdered him as coolly as he murdered Lysander Oates, Gamaliel and Theodore Hunt. Stroud was employed by the jealous Fairclough, who wasn't jealous at all."

"Don't speak in riddles, Inspector."

"I'll try to be plainer then. Fairclough wasn't jealous of his wife. Instead of murdering Hunt, he felt more like kissing him. 'X' didn't know that part of the drama. Fairclough was in love with another woman and his wife's little escapade with Hunt suited him down to the ground. He set a detective, Stroud, on Hunt's trail. Stroud followed Hunt to the Isle of Man, where he took Mrs. Fairclough with him for the outing. Stroud saw them go to Snuff the

Wind. Mrs. Fairclough, under pressure, testified that she never left Hunt whilst they were on the island. She gave Hunt an alibi. So did Stroud. He followed the pair to the mine and saw them leave. He also saw 'X' sitting there with a pair of binoculars watching them. 'X' must have had his second fit of cursing when Hunt turned up at the mine with a woman. All the same, it was better than his not turning up at all. In court, the testimony of Mrs. Fairclough might not have counted for much. A sordid little love affair with the wife of a fellow master. The jury wouldn't have relished that, nor would they have thought much of the testimony of an unfaithful wife.... But it was Stroud who really spoiled it all. He saw 'X'! True, it was the same man in the same cap and dark glasses, unidentifiable, but 'X' for all that. We were able to check that 'X' had hired a car in Douglas, daren't show his English driving licence and hence couldn't drive himself after all. He got over it by giving the paid driver the slip at Foxdale. A man of endless resource is our Mr. 'X'."

"You amaze me, Inspector! All this wealth of detailed investigation! What a pity you were unable to establish the identity of this 'X', as you call him. By the way, if what you say is true, Hunt had a lucky break. Pity Fairclough killed him. He'd only have stood trial for forgery and then, on his release, the money would have..."

"Fairclough didn't kill him; Hunt didn't get the money; 'X' killed Hunt in an effort to silence him and to pin the murders on him. One person knows the identity of 'X', has seen him without his dark glasses and cap, and is coming to the Yard to-morrow to help us identify our man.... "

There was a silence as though Hazlett were half afraid to speak. Then he asked, after waiting expectantly for Littlejohn to mention the name...

"And who might that be? Certainly a triumph for you, Inspector, after all your exemplary work."

"Our friend is a clergyman, the Rev. Caesar Kinrade, Vicar of Grenaby in the Isle of Man. He saw X without his glasses on the 'plane to the island. X was on his way to murder Lysander Oates, was air-sick and his sun spectacles slipped off...."

# CHAPTER NINETEEN

# CATASTROPHE AT GRENABY

The "shadow" deputed to keep an eye on Hazlett posted himself in a dark doorway in Gedge Court opposite the offices of Mathieson & Co., and prepared for a long wait.

"Don't let him out of your sight," Littlejohn had said and Sergeant Holmes understood what that meant. He was known as "Sherlock" among his colleagues and greatly resented it. He could never live up to it! He had, whilst Littlejohn was talking inside with Hazlett, found out by careful inquiries that there was only one entrance and exit to the lawyer's chambers and, as Hazlett was obviously unaware of the trap the police had baited for him, the job of trailing him would be an easy one.

Hazlett, left alone, however, did some quick thinking. To his keen mind the whole scheme sounded suspicious. He knew that the Rev. Caesar Kinrade had seen him on the 'plane and he knew, as well, that if he didn't somehow stop the parson from talking, he would, to say the least of it, prove a dangerous witness for the Crown. But Littlejohn had obviously been trailing his coat when he talked about the identity of "X" being established by this one, very vulnerable person. He had been tempting Hazlett to try to eliminate the Rev. Caesar and thus, once and for all, incriminate himself. Henceforth, his every movement would be watched and if he stirred a step in the direction of Grenaby, he would be in the toils. Hazlett cautiously looked round the window-frame. "Sherlock" Holmes was just visible, a dark shade in the porch opposite. Hazlett grunted to himself, opened his big safe, and took out two brown paper parcels. Instead of going out by the only orthodox way, he went upstairs, let himself out on the roof through a skylight and, crouching on the tiles, made his way to a wooden bridge, a relic of firewatching days, which led across an alley to the next block of offices. Here, with the help of a similar trapdoor, he descended to the street on the other side of the building.

"How was I to know there was a bridge across?" said the very chagrined Holmes over the telephone to Scotland Yard two hours later. "I checked it all before you left and was sure. Else I'd have called for another man...." He had caught Mr. Teale on his way to lunch and asked him if Hazlett was still busy.

"He's gone out.... Must have gone more than an hour ago. When I went up to his room, I found a note saying he'd gone home and would be back about two. He was lunching with a friend.... "

Mr. Hazlett lived in Chelsea and Littlejohn sent a man to his house right away. Meanwhile, there was no time to waste. He had hoped that Holmes would have kept the lawyer in sight, and, on the slightest sign of a move in the direction of the Isle of Man, he would have followed to be in at the finale and at the same time see that no evil befell the Rev. Caesar Kinrade.

"Charter a 'plane for the island, immediately," he said. "There's not a minute to waste." As a precaution, he rang up the parsonage at Grenaby. The housekeeper answered. She sounded flabbergasted.

"Are you back in England already, Mr. Littlejohn?"

"Why? I've never been away since I left you...."

"But you telephoned Mr. Kinrade and asked him to walk down and meet you.... You'd just crossed and were on your way..."

Littlejohn had no time to listen to any more. He ran to the waiting car and told the driver to go like hell for the airport....

Wilmott Hazlett left a note to say he was going home. This he did and stayed there five minutes; just long enough to gather tweed suit, a cap and a fresh pair of dark glasses. Previously he told his housekeeper, quite calmly, that he was going to dine in the West End, at his club to be exact, and then he took his car and made for the club in question. Ostentatiously, he there ordered a careful lunch for two o'clock and said he was going for a nap in the library. The reading-room was empty and Hazlett there took an opportunity of changing his trousers and jacket, stowing them in his bag, assuming his cap and glasses, and sneaking out to his waiting car whilst the coast was clear. Thence he drove madly to the airport.

Hazlett had but a dim idea of establishing an alibi. He didn't take any trouble to test it link by link. His mind was too occupied. He was seized with the obsession, the aching lust to kill Parson Kinrade, just as he had killed others before who had tried to spoil his plan. He'd have killed Littlejohn if he'd had half a chance. In fact, his visit to Scotland Yard had been made with that idea.... He'd had a hunting knife in his pocket. But Littlejohn had been in company with that psalm-singing assistant of his; or at least, he looked like a psalm-singer....

On second thoughts, an alibi was all nonsense. What did he want with an alibi? What had he to remain in England for, at all? A ruined business, a few distant relatives, no friends, no admirers, nothing…. Eire was only half an hour from the Isle of Man. In the parcels in his bag reposed nearly twelve thousand pounds…. Some had gone to satisfy urgent demands in his practice; the rest was intact. He knew a splendid hide-out in the Irish bogs, a little house near a quiet little town. There he might lie low till all had died down and then … well … maybe South America. It had always fascinated him. Meanwhile, if it hadn't been for a silly old dotard of a parson, all this wouldn't have happened. The blood sang in Hazlett's ears as he thought of it and a red mist swam across the road over which he was hurling to the airport.

"Bit of a tall order. Why not take the afternoon B.E.A. service?" asked the man with the charter 'plane. He didn't like the look of the would-be passenger in glasses. He had a furtive way as if he might be up to smuggling something away. All the same, the offer was a good one…. An hour later, Hazlett was landing at Ronaldsway. It was just one o'clock. In Gedge Court, Sergeant Holmes was still watching the offices of Mathieson & Co. from his gloomy doorway and Mr. Teale was putting off his lunch as he feverishly cleared out his drawers ready for leaving the firm for good.

The Rev. Caesar Kinrade was about to begin his lunch when the telephone bell rang.

"It's that nice Mr. Littlejohn wantin' you, parson," said his housekeeper.

"You sound a bit hoarse," said the parson just before he hung up. "A cold? I'll find you something when you get here."

He turned to his housekeeper.

"Lay another place for lunch. Mr. Littlejohn's on his way up; telephoned from Colby. Asked if I'd take a walk down to meet him as he feels like a breath of our fresh air and will send his taxi back at the bridge. I could do with a stretch of the legs myself. We ought to be back in a quarter of an hour.... "

The vicar took his broad brimmed hat and stick and set out on his walk.

On the way over, Hazlett had been doing some careful thinking between the spasms of nausea which attacked him in the air. How to get at Parson Kinrade was a puzzle. On no account must anyone see him and he couldn't be sure of the clergyman being alone. Then, Hazlett remembered a film he'd seen ... They ran-down a man in a car. Made a bee-line for him and stepped hard on the accelerator. It looked like an accident and the speed of travel made the occupants of the vehicle unrecognisable. That would be a virtue, too, if the alibi functioned. Unlikely it would function, but just in case ... .

Hazlett told the charter 'plane to wait and as he left the runway, cast a keen eye on the car park. Nobody heeded him; the Dublin passengers were already assembling and the coming and going of other traffic was occupying everyone's attention. A parson and his wife drew up in a large ancient barouche. He carried a little bag and it was obvious that he was taking a trip and his wife was seeing him off. They parked their car without locking it and the wife, who had done the driving, did not even trouble to remove the ignition key. Hazlett calmly climbed in as soon as the owners were in the airport building and he drove away without anyone worrying in the least.

First, to spy out the land. He asked a schoolboy the way to Grenaby and then drove hard to seek the vicarage. On the way, he noted the stone bridge over the river, the way the road narrowed, the overhanging trees which obscured the road, the absence of traffic and people. He then set out to find a telephone box. He had to drive back to Colby and there, speaking through his handkerchief, he held a cordial conversation with Parson Kinrade, who thought he was Littlejohn. Using his legal persuasiveness to the full, he asked him to take a walk to the bridge and meet him, as he felt like a walk and some fresh air after the trip.

High noon at Grenaby was more ominous than midnight. It was so hot that all the birds had ceased to sing, the trees were silent, a shimmering haze hung over the road like transparent shades trying to materialise. The only sound came from beneath the bridge where the water rippled over the stones. It is a queer, lovely place at any time. It is said that funny things happen there; strange unholy beings haunt the dark river banks, restless spirits wander about the old mill and ruined dwellings....

Charlie Quinney, eighty if a day, emerged from his little cottage by the bridge, carrying a small pail in which to gather water from the stream to give his hens. There were no taps in his house and it was easier to go to the river bank and fill his bucket than pump it from the well....

Charlie's back was bent almost two-double. His long arms hung limply, with their great knotted hands, by his sides; he wore an old felt hat, shirt and trousers, with no collar; and his features were lost in a fortnight's growth of stiff grey whiskers. He sighed heavily as he crossed the bridge. Every day, it grew harder and harder doing for himself. The neighbours, few and far between, were nice enough, but he hadn't quite settled down among them yet. He was a "foreigner" from other parts. He'd only lived in Grenaby fifteen years.... The bent back disappeared down the slope to the stream and Charlie dipped his bucket in the clear water through which the trout shot, alarmed at the commotion....

The sturdy figure of Parson Kinrade, stick in hand, broad black felt shading his eyes, appeared descending the hill. In the distance a car whined, drawing nearer at great speed....

As Charlie climbed the bank and set foot on the road again, the vicar was entering the narrow space between the stone sides of the bridge; the car was flying towards him, dead set to hit him. For a brief second Charlie Quinney stood between the pair of them. He saw what was sure to happen. He could neither cry out, nor reach the parson to fling him aside, nor yet signal to the driver of the car, crouched, intent at the wheel. So Charlie did the only other thing. He flung the contents of his pail at the car. The water struck the windscreen with a noise as if Charlie had thrown half a brick, and spread, momentarily, an opaque mass, between Hazlett and his quarry. The car slewed wildly, struck the parson a glancing blow which threw him clear and prone on the grass verge, and then hit the stone bridge with a fearful impact. The women in the cottages up the hill rushed from the windows whence they had been spying on their vicar's progress, to their doors and then hurried to form a little crowd on the bridge.

Hazlett was sitting at the wheel, crushed, but still conscious.

"Leave me alone! Let me be!" he yelled as they tried to extricate him from the wreck. "My liver's ruptured...."

The doctor confirmed this later, when Littlejohn arrived post-haste at the cottage where Hazlett was lying. He was in the bed of the widow who lived there alone. They'd carried him as gently as they could, but he was too far gone even to take to hospital. Parson Kinrade, little the worse for his shaking, was sitting by the bedside, holding on the patch-work counterpane the hand of the man who had tried to kill him.

"Hast thou found me, oh, mine enemy?" muttered Hazlett as Littlejohn, stooping at the low doorway, entered the room.

Mr. Kinrade nodded a grave greeting to the Inspector and out of the corner of his eye looked sharply at Hazlett. The devil quoting scripture?

"I'm done for, Littlejohn, but I almost gave you the slip.... Even now, you'll never hang me.... In the end, I wanted to show myself that, properly and intelligently done, crime would pay me and I'd leave the law behind and get away..."

"Don't talk," said the doctor, a bony Irishman with pale blue eyes and a tired, kindly face.

"Why not? Silence will do me no good now. I must finish comparing notes with Littlejohn.... Listen to this..."

There was nothing they could do but let him continue. Hazlett's life was fading visibly away and the best thing was to get a confession if he would give it. He had broken his false teeth in the accident and they had removed them. His jaws had sunk and he looked indescribably old...

"...You were right in most of your deductions.... I confess I felt fear in my belly when I knew you were on the case. Just my bad luck...! Why did the fellow have to rob a bank and start the police nosing round the Oates house, just as I'd got it all set...? Give me some brandy...."

Littlejohn took out his pocket flask. He had to hold it as Hazlett drank greedily. The lawyer was too weak even to raise his hand.

"That's better.... It all started when Finloe sent for his deeds after his wife's death.... I had them.... I was curious to know why he was selling the house, so I called with them myself a few days after he asked for them. I went by road that time...in the evening. I had a bit of trouble with the car on the way; it was dark when I got there. The house was in darkness. I approached quietly and waited a while, wondering what to do. Then I heard sounds inside, but still no light appeared. It was a bright night with stars and I could see pretty well. The back door opened and Lysander came out, bearing on his shoulders what looked like a body. He crept down the garden ... I followed him under the hedge .... He put stones in the pockets of the body and threw it in the pond nearby. Then, somebody's dog started a hullaballoo and he almost caught me red-handed ...."

Hazlett paused, closed his eyes and gasped for breath.

"He's done for," muttered the doctor.

"Not yet, Doctor! I'm not leaving you till I've said my say, liver or no liver .... Where was I ....? After that, little more ... I never left the track of Lysander. I found out all you discovered later. I explored every avenue .... I was desperate for money ... spent too much and tampered with some trusts .... I telephoned the bank and wrote to them for information as official solicitor of the Oates family ... the bank had always known me as such and answered me fully. I pieced it all up ... I knew Finloe's Will and guessed what Lysander was up to .... "

Hazlett stopped again, asked for more brandy and then by sheer force of will, continued.

" ... I even followed him to Bishop's Walton ... to Hunt's .... That stumped me for a bit. What was Lysander doing there? Then, I remembered our old days together ... Hunt, expert at forgery .... Yes ... Lysander got all but the house. I got that. Too good to leave behind, especially as I owed so much to trust accounts ..."

"What about Gamaliel?" asked Littlejohn.

"One day ... I followed Lysander on the train ... Gamaliel must have smelled a rat, too ... he was following him as well. Saw me and bolted. After Lysander disappeared, Gamaliel came to see me. Blackmail. Told him what I'd do to him. But the police were on his track. That made me uneasy. I tried to get him, but they put him away in hospital; I followed your man there to hear what was said. I was ready to bolt if he'd told on me. He hadn't the guts or the wits to do it. That signed his death warrant. I went to his shop with a key from my office to see if there was anything incriminating there. Found your colleague's card... Gave me an idea... That's all.... "

"What of Hunt?"

"Very persistent, Inspector. Can't you let me die with just one point unsolved? I wanted to get clear of it all, so thought of Hunt. He was in it up to his neck and was better dead. Full of misery... poor sort of chap... I discovered, in the way you said, how Lysander fled and where... I came over here and..."

Hazlett gathered a new burst of strength. His eyes opened wider and he spoke more clearly. It was as if his own adventures were exhilarating him.

"I killed him, hid him, and took his money. On the way here, I planned about Hunt. Got him to write a letter and arranged it to incriminate him. I stayed on the island till the letter arrived next day. I kept an eye on the mine and the chapel and I'd just planted the letter when Hunt turned up after all, in spite of his letter of refusal. He always was inquisitive. But I hadn't bargained for his bringing a woman. That annoyed me. I could have killed him on the spot. All the same, no jury would have believed an alibi given by his mistress. Little did I think the jealous husband, Fairclough, had set a detective to spy upon her... I slipped there..."

Hazlett made a last effort. He was far gone, but hanging on like death itself. The skin of his face and head tightened, showing the hideous bony death's head beneath.

"...I went back to the bungalow at Netherby to clear things up. I had to watch the post, too.... I did it by daylight. I had the excuse that I was Oates's lawyer. I had a key previously taken from the house. I was busy steaming open letters when suddenly I heard someone insert a key in the lock. My courage failed.... I seized the poker and slipped quickly in the nearest cupboard. A most unfortunate choice, for it contained the electric meter. The intruder had called to check the meter, came straight to my cupboard, and opened it. Where he'd got the key from, I didn't trouble to inquire. There was nothing else to do but kill him.... If he'd told that he'd found me hiding in the house...well...I was fortunate that nobody seemed to notice me or the electricity man enter the house, otherwise my panic would have cost me dear."

The voice was now thick and rattling, and difficult to follow.

"Then...of all things...Hunt came all the way to London to say he'd been caught for forgery! Would I get him off? I could have laughed aloud! Thinking you were still not convinced that Hunt killed Oates and the rest, quite ignorant of the fact that he had a safe alibi, I decided to put the final convincing touches on the case and close it. Hunt never mentioned the detective who followed him and his mistress.... All he said was Fairclough was as jealous as hell. It seemed easy. I put the glasses and cap by which I was known, on Hunt, after I'd followed and killed him. Little did I think I'd been identified already...and of all people by a sleeping parson, or at least, I thought he was asleep...."

Hazlett cackled. It was a death rattle.

"Providence even sent its thunderbolts to protect you, sir, in the shape of a bucket of water! You looked old and sleepy on the 'plane that time .... You were my Nemesis, all the same ...."

He reserved his last words for Littlejohn.

"I'd got it all very nicely cut and dried, Inspector. Foolproof on paper. Just bad luck .... A runaway bank clerk, a sleepy clergyman, and, of all things, a dirty little divorce detective, were my undoing .... Well ... I wasn't as clever as I thought ..."

And thus denouncing himself, Wilmott Hazlett halted in the middle of a sentence and died.

# HALF-MAST FOR THE DEEMSTER

GEORGE BELLAIRS

# CHAPTER ONE
# HALF-MAST

"**A**ny sign of land yet?"

The little man in a cloth cap and an overcoat several sizes too large for him, regarded Littlejohn with pathetic dog-like eyes. His complexion was pale green and he had only roused himself from his stupor in the hope of receiving some good news.

"I can't see anything...."

Littlejohn wasn't feeling very good himself. He had done a fair amount of sea travelling in his time; several trips to the Continent for holidays or to see officials at the Sûreté in Paris. Once he'd been over to New York to consult the F.B.I.... But never anything like this! People said that on certain days you could see the Isle of Man from the mainland; now it seemed at the other end of the earth. This little man with his coat sleeves over his knuckles, made retching noises, hurried to the rail of the ship, was met by a large wave, and retreated soaked to the skin. He didn't seem to mind....

"If I ever reach land, I'll never go to sea again...."

Archdeacon Caesar Kinrade, Vicar of Grenaby, in the Isle of Man, was the cause of it all.

"A friend of mine would like to have a talk with you," he had written. "And besides, if you don't pay me the promised visit before long, I will be too old to show you my beloved Isle. I am, as you know, eighty-three next birthday."

Mrs. Littlejohn wasn't with him. Her sister, who had a Canon of the Church for a husband, and eight children, was moving again, this time to Comstock-in-the-Fen, and there was a vicarage with eleven bedrooms. With her ninth on the way and domestic help hard to get, the Canon's wife had sent the usual S.O.S. to Hampstead....

It was the middle of September and the weather on the mainland had been fine and bright. It had continued so across the Channel just long enough for an excellent lunch to be served and thereupon the *Mona* had started to roll, then to pitch, and then both. Some of the passengers began to disappear down below; those who had been singing to the accompaniment of Sid Simmons and his Ten Hot Dogs, picked-up and broadcast over the ship's loud-speakers, had grown silent. Some lay on the floor and groaned; others were strewn all over the place. The timbers rolled under Littlejohn's feet; a blast of hot roast beef and cabbage rose from the dining-room and swept the deck. Littlejohn struggled to the top deck and looked out at the heaving water and the leaden sky.

"You ought to cross by boat," his wife had said. "It'll blow the cobwebs away...."

As he stood miserably peering ahead, the prospect slowly began to change. It was like the transformation scene at a pantomime, where the electricians by juggling with the lighting suddenly convert the devil's kitchen into the home of the fairy queen. The *Mona* was tossing in tortured gloom, but ahead the sun was shining on calm water, the sky was turning to blue, and, like a backcloth slowly illuminated by unseen floodlights, the Isle of Man with gentle green hills sweeping down to the sea, was stretched out before them.

The man in the big overcoat was at his elbow. He tapped Littlejohn's arm gaily. His complexion had changed to a rosy pink and the brandy he had absorbed rose abundantly on his breath.

"What did I tell you?" he said, as though he'd been a prophet of salvation all the way. "What did I tell you? There she is ... ."

He flapped his sleeve at the Island, like a conjurer who has performed a difficult trick. Having thus justified himself, he made off to the bar to celebrate. People were surging on deck smiling and congratulating one another as though the end of the world had somehow been deferred. As if to cheer them up still more, the *Mona* slid into calm water and blew a wild blast on her siren to those ashore, like a badly frightened cock which crows when danger is past. The echo from Douglas Head threw back the sound.

The man in the overcoat was back.

"What about a li'l drink?" he said to Littlejohn.

The holiday season was drawing to an end, but there was a good crowd waiting on the pier for the arrival of the boat, which glided comfortably into harbour and which, by an admirable piece of practised seamanship, the captain brought gently alongside in a matter of minutes. Someone waved to Littlejohn as he tried to catch the eye of a porter and get rid of his luggage.

The Rev. Caesar Kinrade, Archdeacon of Man, was standing sturdily among a crowd of his friends, his shovel hat riding above the gallant white froth of his whiskers, his blue eyes sparkling. He wore his archdiaconal gaiters, too, but not like an immaculate prince of the Church; they looked utilitarian, like those of his forebears who, riding from parish to parish in the course of duty, found them more convenient on horseback than a cassock. The group round the parson all scrutinized Littlejohn with genial curiosity. The old man, with the native delight in tale-telling, had been treating them to the saga of how Littlejohn and he had between them solved the case of the man in dark glasses, and thus laid the foundation of a firm friendship.

Lying in ambush in the quayside car-park were Teddy Looney and his chariot. The old touring car, looking like a cross between a charabanc and a hearse, had been spring-cleaned and the brass bonnet shone in the sun. Looney grinned and bared a gap in his teeth. He was pleased to see Littlejohn again and glad that the prompt arrival of the boat would get him safely home for milking time.

"Good day, Parson...."

"Now, Reverend! Good to put a sight on ye...."

"Nice day, Master Kinrade. And how's yourself...?"

It was like a royal procession to Teddy's rattletrap. Everybody knew Parson Kinrade and everybody was glad to see him around.

The porter with Littlejohn's bags wouldn't be paid when he found the Inspector was a friend of the Archdeacon, and Littlejohn had to thrust five shillings in the man's pocket to ease his own conscience. The pair of them were almost hoisted into Teddy's tumbril by friendly hands and with a jerk the vehicle made a start. They ran alongside the old quay, bristling with the masts of tiny craft of all descriptions, dirty coasters busy unloading, trim yachts, timber boats from the Continent....

"Hullo, there, Parson...."

The good vicar of Grenaby shook his head at Littlejohn.

"I'll have to stop coming down to Douglas. They all get so excited to see me, and I get too excited, too, at seeing them. I'll be giving myself a stroke or something...."

The old car tossed round the bridge at the end of the quay and took to the country. Beneath the agitation of Teddy's conveyance, Littlejohn could still feel the roll of the deck he had endured for, it seemed, untold hours.

"Take the old road, Teddy...."

The car rattled through Port Soderick village, raced down Crogga Hill, turned on two wheels at the bottom, and snorted up the other side. They reached the top with difficulty and there stopped, for the contraption seemed to have caught fire. Dirty smoke oozed from under the bonnet, which Teddy opened to disclose a lot of dirty rags, smouldering with choking fumes.

"Forgot to take out me cleanin' cloths," he said, scattering them over the stone wall which skirted the road.

The parson, who hitherto had seemed half asleep, happy to let Littlejohn enjoy the scenery on the way in peace, suddenly roused himself.

"Let us out of this, Looney. We'll stretch our legs and if you can get going again, you can catch us up. Come on, Littlejohn, stir your stumps. I've something to show you...."

They strolled to an eminence in the road and the old man pointed in the direction of the sea.

"There! Did you ever see the likes of that?"

Difficult to believe the ocean had ever been rough, for now it stretched like a sheet of green glass as far as you could see. Between the road and the sea, undulating fields, divided by sod hedges, with gorse flaming on top of them and with clean white farmsteads dotted about them. Beyond, a long spit of land, like a granite spur, jutted out, with a ruined chapel and a fort at one side and a lighthouse on the other, and in the middle of the base of this triangle of rock, the towers of King William's College, in the old island capital of Castletown, rose strong and grey.

Parson Kinrade fished in the tails of his coat and brought out an old pipe, which he filled from a pewter tobacco-box, after telling Littlejohn to help himself. They leaned their elbows on the wall and smoked, and Looney who had drawn up beside them, knew better than disturb them.

"We've to call at Castletown," said the Archdeacon at length. "The court's sitting there to-day and I've promised we'll pick up the Deemster when it's finished.... Know what a Deemster is?"

"A judge here, isn't he?"

"More than that, Littlejohn. A very ancient office ... very ancient and stands in eminence next to that of the Governor of the Isle himself. In this small place, the Deemster's all His Majesty's mainland judges rolled into one. Civil, Criminal, County Court, Quarter Sessions.... All rolled into one. Judge of Appeal, too, against the decisions of his colleague, the other Deemster, when he sits with a judge from over the water to help him...."

"A busy man!"

"That's right. And before the laws were written or decisions recorded, he'd to remember the law.... Breast Law it was then, as if cherished in his heart.... They only take civil cases in Castletown now. First-Deemster Quantrell's sitting to-day. I'm calling to bring him with us for dinner at Grenaby. He wants to meet you. He's in trouble. Somebody's tried twice to murder him."

The parson dropped his last sentence like a bombshell and then was silent. It seemed impossible to think of murder in such a place. The birds were singing; the gulls were crying; a man, a woman and a sheep-dog climbed the road over the hill opposite and vanished; a small train puffed past in a cloud of steam and whistled; and, out at sea, a yacht with white sails spread, slid quietly round the granite spur of Langness and was gone.

Littlejohn pushed his hat on the back of his head, rubbed his chin, and smiled.

"My wife's last words were 'Keep out of mischief,'" he said. "By which she meant, I always seem to run into trouble if I go on holidays without her."

Parson Kinrade tapped his pipe on the wall.

"Oh, come now. I'm not intending this to be a busman's holiday. You're here because I wanted to see you again. But whilst you're with us, I thought you might perhaps help and advise a good man who's in trouble."

"Only my joke. Of course, I'll do anything you want. But aren't the local police good enough? They might take it to heart if—how do you say it?—if 'a fellah from over' started trying to teach them their business."

The vicar patted the moss on top of the wall and then turned his far-seeing eyes on the Inspector.

"This is only a little island, Littlejohn. News travels fast. They love a little gossip and the police aren't above joining in. Once it got abroad that somebody was out to murder a Deemster, where would he be? The law is above everybody else. It's safe and impregnable. Or that's the illusion that's to be created about it if people are to respect it. 'That's the man somebody's after murdering,' would think every male-factor brought before him. It just wouldn't do, Littlejohn. That's why Deemster Quantrell's told nobody but me and I said you were the man to share the secret and put it right in secret. Understand?"

"I understand. How did it happen?"

"Simply enough. His Honour drives his own car. The roads are good here and one tends to develop a fair turn of speed. Even Teddy there…. The hills are pretty steep and there are bends and drops at the bottom of them. Fortunately the Deemster's steering went wrong too soon. It broke as he drove it out of his garage. Whoever'd sawn into it, did it a bit too much ... ."

"*Sawn* into it? Are you sure?"

"His Honour's no fool. In his young days he mended his own motor-bike and then his car. It was sawn, all right. He guessed then that somebody was up to no good. He kept it quiet for his wife's sake and, lest some local tittle-tattler should get talking, he sent for new parts and a mechanic from the mainland to fit them."

"But who could have wished to ...?"

"That's just it. Who could? Deemster Quantrell's a member of a very old Manx family, always highly regarded, which has given to this land dozens of fine men; deemsters, doctors, lawyers, parsons. Everybody loves the Quantrells. And as for criminals he's sentenced .... Do the mainland judges get murdered for their judgments? No, they don't. And any fierce sentences Deemster Quantrell ever gave were in the past, long ago. There hasn't been a murder trial here for untold years and most of the real bad criminals go across to the mainland and commit their evil deeds and get their just dues across the water ... ."

"What about the second attempt, sir?"

"Two bricks off a block of property being pulled down in Douglas. *Two*, I said. Like the barrels of a shot gun. Bang down comes one and misses His Honour's head by inches. Then another. And nobody up on the building, because it's dinner time for the men."

"Is he sure it was deliberately done?"

"No wind blowing; no children playing on the site. Just nobody about. Deemster Quantrell sent a policeman to look into it. He said he'd seen something fall down. He didn't tell the officer it had nearly fallen *on* him.... That settled in his mind that somebody was out to give him trouble, to put it mildly...."

Littlejohn knocked out his pipe and shook his head.

"It looks like deliberate attempted murder. It's as well we're going to meet the Deemster. Maybe I can do something."

"I'm sure you can. Quietly, circumspectly, you'll put things right. We'll talk it over after dinner, and then you can decide what to do for the best. Well ... I see Teddy's getting mad at the thought of his unmilked cows. Let's be getting along."

They followed the undulating road, with broad panoramas of hills and the sea until, with a quick turn, it joined the main highway to the village of Ballasalla, beyond which the view opened to reveal the ancient island capital of Castletown with its old granite castle standing like a bastion ahead of them. As they slowed down to pass the busy airport of Ronaldsway, the parson gripped Littlejohn's arm and pointed ahead.

On the topmost tower of Castle Rushen stood a flagstaff, and they were slowly hauling up the flag.

Teddy Looney turned in his seat.

"They seem to be celebratin', sir...."

"Wait!"

The limp flag had stopped half-mast and a puff of wind caught it, revealing the emblem of the Island, three legs, in armour, and spurred, in gold on a red ground.

"Half-mast?"

"Hurry ahead, Looney," cried Parson Kinrade. "I hope it isn't, but it looks as if...as if..."

"Half-mast for the Deemster, sir?"

Littlejohn finished it for him, and they sat in silence until Looney braked at the roundabout leading to the by-pass road at Castletown.

"Go along into the town, Looney...."

But the parson needn't have said it. Standing at the junction was a policeman with a bicycle, who jumped with interest at the sight of Looney's car. He hurried across and held up his hand. He saluted smartly as he saw the Rev. Caesar Kinrade.

"Afternoon, Archdeacon. The sergeant said I was to look out for you on your way back from Douglas, and say he'd like to see you, if you don't mind...."

"I was coming in any case...I promised to pick up the Deemster...."

The constable's face assumed a look of reverent awe, as though he were already marching in the funeral procession.

"The Deemster died half an hour since. That's what the sergeant said he wanted to see you for.... And..."

The bobby turned to Littlejohn, gave him a look of admiration and fellow-feeling, and saluted again, a feat which required considerable contortion, because the officer's head was thrust through the open window of the car.

"And are you Inspector Littlejohn, sir, of Scotland Yard?"

He uttered Scotland Yard in tones a pilgrim would use of Mecca.

"Yes, Constable..."

"I was to bring you along, too."

"Why?" asked the parson curiously. "Nobody knows he's here.... Or do they?"

The constable cleared his throat.

"Beggin' your pardon, Archdeacon, but I shouldn't be talkin' like this. The sergeant said to bring you right away.... But they found a note the Deemster must have just started to write before he died. It said, 'My dear Inspector Littlejohn...' and then it finished. So the sergeant said you was to come as well, *if* you please...."

He flipped a thumb at Teddy Looney to indicate he had better be driving along, and mounted his bicycle to escort them.

"Here, here," called the Archdeacon. "How did he die? Was he murdered...? Shot...? Stabbed...? What?"

He couldn't wait.

The constable looked at the ancient whiskers reproachfully.

"Oh, come, sir. Not that. He had a seizure in his room in the court. They found him dead when they went to call him after the lunch adjournment.... They thought at first he was asleep...."

And to speed up progress, the bobby put on a spurt, pedalled ahead, and waved to Teddy Looney to get a move on.

# Want another Perfect Mystery?

## Get your next Classic Crime Story for FREE ...

Sign up to our Crime Classics newsletter where you can discover new Golden Age crime, receive exclusive content and never-before published short stories, all for FREE.

From the beloved greats of the golden age to the forgotten gems, best-kept-secrets, and brand new discoveries, we're devoted to classic crime.

If you sign up today, you'll get:

1. A free novel from our Classic Crime collection.
2. Exclusive insights into classic novels and their authors and the chance to get copies in advance of publication, and
3. The chance to win exclusive prizes in regular competitions.

Interested? It takes less than a minute to sign up. You can get your novel and your first newsletter by signing up on our website - www.crimeclassics.co.uk

53077807R00173

Made in the USA
San Bernardino, CA
12 September 2019